Praise for *Sharpe'*

"Gripping action that's not for the
—*Kirkus Reviews* (starred review)

"Cornwell again makes writing flawless historical prose seem effortless."

—*Library Journal* (starred review)

"Cornwell, who recently wrapped up his Last Kingdom series, which focused on the early history of Britain, has never let his fans down, and regular readers of the Sharpe novels have been eagerly awaiting this one's arrival."

—*Booklist*

"All the favorite ingredients of a Sharpe novel are here: the supporting characters whose names begin with *H* . . . meticulous descriptions of the loading, firing, and effect of the Baker rifle; soldiers' wit and toughness . . . and most of all the author's expert focus on putting us, through Sharpe's eyes, always at the center of gripping action. . . . Cornwell continues to be the master of military historical fiction—long may he remain so."

—*Historical Novels Review*

"Sharpe fans will find *Sharpe's Command* up to snuff with the other novels in this series, with Sharpe's old comrades in arms, like rifleman Daniel Hagman, Major Hogan, and the Irishman, Sergeant Harper, very much present. Meanwhile, newcomers may take delight and relief in exchanging the problems and mores of our present age for those of another place and time. Enjoy!"

—*Smoky Mountain News*

Books by Bernard Cornwell

1356
The Fort
Agincourt

Nonfiction

Waterloo

The Saxon Tales

The Last Kingdom
The Pale Horseman
The Lords of the North
Sword Song
The Burning Land
Death of Kings
The Pagan Lord
The Empty Throne
Warriors of the Storm
The Flame Bearer
War of the Wolf
Sword of Kings
Uhtred's Feast

The Sharpe Novels (in chronological order)

Sharpe's Tiger
Richard Sharpe and the Siege of Seringapatam, 1799

Sharpe's Triumph
Richard Sharpe and the Battle of Assaye, September 1803

Sharpe's Fortress
Richard Sharpe and the Siege of Gawilghur, December 1803

Sharpe's Trafalgar
Richard Sharpe and the Battle of Trafalgar, 21 October 1805

Sharpe's Prey
Richard Sharpe and the Expedition to Copenhagen, 1807

SHARPE'S RIFLES
Richard Sharpe and the French Invasion of Galicia, January 1809

SHARPE'S HAVOC
Richard Sharpe and the Campaign in Northern Portugal, Spring 1809

SHARPE'S EAGLE
Richard Sharpe and the Talavera Campaign, July 1809

SHARPE'S GOLD
Richard Sharpe and the Destruction of Almeida, August 1810

SHARPE'S ESCAPE
Richard Sharpe and the Bussaco Campaign, 1810

SHARPE'S FURY
Richard Sharpe and the Battle of Barrosa, March 1811

SHARPE'S BATTLE
Richard Sharpe and the Battle of Fuentes de Onoro, May 1811

SHARPE'S COMPANY
Richard Sharpe and the Siege of Badajoz, January to April 1812

SHARPE'S SWORD
Richard Sharpe and the Salamanca Campaign, June and July 1812

SHARPE'S ENEMY
Richard Sharpe and the Defense of Portugal, Christmas 1812

SHARPE'S HONOR
Richard Sharpe and the Vitoria Campaign, February to June 1813

SHARPE'S REGIMENT
Richard Sharpe and the Invasion of France, June to November 1813

SHARPE'S SIEGE
Richard Sharpe and the Winter Campaign, 1814

SHARPE'S REVENGE
Richard Sharpe and the Peace of 1814

SHARPE'S WATERLOO
Richard Sharpe and the Waterloo Campaign, 15 June to 18 June 1815

SHARPE'S ASSASSIN
Richard Sharpe and the Occupation of Paris, 1815

SHARPE'S DEVIL
Richard Sharpe and the Emperor, 1820–1821

SHARPE'S COMMAND

Richard Sharpe and the Bridge
at Almaraz, May 1812

BERNARD CORNWELL

HARPER

NEW YORK · LONDON · TORONTO · SYDNEY

HARPER

Originally published in Great Britain in 2024 by HarperCollins Publishers.

A hardcover edition of this book was published in 2024 by HarperCollins Publishers.

HarperCollins books may be purchased for educational, business, or sales promotional use. For information, please email the Special Markets Department at SPsales@harpercollins.com.

FIRST U.S. PAPERBACKS EDITION PUBLISHED 2025.

Library of Congress Cataloging-in-Publication Data has been applied for.

ISBN 978-0-06-321931-1 (pbk.)

25 26 27 28 29 LBC 5 4 3 2 1

SHARPE'S COMMAND
*ist Clemens Amann gewidmet
mit tausend Dank für
seine Großzügigkeit*

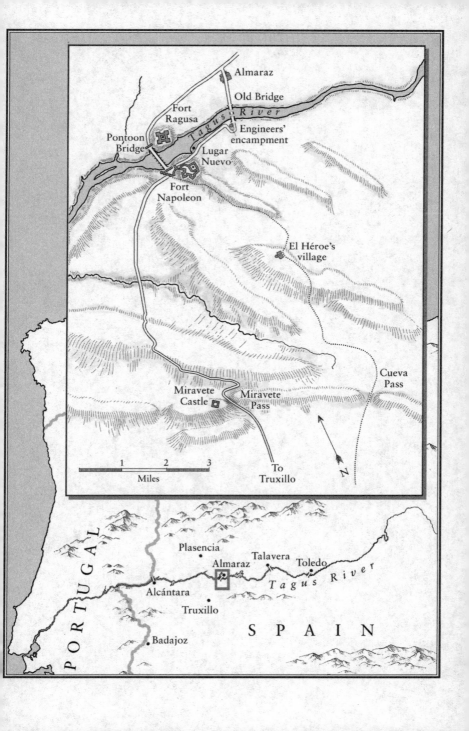

CHAPTER 1

Sharpe was thinking about breakfast when he was hit.

The choice was between salt pork or salt beef, neither with any bread and both tough as boiled boot leather. He was about to choose the pork when the shot sounded, but so far away that he thought it unimportant. He dismissed the distant shot as a hunter in the far hills, and almost immediately the hunter's shot hit him.

It struck his upper left thigh, glanced harmlessly onto the metal scabbard of his heavy cavalry sword, and dropped to the ground. He stumbled from the impact, cursed and rubbed his thigh, which would be bruised.

Sergeant Harper stooped to recover the ball. "Bloody fine shot, sir," he said.

"Bloody stupid shot," Sharpe retorted. He was gazing northeast and could just see a puff of smoke drifting in the almost still air. The smoke came from the rocky crest of a hill that had to be almost half a mile away.

He rubbed his thigh. He knew he was lucky, indeed his men

called him "Lucky Sharpe," but still shooting a musket at a target a half mile away was stupid. The ball had been slowed by the air until it was almost spent and lacked the power to pierce even the cloth of his overalls. It had smarted and would leave a bruise, but that was a lot better than a lump of lead deep in his muscles. "Bloody Crapaud," he said angrily. "I'll have some pork."

"Wasn't a Frenchman," Harper said. He tossed the musket ball to Sharpe, who caught it one-handed. "That's one of ours."

The ball was still warm. It was smaller than a rifle bullet, but larger than the ball fired by a French musket. The difference in sizes was minute, but Sharpe had been a soldier for nineteen years. He had enlisted in the 33rd when he was sixteen and since then he had fought in Flanders, India, Portugal, and now Spain. He had been promoted to sergeant in 1799 and four years later had been commissioned as an officer. Now, in the spring of 1812, he was a major and wore the green jacket of a rifleman. Nineteen years of battle and every one of them as an infantryman, Sharpe knew that Harper was right. The spent musket ball, fired at such a ridiculous range, was British.

"Here comes Cupid," Harper said in warning.

"Don't call him that," Sharpe said irritably.

"Everyone else does," Harper responded, "you do!"

"Sir! Sir!" Lieutenant Love stumbled in his hurry to reach Sharpe. "Are you hurt, sir? Is it serious?"

"It's nothing, Lieutenant," Sharpe said dismissively. "A spent round."

"So the French are barring the road," Lieutenant Love said, gazing at the distant skyline, "that is grievous news, sir."

"It's not the bloody Crapauds," Sharpe said, "that was fired by a *partida*." He used the Spanish word for the guerrilla fighters who dogged the French all across Spain. He tossed the musket ball away and turned back to the trees where his men had spent the night. "Dan! See anything up there?"

Daniel Hagman gazed at the distant crest where the puff of smoke had thinned and was drifting eastward, then suddenly a dozen eruptions of smoke showed along the rocky skyline. The balls went God knows where and the volley's ragged sound arrived an instant later. "They don't like us, Mister Sharpe," Hagman said, amused.

"Oh my Lord almighty!" Lieutenant Love had dived behind the nearest tree trunk. "*Partidas*? Really?"

"Really," Sharpe said flatly, then looked back to Hagman. "Say hello back to them, Dan."

"A pleasure," Hagman said. He lay on his back, propped his rifle barrel between his feet and sighted along the barrel. Sharpe saw him edge the weapon a touch to the left and knew Hagman was compensating for the small wind. "Want the bugger dead, Mister Sharpe?"

"I want them scared."

"Scared it is," Hagman said and pulled the trigger.

The rifle's sound was crisper than a musket's and, unlike a musket, its bullet would be lethal at a half mile. "I reckon he needs new britches, Mister Sharpe," Hagman said, standing and fishing a new cartridge from his pouch.

"But aren't the *partidas* on our side?" Lieutenant Love had crept out from his sheltering tree. "Are they not our allies?"

"They are, Lieutenant, but those buggers don't know which side we're on."

Lieutenant Love peered anxiously at the distant skyline where small drifts of powder smoke showed against the sky. "They suspect we may be French?" Love sounded disbelieving.

"That's what the buggers think, Lieutenant."

"But . . ." Love began.

"They think the British wear red," Sharpe interrupted him. He led sixteen men, all but one of them riflemen wearing the dark green jacket of the 95th Rifles, while Lieutenant Love sported the dark blue coat of the Royal Artillery. "They think you're a Crapaud officer and the rest of us are dragoons. Crapaud dragoons wear green."

"But dragoons have horses, sir!"

"Dragoons are mounted infantry," Sharpe said, "or supposed to be."

"Then we're in a pickle, sir," Love said. He straightened and stared belligerently down the long road that climbed to the far ridge. "There's no cover between us and that hilltop! How can we approach without being slaughtered? Oh, if only I had a nine-pounder!"

"You don't," Sharpe said with a deal more asperity than he had intended, but in truth Lieutenant Courtney deVere Love was wearing Sharpe's patience thin, a patience already scraped almost bare by this journey deep into enemy-held Spain. Another fusillade of musketry sounded, though none of the balls came close to Sharpe or his men.

"I have a thought, sir?" Love said, holding the hilt of his light cavalry saber.

"Try me," Sharpe said.

"I have a spare white shirt, sir," Love explained eagerly. "Allow me to fix it to my saber's tip and it will serve as a flag of truce."

"You think the *partidas* will honor a flag of truce?"

"They are supposedly Christians!" Love said fiercely. "Even if they are Romanists."

"Lieutenant," Sharpe forced himself to sound patient, "I don't care if they're a band of bloody Methodists. If you walk out there waving a white flag they'll take it as a sign of weakness and wait for you to get in range and then kill you."

"Surely not, sir! Aren't these the very fellows we've been sent to meet?"

"Probably," Sharpe allowed, "but they don't know that. And they see a blue uniform and they'll use you for target practice. And you're a big fellow." Lieutenant Love was at least a foot taller than Sharpe, though hardly big because he was as thin as a ramrod. "I'd hate to lose you," Sharpe added unconvincingly.

Lieutenant Love looked crestfallen. "Then what do we do?"

"Whatever Mister Sharpe suggests," Harper said firmly.

"We go round the buggers," Sharpe said, "but first we pull back into the trees."

"But I need to inspect that road," Love pleaded, pointing to where the road climbed the ridge where the muskets still fired, their bullets either falling far short or flicking through the leaves of the low scrubby trees that grew in a shallow valley where a dry streambed led east.

"You will inspect the damn road," Sharpe said, then ordered his men back into the cover of the trees. Their disappearance prompted an end to the desultory and useless musket fire from the distant ridge.

"Will they follow us?" Lieutenant Love asked nervously.

"Not if they've got a lick of sense," Sharpe said. "They think they've driven us off and they'll wait to make sure we don't come back. And they reckon they're in a perfect defensive place. Which they are."

"So . . ." Lieutenant Love began.

"So we push them off the ridge," Sharpe said. He was leading his men eastward along the rocky bed of the dry stream. It fell, still shrouded by trees, into a much wider and deeper valley that ran south to north. Sharpe turned northward, first going to the valley's bottom where a stream foamed over rocks. "Keep your head down, Lieutenant," he told Love.

"Down?"

Sharpe was following the stream northward, which meant that the ridge where the muskets had been fired lay to his left. The valley was deep enough to hide that ridge and Sharpe did not want the men there to see any motion in the valley. "You're tall," he told Love. "If you can see the ridge's crest then men up there can see you."

"Ah!" Lieutenant Love half crouched. "You plan to go round them, sir?"

"I plan to teach the buggers not to waste ammunition," Sharpe said grimly. The fact that the fools had shot British ammunition had persuaded him they were partisans, and probably the very partisans he had been sent to meet, though there was still a remote chance that the muskets had been fired by the French. Sharpe had been assured that he could expect to meet no Frenchmen on these barren hills. There was indeed plenty of French infantry, but they were in forts that were still six or seven miles away, and reports from the *partidas* indicated that they only left their strong forts to forage, and even that rarely. But even an occasional French forage party would not be armed with British muskets, which meant the shots must have been fired by the *guerrilleros*, the Spanish partisans who hated the French and waged a cruel and galling war against the occupiers. "We just have to find the buggers and convince them we're on their side," Sharpe said.

He led his men a half mile northward. "I never did get my breakfast," he said to Sergeant Harper.

"I ate it," the big Irishman said, "that's why I joined this bloody army, to get fed."

"I hope it choked you."

"Seemed a pity to waste it," Harper said, grinning.

Sharpe looked back along his file of resting men. "Dan! Here!"

Daniel Hagman, a poacher from Cheshire, came to Sharpe's side. "Mister Sharpe?"

"The ridge is up there," Sharpe pointed westward. "I want you to have a look-see, Dan."

"Pleasure, Mister Sharpe."

"You want my glass?"

"No need."

"Off you go."

Hagman began scrambling up the valley's steep side. "Can I go with him, sir?" Lieutenant Love asked eagerly.

"Wait here, Lieutenant. Rest."

"I really do need to see that road, sir," Love appealed.

"You'll see it, Lieutenant. Within an hour you'll walk it."

"I do pray so, sir."

"Pray on, Lieutenant," Sharpe said curtly, then looked up to see that Daniel Hagman had settled beside a rock and was gazing intently upward.

"Wait here, Pat, I'll be back," Sharpe said, then looked at Love. "Stay with Sergeant Harper, Lieutenant."

"Of course, sir," the lieutenant said meekly.

Sharpe clambered up the slope, keeping to the grass so that the metal scabbard of his heavy cavalry sword did not clash against a rock. He climbed the last few paces slowly and carefully, then dropped beside Hagman and eased his rifle over a clump of coarse foliage.

"Forty-three horses, Mister Sharpe," Hagman said, "and the buggers are on the ridge above."

Sharpe could see them above, a line of men stretching away from him high on the rocky ridge. The men were ragged and dressed mostly in old Spanish uniforms that were much patched and faded by the sun. To their north, behind the ridge, a group of horses were picketed. He looked back to the men, all of whom had muskets. "They still think we're south of them."

"That's the way they're looking," Hagman said. "Spaniards."

"Aye, they're *guerrilleros*. Probably the ones we're sent to meet."

"So I shouldn't shoot at them again?"

"Best not, Dan."

Sharpe spent some minutes staring at the hill above him

and reckoned he could climb up the southern edge of the ridge's flank and stay out of sight of the men lining the long skyline. "I'm waiting to see if they bugger off," he told Dan.

"I think they're half asleep, Mister Sharpe."

"I'll give them a few minutes." Sharpe suspected these were the men he had been sent to contact, but rather than startle them and provoke more musket fire he would prefer to wait till they had withdrawn and he could contact them more peaceably. "Have a nap, Dan," he said. "I'll watch. Just don't snore."

He waited.

"What's he waiting for?" Lieutenant Love asked.

"He's putting them to sleep, sir," Harper said.

"Sleep?"

"Easier to kill when they're asleep."

"Kill!" Love sounded outraged. "Those men are probably our allies!"

"Aye, sir, but they shot at Mister Sharpe, and no one does that without getting a good kicking."

"He must forgive their mistake!"

"He's not a very forgiving officer, sir."

"If Major Sharpe causes harm to our allies, I will be forced to make a report."

"Won't do any good, sir."

"Sergeant—" Love began.

"The thing is, sir," Harper interrupted him, "Mister Sharpe is in Nosey's good books."

"Nosey? Oh, you mean Lord Wellington."

"Whenever Nosey's in trouble, sir, he sends for Mister Sharpe, on account that Mister Sharpe is a devil."

"A devil?" Love sounded shocked.

"You've not seen him fight, sir. He's a bloody savage in a fight."

Lieutenant Love looked troubled. "I've no doubt he's effective, Sergeant, but essentially this is a reconnaissance and a diplomatic mission to allies. It calls for subtlety and forbearance."

"But they sent us, sir, and essentially that means they want someone properly buggered."

"Do watch your language, Sergeant."

"Of course, sir, bloody sorry, sir."

"We come, we look, and we go," Love said, "no need for picking unnecessary fights."

"They have exploring officers to do the looking, sir, but Nosey picked Mister Sharpe, and that means he expects someone to get hurt. Probably wants it."

"But our orders are to come, look, and leave without the enemy realizing we're here."

"We'll do the reconnaissance, sir, don't you worry about that, but Mister Sharpe will let the enemy know we're here."

"He'll disobey orders?" Love sounded incredulous.

"He's Mister Sharpe, sir, and that's what he does. He's the best soldier in our army, sir, which is why Nosey likes him."

Love shook his head. "Intelligence tells us there are at least a thousand French troops not far from here. And we are sixteen men. Major Sharpe is not a fool."

"No, he's not," Harper agreed, "and it makes me feel sorry for the Crapauds because they don't know he's coming. And he is coming, sir, right now." Harper nodded up the hillside where Sharpe was scrambling back down toward the stream. "Lord Wellington's devil himself, sir."

Sharpe gathered his men on the stream bank. "You filled your canteens?" he asked and, when they all nodded, he jerked his head up the slope to where Hagman lay. "We're going up there, lads," he said. "Single file. Sergeant Harper and I lead, Sergeant Latimer and Lieutenant Love at the rear." From the corner of his eye Sharpe saw Love about to protest, so hurried on. "We go silent!" He stressed the word. "Make sure your rifle butts don't hit a rock, and be bloody sure they're not cocked. The idiots at the top of the hill are supposed to be on our side so we keep them alive."

"Pity," someone muttered.

"Let's go," Sharpe said, but before he could start back up the slope Lieutenant Love intercepted him.

"Shouldn't I be with you, sir?"

"What happens if one of those buggers shoots me, Lieutenant?"

"Surely that won't happen, sir."

"They've already tried once. If I die, you're in charge." And God help my men in that case, Sharpe thought. "And one of us must survive, which is why you're in the safest place. And if the buggers do put a ball in my skull, Lieutenant, you listen to Pat Harper. He'll know what to do."

"We'll do our duty, sir!" Love said.

"And you bury me with my sword, Lieutenant. Where I'll be going, I'll need a good weapon." He left Love looking

11

shocked and climbed to where Harper was waiting. "Bloody Cupid," he grumbled. "I told him to listen to you if I get killed, but if I were you, I'd slit his scrawny throat before he gets all of you slaughtered."

"Be a pleasure, sir," Harper said.

The two climbed the slope, going slowly in their care to be silent. "So who's the fellow we're meeting?" Harper asked.

"Calls himself El Héroe."

"The hero! He's not very good."

"Supposed to be one of the best guerrilla fighters in Spain."

"A real hero, is he?"

"Buggered if I know, Pat. Probably not."

"Just wishful thinking then." Harper was carrying his rifle in his right hand while over his left shoulder was slung his seven-barreled gun, a monstrous weapon designed for the Royal Navy. Its seven barrels were bunched together and fired by a single flintlock that sparked the explosion that would gout seven half-inch pistol balls. The navy had wanted it to clear enemy sharp-shooters from their rigging, but the gun's recoil had broken men's shoulders and only the strongest sailors could use the weapon. Harper was huge, almost as tall as Lieutenant Love and twice as broad, and totally capable of firing the massive weapon.

"Is that toy loaded?" Sharpe asked.

"Of course."

"Maybe we'll use it to wake the bastards up."

El Héroe might be reputed to be one of the finest *guerrillero* leaders in Spain, but he had set no sentries to watch his flank and if Sharpe had been leading a company of French Voltigeurs he would have found El Héroe's men easy meat.

They climbed higher and, looking to his right, Sharpe saw a silvery glint somewhere in the hilly land to the north. The River Tagus, he thought, sliding westward in its journey to the sea. "That's where we're going," he spoke softly to Harper, pointing at the distant river.

"Another day's march then," the Irishman said.

"Much less." Sharpe pushed on ahead, passing the place where he had watched with Hagman, then cautiously clambering up the flank of the ridge where the partisans waited. He stopped between two vast gray rocks where he could peer over the crest and see the *guerrilleros* still lining the long ridge. The nearest was some twenty paces away, a young man with long black hair and a dull red jacket. The young man was holding a British musket. It was cocked.

Sharpe ducked back and waited as his men assembled. Then, very obviously, he cocked his rifle. The two clicks sounded unnaturally loud to him and were followed by the same noise as his men pulled back their dogheads, but no sound came from the *guerrilleros* who still waited and watched the country to the south.

"Wake 'em up, Pat," Sharpe said.

Harper exchanged his rifle for the volley gun, braced it at his hip, cocked it, and pulled the trigger. It sounded like a small cannon firing and belched a cloud of thick powder smoke as the seven bullets seared into the sky.

"Up, boys," Sharpe said and led his men onto the ridge's top, where they made a line with rifles at their shoulders. The *guerrilleros* were scrambling backward from the crest, panicked by the noise, and now turned toward the riflemen.

"*Somos Ingleses!*" Sharpe bellowed. "*Ingleses!*"

"*E Irlandés*, you dozy bastards!" Harper shouted.

"Rifles down, lads, make them safe," Sharpe ordered, then shouted again, "*Somos Ingleses! Somos amigos!*"

One man panicked and fired his musket, but he was over a hundred paces away and the ball went high. "*Amigos!*" Sharpe bellowed. "*Ingleses!*"

Someone shouted from along the ridge and the *guerrilleros* lowered their muskets, though a few still stared suspiciously at the green-jacketed men who had suddenly appeared on their flank. The man who had shouted at them to be calm kept calling, telling them to hold their fire, then, accompanied by four companions, he started walking toward Sharpe.

"That has to be the hero," Harper said, amused.

The man was an extraordinary figure, immaculate in a bright yellow uniform crossed by two white sashes. He wore thigh-length boots, had a saber scabbarded at his side, the pommel of the hilt looked like a lump of gold, cast into a lion's head. There was a gold-edged scarlet strip about his waist and his black cocked hat had a high white plume that nodded as he walked. "Dragoon uniform," Harper said.

"Looks like a clown to me," Sharpe grunted.

The yellow coat had scarlet turnbacks and was lavishly embroidered with silver lacing. A golden star hung from a blue ribbon about the man's neck and the broad white sashes of white silk were tasseled in scarlet. His cavalry breeches had a scarlet line down each side, tucked into the tall black boots that were polished and furnished with golden spurs that kept snagging in the coarse grass. He was a tall man, not young, but not old either. Sharpe guessed El Héroe, if it was indeed him, must be around forty years old. "Handsome bugger," Harper grunted. And that was true. El Héroe was as tall as Sharpe, well built and had a confident face, bright blue eyes, and a firm jawline. He stopped some five paces from Sharpe.

"*Quién eres?*" he demanded brusquely.

"Major Sharpe, 95th Rifles," Sharpe said. "And you are?"

"*Yo soy* El Héroe," El Héroe announced grandly. "*Hablas español?*"

"Not a word," Sharpe lied.

"Fortune for you," El Héroe said slowly, "I have the English. You bring me rifles?"

"I bring you riflemen."

"I demanded rifles!"

"And you got them," Sharpe said, "with men trained to use them."

"You are major?"

"I am."

"I am general. You obey me."

"That's usually how it works," Sharpe said.

"You give me rifles, Major."

"No," Sharpe said.

El Héroe laughed and it seemed genuine amusement. "You disobey first order, Major, I like you! You bring money too?"

"Gold," Sharpe said.

"You give it now," El Héroe demanded.

"When I'm ready," Sharpe said. He instinctively disliked El Héroe. Part of that dislike, he knew, was a sergeant's mistrust of officers. The army, Sharpe had long concluded, was run by the sergeants; men who knew their business but who were commanded by younger men who knew less of soldiering yet who expected instant obedience. Sharpe had been a sergeant himself. "You'll get the gold," he told El Héroe, "when you've shown me what you want doing."

"I want you to kill Frenchmen!" El Héroe paused, astonished by the tall, lanky figure of Lieutenant Love. "Who are you?"

"Lieutenant Love, sir, Royal Artillery."

"You bring cannon?"

"No, sir."

"Then why you come?" El Héroe dismissed Love and looked back to Sharpe. "We go kill Frenchmen, Major. You have horses?"

"We're infantry," Sharpe said caustically, "we have shoes."

"Then follow me!"

Sharpe followed.

It had begun ten days before inside Badajoz, the Spanish border city that the British had captured. Sharpe still had nightmares of that attack, of the ditch of steaming dead, of the fires in the night and the screams of the dying. The South Essex, the redcoat battalion to which Sharpe's riflemen were attached, had been ordered to remain in Badajoz, where Sharpe had received an order to report to Major-General Sir Rowland Hill.

"Daddy" Hill he was called, a nickname that sprang from the affection soldiers felt for the man. Sharpe had met Hill once and been surprised that Daddy Hill was young, no older than Sharpe himself, who reckoned he was thirty-five. He was not sure because he had been born to a London whore who was long dead, and he had been raised in a workhouse where birthdays were neither known nor celebrated. Men reckoned they could tell the age of a horse by its teeth and Sharpe reckoned his teeth were still young so thirty-five seemed about right.

General Hill had quarters in a house that overlooked a small square. The house was guarded by three men wearing the red coats and yellow facings of the 29th, a Worcestershire regiment. One of them, a sergeant, looked askance at Sharpe, noting the red officer's sash but also the faded and patched jacket and the rifle hanging at Sharpe's right shoulder. Sharpe might also carry a sword, but a longarm was no officer's weapon. "You have business here?" the sergeant demanded brusquely.

"The scruffy rascal has business here, Sergeant!" a voice called from an upper-floor window. "Major Sharpe! Welcome!"

Sharpe looked up and grinned. It was Major Michael Hogan who had called down. "Sweet Christ," Sharpe said, "if you're here there must be trouble."

"I'm trying to win the war, Major! And astonishingly I need your help. Come on up."

"Sorry, sir," the sergeant said in a low voice. "Didn't recognize you. If I'd known you were Major Sharpe, sir." He left it at that.

"I don't recognize myself sometimes, Sergeant," Sharpe said. "Straight through?" he asked, gesturing at the house.

"And up the stairs, sir."

The stairs led to a wide parlor. A crucifix hung on one wall, the ceiling was crossed by dark wooden beams, the floor was wide polished planks. A big round table stood between windows overlooking the plaza, the table covered with maps over which Major Hogan stood, grinning broadly. "Ah, it's grand to see you, Richard! You're looking well, but a bit thin. The army's feeding you properly?"

"It'll be a cool day in hell when they start to do that. You look well yourself, sir."

"None of the 'sir' business," Hogan said. "We're the same rank. And you deserve it, Richard."

"I wouldn't know about that," Sharpe just managed to avoid adding "sir." "And you're well?"

"I thrive like the wicked," Hogan said happily. "A glass of wine? It's General Hill's wine and he won't mind." He poured a glass for Sharpe. "The general's in the necessary. He ate something he shouldn't."

"And you're on his staff now?"

"Bless you, no. I was sent down by the Peer," he meant the Viscount Wellington, "I am a mere dogsbody, not a hero like you." Hogan brought the glass of wine to Sharpe. "It is grand to see you. And I was in Elvas yesterday and saw your Teresa. She's looking splendid and your daughter's thriving: a fine bonny baby! You're a lucky man, Richard."

"I am," Sharpe said. His heart had leaped at the mention of Teresa's name. He had married her, fathered a daughter on her, but after the horrors of Badajoz she had gone to relatives in the Portuguese town of Elvas. "I've not seen Teresa for a fortnight," Sharpe said awkwardly. "They've kept us busy."

"Doing God's work?"

"Burying and burning the dead seems more like the devil's work."

"You're the ideal man for that," Hogan said cheerfully, "and you might see Teresa sooner than you think. I've work for you both."

"Work?"

"We'll let the general explain," Hogan said, straightening one of the maps on the big table. "A fellow called Lopez made most of these maps, and a fine imagination he has! He adds roads where he thinks they ought to be. Still, they're the best we have till we make our own." He touched Sharpe's elbow as he heard footsteps outside. "Remember, Daddy doesn't like swearing." He turned as a door opened into the room and General Hill entered, followed by an aide. "You're looking better, sir," Hogan greeted him.

"You lie, Hogan, you lie," Hill said. He looked pale. He was a stout, amiable man, noted as much for his kindness as well as his stoicism in battle. He smiled at Sharpe. "You must be Major Sharpe. We met, didn't we?"

"Before Talavera, sir, yes."

"I remember. It's good to see you again, Major. This is Captain Pearce, one of my aides." The captain gave Sharpe a respectful nod, but looked somewhat shocked by Sharpe's ragged appearance. Hill grinned. "You're an odd duck, Major."

"I am, sir?"

"A rifleman serving in a county regiment? How did that happen?"

"By accident, sir. We were attached to the South Essex for a temporary duty and have just stayed there."

"Well, I'm detaching you and your men for another temporary duty. How many Greenjackets do you have?"

"Fifteen, sir."

Hill grimaced. "Is that enough?" He offered the question to Hogan.

"If Major Sharpe leads them, sir, it's more than enough. And we can reinforce him with *Señora* Moreno's partisans."

"Not sure I like the idea of sending a woman to war, Hogan."

"The woman would disagree with you, sir. Teresa is deadly."

"The world changes," Hill said, "it does indeed, but let's set about changing it a little more." He crossed to the table and gazed down at the map, which showed all of Portugal and most of western Spain. Much of the map was empty white space on which the major towns showed black, joined by a spidery network of roads. "Spain and Portugal," Hill said proudly, almost as if he owned the countries.

"Looks mostly empty," Sharpe said.

"It's filled with nasty Frenchmen," Hill said, "and you're going to help me evict them." He picked up a piece of charcoal and ran it over the thin dotted line that showed the border between Portugal and Spain. "We possess Portugal and the Frogs have Spain. We must take it from them."

"Indeed, sir," Sharpe said, only because Hill had evidently expected some response.

The general leaned over the map and used the charcoal to draw a line from the Atlantic coast of Portugal deep into the heart of Spain. "The River Tagus, Sharpe. The longest river in

Spain, and it divides the western half of the peninsula and it's a wide river!"

"I've seen it, sir," Sharpe said.

"So you know it ain't easily crossed," Hill said. "You need a bridge or a fleet of boats and luckily for the Frogs the Romans left good bridges. Here at Toledo"—he stabbed the charcoal down—"here at Almaraz and here at Alcántara."

"The Almaraz bridge wasn't Roman," Captain Pearce put in. "Much later, sir."

"You are a constant source of knowledge, Horace," Hill said good-naturedly. He used the charcoal to ring the bridges. "Those bridges are important, Major. They link the French armies in the north of Spain with their forces in the south. They can forget Alcántara, it's broken, as is the bridge at Almaraz, but the clever buggers have built a pontoon bridge there instead. They can keep Toledo for now." He drew another charcoal ring round the central bridge, which was evidently at the place called Almaraz, then sketched quick lines in the country to the south. "Marshal Soult is down here, Major, with fifty thousand troops, while up here"—he sketched more hatched lines in the country north of the bridge—"is General Marmont with another fifty thousand unwashed rascals. If the Peer," he meant the Viscount Wellington, "decides to attack Monsieur Marmont, what will Monsieur Soult do?"

"March to help him," Sharpe guessed.

"And then the rascals will outnumber us three to one and we'll all end up buried," Hill said cheerfully. "And if the Peer decides to spank Soult? The same thing, Marmont marches south, so our job is to make it doubly difficult for either to help the other."

"By blocking the river."

"Precisely. The Peer said you were a very intelligent fellow."

Had Wellington really said that, Sharpe wondered, then forgot the question as Hill drew another circle round the bridge at Alcántara. "They can't use this bridge, it's shattered. We don't mind if they use Toledo, because it's a long march inland and it will take two weeks for an army to get from one side of the river to the other. Even longer if they send some troops through Talavera." The general sketched a quick circle even farther inland from Toledo. "You captured an eagle there, yes?"

"I did, sir."

"Then you're a fine fellow, Sharpe! So the scoundrels can have the bridges at Toledo and Talavera, but we have to take away their pontoon bridge at Almaraz." He stabbed the charcoal down so hard that it shattered, scattering black scraps across the pristine map. "The trouble is the Frogs aren't complete idiots. They know the value of the Almaraz bridge so they're protecting it with two forts and outlying bastions. Tough little nuts with stone walls and emplaced cannon. Horace?"

Pearce immediately obliged by producing another map, this one a crude pencil-and-ink plan that showed the river at its center. The bridge of Almaraz was shown as a line of small boats, while just upstream was a second bridge, with a gap in it. "The old stone bridge," Hill said, tapping it, "also destroyed, though we hear the French are trying to repair it." He moved the charcoal to the pontoon bridge and tapped it on an inked square to the south. "Fort Napoleon," he said, "with probably seven or eight cannon and a garrison of three or four hundred men." He tapped another square north of the river. "Fort Ragusa, with the same kind of garrison. Both forts overlook the pontoon bridge, so we can't get to the boats without coming under fire. Besides which there are two smaller defensive works right at the end of the bridge, one to the south and one to the north."

"*Têtes de pont* bastions," the aide murmured.

"Thank you, Horace," Hill said with an edge of sarcasm. "We'll approach from the west," Hill was talking to Sharpe again, "but up in the hills here there's an old castle called . . ." he hesitated.

"Miravete," the aide murmured.

"Miravete," Hill went on as though he had not needed the reminder, "which the Frogs have fortified and added cannon to stop any approach from the west. "And Miravete Castle is a tough nut, eh Hogan?"

"It will need siege guns," Hogan said.

"Which we must drag a hundred miles. But I'm ordered to destroy the pontoon bridge," he went on. "And to get to the bridge I must first reduce Miravete Castle, which will give plenty of time for the French to reinforce the forts at the river. So in an ideal world, which the good Lord knows this one is not, I need to get the guns past the castle so I can engage the forts first. Any thoughts, Sharpe?"

Sharpe stared down at the sketch map. "There must be a way round the castle, sir?"

"There is. There's a guerrilla leader in those hills, fellow who calls himself El Héroe, who says there's a track that avoids the castle. He reckons we sneak by on that track and attack Fort Napoleon without waking up the wretches in Miravete."

"And El Héroe is reliable?" Sharpe asked.

"He claims to be the best guerrilla leader in all Spain," Hogan said. Sharpe detected skepticism in his old friend's voice.

"Really?"

"He told us so himself," Hogan said. "But truth is we know very little about El Héroe. One of our exploring officers met him and reported that El Héroe has a grand opinion of himself, which may or may not be justified. He loves money, we know that, and we pay him well for his information, which has proved useful. He promised he would help us."

"For a price," Horace put in drily.

"For a price, indeed," Hogan agreed. "Our hero wants British rifles and a thousand guineas in gold. In return he'll destroy the works at the old bridge."

"The works, sir?"

Hill moved a charcoal-stained finger to the old bridge that lay just upstream of the pontoon bridge. "That's the old bridge. The northern span was blown by the Spanish three years ago to stop the Frogs from crossing the river. El Héroe tells us the Frogs have an encampment there and it's manned by engineers who are trying to repair the bridge. Not much point in us blowing up their pontoon bridge if they can rebuild the old bridge. So we need to know about that encampment and how well it's defended."

"How far is the old bridge from the new one?" Sharpe asked.

Hill looked at Captain Pearce. "Just over half a mile," the aide said.

"But if we capture their forts," Sharpe suggested, "the works at the old bridge will be indefensible."

"And to capture their forts," Hill said firmly, "I need artillery. Heavy artillery, and I have to move it a hundred miles, then get it past Miravete Castle to the river. I need to know if that's possible."

"Eminently possible as far as Miravete Castle," Hogan said. "It's the last few miles to the river that we don't know about. If we can't capture the castle immediately, we can't use the main road to the bridge, which means dragging the guns over hilly country, which might not be feasible."

"So you want an opinion on that, sir?" Sharpe asked.

"We do, which is why an artilleryman will accompany you. A Lieutenant Love."

"Cupid," Hogan put in mischievously.

"Lieutenant Love," Hill said sternly, "will provide an expert opinion on the viability of hauling heavy guns to attack Fort Napoleon. Your job, Major, is to protect the lieutenant and to gauge the ability of the river forts to resist our assault. It would be best if the French knew nothing of your presence."

"And you must judge whether El Héroe's men are of any use to us," Hogan added.

"And I'm afraid he won't be happy with you," Hill's aide put in. "He demanded a thousand golden guineas and we're sending him a hundred. He also demanded fifty Baker rifles, and we're sending fifteen riflemen instead."

"And one other thing, Richard," Hogan put in quietly. "We haven't told El Héroe that we plan an attack on the bridge, and we don't want him to know. Let him think you're on a reconnaissance, nothing more. If he knows we're coming in force he'll tell his men and the news will spread fast."

"And undoubtedly reach the enemy," Hill said dourly.

"I'll keep quiet, sir," Sharpe promised, "but it sounds as if you don't really trust El Héroe."

"We don't know him," Hogan admitted, "but if he's no good, you'll have La Aguja's men instead."

"And La Aguja herself?" Sharpe asked. The nickname meant "the needle."

"If there are Frenchmen to kill, I won't be able to keep Teresa away. It'll be simple, Richard! March a hundred miles behind enemy lines, have a sniff round the enemy forts, and come back to tell us what you discover! What can go wrong?"

Sharpe said nothing.

El Héroe mounted a fine white stallion. The horse, even to Sharpe's inexpert eye, was superb. The saddle looked new, the bridle was trimmed with silver. The rest of El Héroe's men were mounted on ragged, swaybacked beasts, but the hero had a horse that lived up to its rider's name. "A fine beast," Sharpe remarked.

"I have four of them! Captured from the French, Major. This one was ridden by a colonel, like me."

"You're a colonel now?"

"I was colonel of the *de la Reina* Dragoons, Major. Now I am general. You call me *señor*."

Many of the *guerrilleros* had been in the Spanish armies that had been broken by the French invasion; indeed, most of El Héroe's men were in the tattered remnants of their old uniforms, now much repaired with plain brown cloth. "Where are the *de la Reina* Dragoons now?" Sharpe asked, deliberately not adding *señor*.

"I hope fighting the enemy," El Héroe said airily, "but I do more damage here."

"How many men do you have?" Sharpe asked.

"Hundreds!" El Héroe answered. "You see a few here, but if I snap my fingers, more will come. I have men in every town and village! How else did I know you were coming? My men in Jaraicejo saw you and sent me warning."

That at least explained why El Héroe had laid his ambush on the main road, but did nothing to persuade Sharpe that the man could summon hundreds of troops. He was about to ask more, but Lieutenant Love stepped past him.

"*Señor!*" Lieutenant Love stood close to El Héroe's horse. "I need you to show me the road that leads round Miravete Castle. It is most urgent!"

"Why urgent?" El Héroe asked.

"Because my general asked me, *señor*," Love replied, evidently trying not to betray General Hill's plan to attack the forts.

"Why does he ask?" El Héroe responded. "He plans to come here?"

"No, no," Love said, reddening.

"The general needs to know about every crossing of the Tagus," Sharpe said, hoping Lieutenant Love's words had not betrayed Hill's intent. "And we need accurate maps. We're doing this all along the frontier."

"I will show you the road round Miravete," El Héroe said,

"but you give me gold and rifles first. Now come." He spurred ahead, following a track that led east and north around a high hill that Sharpe supposed overlooked the Tagus. El Héroe had sent no scouts ahead, evidently confident that the French had no patrols in this high country.

Sharpe was not so confident. The morning had been broken with a fusillade of musketry fired by El Héroe's men and that sound had surely carried to the forts beside the river. One musket shot could be ignored as the sound of a hunter, but a crackle of musketry meant soldiers, and if Sharpe were guarding the pontoon bridge, he would have responded by sending men to discover the source of the sound, but El Héroe had dismissed the worry. "They fear me!" he had assured Sharpe. "They stay in their forts and I rule the land!"

"He's a confident bugger," Harper said to Sharpe.

"He's a hero, Pat."

"Aye, and who gave him that name?"

"His men?"

"More like he gave it to himself," Harper said. He was searching the northern skyline, looking for any sign of French troops. "And he's a gaudy bugger, isn't he? Not trying to hide himself."

"Says he doesn't need to. Says he rules the land."

"Aye, and I'm the King of Donegal."

"He might be right," Sharpe said cautiously. If General Hill was correct, the French had close to a thousand men in the forts around the bridges, most at the pontoon bridge and a smaller garrison at Miravete Castle, and those men were either infantry, artillerymen, or engineers. "Reckon six to seven hundred Crapaud infantry," Sharpe said, "and to patrol these hills you'd need to send out at least two companies, and El Héroe can probably confront them with twice that number. You'll lose men every day and you don't have that many to begin with. I reckon the Frogs are bottled up."

"El Héroe," Harper said caustically, "if he fights like he did this morning the Frogs can ignore him."

"Those were warning shots," Sharpe said. "He was hoping we'd turn away."

"No stomach for a fight then."

"We'll see," Sharpe said. In truth he shared Harper's mistrust of El Héroe, but knew that he must rely on the *guerrilleros* to assist his reconnaissance of the forts and he did not want his men infected by that mistrust.

El Héroe led them to an upland village, a place of small houses and stone-walled sheep pens. "We stay here," El Héroe said. "And now the gold, Major?"

The guineas were distributed among Sharpe's riflemen and Sharpe did not doubt that a few had been filched from their calfskin bags. Indeed, he had slid a couple into his own cartridge pouch, but what remained made a glittering pile on a plain table in the house El Héroe had given to the riflemen as their quarters. The pile was big enough to satisfy El Héroe, who rubbed one of the guineas between finger and thumb before biting it. "I take this now," he announced grandly, gesturing at the piled coins, "and buy cannon."

"You'll take it when the job's done," Sharpe said. "You help me look at the French defenses and then I pay you gold."

"I order you," El Héroe said flatly.

"And I disobey your orders," Sharpe said. "The gold is payment for your help, and I'll pay it when we're done." He turned to Latimer. "Bag the gold, Sergeant."

El Héroe watched sullenly as the gold was returned to the small bags. He had kept one coin and now pushed it into a pocket of his yellow coat. Sharpe reckoned he had pushed his luck enough already so let the man keep it. "I want to see the old bridge," he told El Héroe.

"You go that way," El Héroe gestured vaguely northward. "Follow the track and you come to the river. I take you in the morning."

"Is that the track that avoids Miravete Castle?" Sharpe asked.

"It is," El Héroe said, then pointed to the village street through the open door. "That is the road. It begins south of the castle and goes to the river."

"Then I go today," Sharpe said.

"Not today, I forbid it."

"Why not today?"

"If the French see you? They will know trouble comes."

"They won't see me," Sharpe said curtly. "Pat? Dan? With me." He dropped his knapsack on the floor, then took from it his telescope, a beautiful precision instrument made by Matthew Berge of London and a gift from the Viscount Wellington, whose life Sharpe had saved in India.

El Héroe eyed the telescope. "I will buy it from you, Major."

"You will not."

"Allow me?" He held out a hand. *"Por favor?"*

It seemed churlish to refuse so Sharpe reluctantly handed him the glass which El Héroe carried outside. He pulled the tubes open and trained the telescope on a distant crest. "It is magnificent," he said.

"Made in England," Sharpe said.

"I have one made in Madrid," El Héroe announced, still gazing eastward, "and better than this, but heavier. Too heavy." He closed the glass and peered at the engraved plate on the outer barrel. "In gratitude, AW," he read aloud. "Who is AW?"

"A man whose life I saved," Sharpe said.

"AW?" Lieutenant Love interjected, "surely that's not—"

"It's not," Sharpe said abruptly.

"He is a rich man?" El Héroe asked.

"Very rich," Sharpe said. He held out his hand for the glass, but El Héroe was reluctant to let go of it.

"Your rich friend can give you another," he insisted.

"Buy your own," Sharpe said.

"Sell me this one!"

"No," Sharpe said, and reached for the glass, which El Héroe jerked away, then went very still because Harper had just cocked the volley gun, the two clicks echoing from the stone walls of the village church that stood on the far side of the road.

"Sergeant . . ." Lieutenant Love took a half step toward Harper.

"Kill the bugger, Pat," Sharpe said harshly. He knew the massive gun was not loaded, but when Harper put the gun's butt to his shoulder, El Héroe reluctantly handed the telescope back.

"I shall demand one from the British," he said, "along with rifles. Why you no give me rifles?"

"I'm giving you something better," Sharpe said, "rifles with riflemen."

He pushed the telescope under the flap of his cartridge pouch. "You'll feed my men tonight?"

"There are women in the village," El Héroe said airily, "and they will cook."

"Food and wine," Sharpe said.

"Such things cost money," El Héroe said.

"You already have a golden guinea," Sharpe said, "and that'll pay for tonight's rations. You'll get the rest of the gold when we're finished here." He challenged El Héroe with a glare, and when there was no response, he glanced up and down the small street. "Do the French know this is your village?"

"Of course they know."

"Then why don't they attack?"

"They fear me, of course!"

"You have sentries?"

"There are men watching all round, but the French will not come. They fear me!"

"Then tell your sentries to expect us back after dusk and to hold their fire."

"You must not go," El Héroe insisted. "It's not safe for you. Maybe tomorrow?"

"Just make sure your sentries are warned," Sharpe said.

"And I have warned you," El Héroe retorted and then, with a swift and reluctant nod, he led his few companions back down the village street.

"You're not really thinking of going, are you, sir?" Lieutenant Love asked nervously.

"On the one hand," Sharpe said, "that gaudy bugger tells me the French don't dare patrol the hills, then he claims it's unsafe. There's only one way to find out and that's to go look. So we go."

"And if there are French patrols, sir?"

"Of course there are. The Crapauds aren't idiots." Sharpe turned and shouted for Sergeant Latimer to come out of the house. "You're in charge," he told Latimer. "Make sure you keep the rifles safe." He looked at the small house. "Hide the gold in the chimney. If El Héroe asks for it, say I took it with me. And don't interfere with the women here."

"Women, Mister Sharpe?" Latimer brightened.

"Leave them alone. We're here to fight the Crapauds, not El Héroe's men. And put pickets front and back of the house. If you see Frogs, get the hell out. We don't want them to know we're here, so go back the way we came and I'll find you."

"Am I coming with you?" Lieutenant Love asked Sharpe.

"You are," Sharpe said reluctantly. He did not want Love's company, but the lieutenant had been sent to make a judgment on the practicality of the country to bear heavy artillery, so he had better be given every chance to form his opinion.

"What if that Spanish bastard asks me to give him the gold, Mister Sharpe?" Sergeant Latimer asked nervously.

"Tell him to bugger off."

"But politely," Lieutenant Love added.

"Rifleman Harris speaks Spanish," Sharpe said, "and he doesn't know how to be polite. Pat? Dan? You're with me, so let's go. But leave your shakos here." He took off his own shako and tossed it into the house.

"Why no shakos?" Love asked as he walked beside Sharpe with Sergeant Harper and Rifleman Hagman following.

"The easiest way to spot a Crapaud is by their shakos," Sharpe said. "Frog shakos widen to a broad flat top, ours are tall and narrow. Some bloody Frog sees our shakos and he'll know we're British."

"Ah," Love said, "and my hat?" He touched his shako with its distinctive white plume.

"Leave it here," Sharpe said, "and maybe lose the saber too."

"My saber!" Love sounded shocked.

"It tells the enemy you're an officer, which means they'll shoot you first."

"Then I'd best get close to them, sir."

"Close?" Sharpe looked at Love as though he were mad.

"Every artillery officer knows one thing, sir: the closer the target is to the gun, the safer it is." He paused, searching Sharpe's face. "It's a jest, sir."

"I'll remember that, Lieutenant," Sharpe said sourly.

He led the three men north. He had chosen Harper and Hagman because they had the best eyesight of any of his men, and the day was already advanced, the shadows long. They followed the track from the village, which soon shrank to a path just wide enough for one man. A sheep track, Sharpe reckoned, which led along the flank of a hill, dropping steeply to his left and rising to his right. "Lieutenant," Sharpe called back, "what's the width between the wheels of a nine-pounder carriage?"

Love paused, plainly unsure of the answer. "I'd say between five and six feet, sir?"

"And this path is twelve inches wide," Sharpe said.

"Possibly the guns could be drawn along the spine of the hill?" Love suggested.

"Let's look," Sharpe said, and they climbed up to the ridge, which was obstructed by gullies and rocks that would plainly not provide a path for wheeled artillery. Love kept pausing to pencil notes into a small notebook, then hurrying to catch up with Sharpe, who pressed on north. The new height offered a view of the Tagus valley stretching east and west, the river's water glittering under the lowering sun. "The old bridge," Hagman said after a while, and Sharpe looked to his right and saw a massive stone bridge spanning the wide river with two immense arches, the farthest of which was shattered to break the roadway.

"They did a proper job of work on that," Harper said admiringly. The bridge was high above the river, its broken roadway that carried the road between the hills on either bank at least a hundred feet above the water.

"I don't see a pontoon bridge," Sharpe said.

The new temporary bridge was evidently hidden by the spur of the ridge, but Lieutenant Love was still gazing at the broken bridge. "May I borrow your glass, sir?" Lieutenant Love asked.

Sharpe handed the telescope to Love, who used Hagman's shoulder as a rest so he could examine the shattered span. "There are French engineers there, sir. They're constructing a form."

"A form?"

"A wooden structure inside the broken arch, sir. When it's complete it will support a new roadway."

"Then that's one of our targets," Sharpe said grimly, then looked to the left. "I still don't see the pontoon bridge."

"We need to walk on," Lieutenant Love said, "the forts aren't in sight yet." He collapsed the telescope and looked at the engraved brass plate. "AW, sir?" He hesitated. "Arthur Wellesley?"

"He was Sir Arthur back then," Sharpe grunted.

"Then may I inquire why he was grateful to you, sir?" Love asked, giving the glass back to Sharpe.

"I've forgotten," Sharpe said.

"He saved Lord Wellesley's life, sir," Harper said.

"How, pray?"

Sharpe said nothing, just started walking northward again.

"His Lordship was surrounded by heathens, sir," Harper said, "his horse dead and a long ways from friendly troops. Mister Sharpe killed the heathens, sir, every last one of the buggers. He's good at that." He hesitated. "Which is why, if you do write a protest, sir, His Lordship will likely use it to wipe his bum."

"We must catch up with Major Sharpe," Love said hurriedly.

Sharpe had stopped on a spur of rock that overlooked the valley of the Tagus. To his right was the broken bridge, while to the left were the pontoon bridge and its guardian forts. Harper gazed down at the nearest fort. "God save Ireland," he murmured, "but that's a proper bastard."

"It's not going to be easy," Sharpe said mildly, taking out his telescope again. The fort was indeed formidable, built atop a small hill. A ditch had been excavated around the hill's summit, and within the ditch was a stone-built square fortress with a tall lookout tower. Sharpe could see the muzzles of cannon in the fort's embrasures. A French flag hung in the windless air on top of the tower.

"Those are big walls," Harper said. "Glad it's not us who has to take them."

"Cannon there too," Hagman said.

"A right bastard," Harper said.

Sharpe said nothing. He was gazing through the telescope and saw nothing to contradict Harper's gloomy assessment. There were dozens of blue-coated French infantry on the battlements and presumably more in the courtyard.

"So that's Fort Napoleon," Lieutenant Love said.

"He's welcome to it," Harper grunted, "let him keep it."

"And there's another on the far bank," Hagman said, "just as bad."

"Fort Ragusa." Sharpe raised the glass and saw that the northern fort was slightly smaller than Fort Napoleon, but just as formidable with a ditch, a stone wall, and cannon mounted in the embrasures. Between the two forts were two smaller bastions, the ones General Hill's aide had called *têtes de pont.* They were small stone forts, little more than stout barricades that guarded the ends of the bridge and were equipped with cannon and manned by blue-coated infantry-men. Between them stretched the pontoon bridge, a long line of anchored barges spanning the river and overlaid with a plank road. Sharpe counted twenty pontoons, which were not quite enough to span the river so the French had put two local boats, perhaps ferries, in the center of the bridge. The line of boats bowed slightly to the west, pushed by the river's current and straining the anchor cables. The river looked to be about five hundred yards wide. "Easiest thing to do," Harper said, "is put some cannon up here and bomb the shit out of the bridge."

"Then they just repair it," Sharpe said. He was gazing at a small village that lay close to the pontoon bridge on Fort Napoleon's bank. The village might be small, but it contained large warehouses and a quay where a single riverboat was tethered. He could see more French infantry there. "That's a supply depot," he muttered.

"Lugar Nuevo," Lieutenant Love offered, "it is indeed a supply depot, sir, quite an important one, I'm told."

Sharpe turned the glass eastward and trained it on the old bridge and saw a small encampment built against the massive wall that carried the roadway from the southern hills to the first arch. Supposedly that was where the French engineers were working to repair the old bridge, but the encampment was too far away to see any detail. There were men there, he could see the smoke of fires, but he could not make out any detail. "We have to get closer."

"The enemy can see us here," Love said nervously. "We're on their skyline."

"They don't see red coats or British shakos," Sharpe said, "and they know El Héroe's men are in these hills." He collapsed the telescope. "I want a closer look at the old bridge."

"We can see it from here, sir," Love pointed out.

"Best place to look is from the bridge itself," Sharpe said.

They scrambled down the hillside, then walked north on the narrow track which, after half a mile, joined the main road that led from Miravete Castle to the bridge. Sharpe half expected there would be French sentries on the old bridge, which was high enough to give good views up and down the river valley, but the broken roadway was deserted. It seemed fool-hardy to walk onto the bridge itself, but it was unguarded and so Sharpe led them some forty or fifty yards along the road, then he leaned over the western parapet and found himself staring straight down into the encampment, which he saw was filled with enormous carts, each one as long as a barge. "Pontoon carriages," he said, "but no spare pontoons."

"And not many men," Harper added.

"Just a dozen of the dozy buggers," Hagman said.

Sharpe, careless that the men below might see him, leaned over the parapet and trained the glass. Hagman was right, there were only a dozen men visible and they were relaxing in the afternoon's last light. Five were sitting round a fire. They were handing two bottles around, while one used a length of wood to light a cigar. He could hear the laughter. One man was standing on a makeshift firing platform gazing upriver toward the bridge of boats and he appeared to be the only sentry. Two men were bringing a cooking pot to the fire. He swept the glass around the small encampment that was ringed with a wooden palisade, all except its northern flank, where the riverbank was a shallow shelving beach. That made sense as the best place to launch the heavy pontoons that were then floated downstream to where the engineers had decided was the best place to make the temporary bridge. He moved the glass around the camp's edge and saw cannons pointing west-ward. Big cannon. So presumably there were gunners in the encampment as well as infantry. There were muskets stacked beside a large hut that was presumably their living quarters. He counted twenty-four muskets. "Officer coming," Harper murmured, and Sharpe looked up from the glass to see the Irishman pointing downriver. A lone French officer was approaching the encampment on a horse, calmly and slowly walking the beast along a riverside path that led from Fort Napoleon. "And the bugger has seen us," Harper said.

"Wave at him."

"Wave?"

"He'll think we're his men."

"I can shoot him," Hagman offered.

"Wave!"

They all duly waved and the man raised a nonchalant hand in reply and kept his horse at the slow walk.

"Good Lord!" Lieutenant Love exclaimed excitedly.

"Good Lord?" Sharpe asked.

"We just waved to the enemy, sir! That's extraordinary!"

Sharpe handed the telescope to Love. "Have a peer at the cannon down there, Lieutenant," he said, "and tell me what they are."

Love leaned over the parapet and Sharpe heard the lieutenant hiss. "Bad news?" he asked.

"Iron cannon, sir, painted black, and big! I do believe they're twenty-four-pounders! Garrison guns and very nasty. Probably captured from the Spanish. Oh! And that's interesting."

"What?"

"They have some old four-pounders. I swear that's what they are, but I've never seen one before!"

"Bugger the four-pounders," Sharpe said, "it's the big ones I don't like."

"Those fours," Love said, "can throw canister. It's what they're best at."

The cannons commanded every approach to the encampment, pointing north and west, and were presumably there to destroy any attempt to assault the small garrison that protected the engineers repairing the bridge. Sharpe was tempted to go farther south along the bridge to peer down the roadway's broken edge, but he had seen enough and so instead reached to take the telescope from Love. "Time we went," he said.

"Listen!" Harper urged. Sharpe went still and listened. He could hear the voices of the men round the fire, then heard what must have alerted Harper; the sound of women laughing too.

"Dear God," Harper said, "they've got frows with them!" He bent over the parapet again. "They must be in that hut!"

"And men are leaving Fort Napoleon," Hagman said.

Sharpe used the glass and saw a file of men leaving the distant fort. He counted twenty-one, all of them going southward toward the higher hills; toward El Héroe's lair. "They're far enough away," he said, "and we'll stay clear of the bastards. Come on, lads."

None of it made sense to Sharpe. He was not surprised there were women in the enemy camp; soldiers picked up women like dogs found fleas, but the nonchalance of the lone officer was more than strange. The French sent messengers between their armies in Spain and each messenger needed hundreds of cavalrymen to escort him safely through the land dominated by the *guerrilleros*, yet here a Frenchman thought it safe to wander the mile-long path between the bridges. Maybe the Frenchman was right and the path was simply too close to the forts to offer any partisan a safe retreat into the hills, but still the Frenchman's confidence worried him.

They were retracing their steps, walking along the low ridge that carried the old road away from the broken bridge. "Did either of you count the pontoon carriages?" Sharpe asked, mentally blaming himself for not having counted them.

"Twenty," Hagman said, "big buggers!"

"They have to be big to carry the pontoons," Sharpe said, "and they must weigh two or three tons each."

"A lot of horses."

"Which we can't see, so they were taken away," Sharpe decided.

"Why don't they keep the carriages in the fort?" Harper wondered.

"Too big," Sharpe said, "and they'd just clutter up the courtyard. That fort isn't big enough. So they're keeping the carriages where they launched the pontoons." He thought for a heartbeat. "And the buggers didn't have much masonry there."

"Masonry?" Harper asked.

"They're supposed to have engineers repairing the bridge. There's not a lot of stone being worked on the bridge."

"There was plenty on the three stacks, Mister Sharpe," Hagman added. "It was all cut and ready."

"They'll mostly use timber for the repair," Lieutenant Love suggested. "It would be much quicker than cutting more stone."

Sharpe nodded. "Probably, but whatever they're using, they're not bothering to guard it properly."

"Dozy buggers," Hagman said happily.

Sharpe glanced behind as they walked away from the bridge. "We'll be coming back here," he said.

"Tonight?" Harper asked enthusiastically.

"I'll let them live another few days," Sharpe said, knowing he had to report to General Hill within a week or so, and only after that could he look forward to taking the war to the two forts and the old bridge.

"You're a living saint, so you are," Harper said.

The living saint was thinking about the twenty-one men seen leaving the fort. "There's a castle over there," Sharpe said, waving southwest. "I'm reckoning they're heading for it."

"Not in our way then?" Harper asked.

"They'll be going away from us," Sharpe said.

"They're not," Hagman said. "Buggers are on that hill." He nodded westward across a shallow valley where a small stream fell to the Tagus. He was nodding toward the hill from which Sharpe had first seen the pontoon bridge.

Sharpe looked, saw nothing. "You sure, Dan?"

"Can't mistake a fat Crapaud hat," Hagman said. "Buggers are just the other side of the crest."

"Between us and the hero," Harper said. "Reckon they were sent to capture us."

"Or kill us," Hagman added darkly.

"Oh good Lord," Love said nervously. He touched the hilt of his holstered pistol. "Twenty-one of them?"

"Against three riflemen," Sharpe said nonchalantly, "so seven each."

"Sir!" Lieutenant Love began.

"Don't worry, Lieutenant," Sharpe interrupted, "we'll leave one for you."

To his left there was a low hill crowned with rocks. "Up there, lads," he said, "and let's see if they want to play games."

They scrambled up the bare slope and dropped behind the summit rocks. The sun was about to fall below the western horizon. Not much time till full dark, Sharpe thought, but time enough if the damned French wanted to play. He cocked his rifle and waited.

CHAPTER 2

It was not, Sharpe decided, a bad place to be. He had thought the rocky crest was the top of a hill, but once there he saw it was the head of a spur jutting from the larger hill behind. Still, the slopes of the spur were steep, the summit rocks gave good cover, and the French would be forced to approach across the valley where the small stream tumbled. They could try to outflank him by going either north or south, but he would see them unless the night fell. For now the French had gone to ground, sheltering on the far crest. "Two hours' dusk and twilight left," he muttered.

"Not much light," Harper responded.

"There's enough for now," Sharpe said. He was lying between two rocks, his rifle pointing across the valley, which he reckoned to be about four hundred paces across. Far too wide for a musket to be effective from the farther side, but well within killing range of the Baker rifle. How long, he thought, would it take the French to cross the valley? If they ran, and he reckoned they would have to run to stand any chance of reaching him, it would be three minutes, maybe four, with the last hundred paces steeply uphill. Call it four minutes, which meant three riflemen could loose off four shots each. Even if only half of the shots were effective, the French would have lost six men. That would discourage them.

Sharpe was on the right of the rocks with Lieutenant Love, Harper was six paces away, and Hagman about ten paces farther south. "Dan!"

"Mister Sharpe?" Hagman was always punctilious.

"If you can see the buggers, take down the guys on their right! Pat? Chew up the center of their line."

"Seven men each, eh?" Harper said. He was prone like Sharpe and had his volley gun lying next to his rifle. Reloading the rifles would be slow because it was awkward to charge a barrel while lying flat, so Sharpe reckoned he might only get off three shots before the enemy were among the rocks with their bayonets. He looked to his right, looking for more men coming from the encampment by the bridge, but nothing showed there except the river surging past the great stone pier that supported the broken roadway. "Can you see them, Dan?" Sharpe called.

"I can see one bugger, rest are hiding, Mister Sharpe."

"Kill your bugger."

"Pleasure, Mister Sharpe."

"Is that wise, sir?" Lieutenant Love asked in a whisper. He had drawn his pistol and was ramming a bullet down its small barrel.

"Wise?" Sharpe asked.

"Why provoke them, sir?"

"You think they'll just go away if we do nothing?"

Love hesitated, then admitted, "I don't know, sir."

"They want to kill us," Sharpe said, "or at least capture one of us. So we have to dissuade them. And the best way to do that is to kill them."

"Twenty-one of them!" Love protested.

"Hush, Lieutenant." Sharpe heard a sound as Hagman rested his rifle on a low boulder, then the double click of the doghead being pulled back to full cock. He stared across the valley. The sun had sunk beneath a rill of cloud, but still the light in the west made it difficult to see anything on the far ridge. It was a low ridge and the French were concealed behind it. Or perhaps they had sent men south to outflank him? He looked that way just in time to see the jet of smoke from Hagman's rifle. The noise echoed back at Sharpe. "Twenty men now, Mister Sharpe," Hagman called.

"You sure, Dan?"

"Unless the bugger can live with a ball in his noggin."

"You've got another six to finish off, Dan," Harper called.

Hagman had rolled onto his back, pulled the rifle down until the muzzle was at his neck, and was pouring powder from a cartridge into the rifle's barrel. He had torn open a dozen cartridges and laid them on a flat rock next to their bullets, each of which rested on a small square of leather. He folded a leather patch round one of the bullets, pushed it into the rifle's muzzle, and rammed it down, then rolled back, thrust the rifle forward, and used his powder horn to prime the lock. "Ready, Mister Sharpe."

Sharpe copied him, tearing open four cartridges and taking four leather patches from the small brass-lidded compartment in the rifle's stock. He laid the patches on a flat rock and put a bullet on each one. It would make reloading much faster. He looked back across the valley, then leftward to see if the enemy was trying to outflank him and right to see if reinforcements were coming from the bridge. He saw nothing. So twenty men left.

"I almost feel sorry for them," Hagman said.

"Why sorry, Dan?" Harper asked.

"Silly buggers have probably never fought riflemen. Don't know what's waiting for them. And they're just lads from the farms."

"Why are you here?" Sharpe asked.

"Here, Mister Sharpe?" Hagman asked. "To throw the buggers out of Spain."

"And will we do that by shooting them, or by feeling sorry for them?"

"They're only lads," Hagman said.

"And they won't waste pity on you." Sharpe looked south again. He reckoned the French would have to go at least half a mile that way before they could cross the stream unseen. That is what he would have done if he were leading the Frenchmen. Go south and work his way behind the rocky spur and assault from behind. Then it would be quick and brutal bayonet work at nightfall. "Soon as it's real dark," he called, "we'll keep moving south."

Still there was no movement ahead or to either side. Sharpe assumed the men on the opposite ridge were led by an officer, and was that man waiting for twilight? Sharpe's instinct told him that the men opposing him were not a real threat.

They outnumbered him and a charge across the valley would mean some men inevitably reaching his position, and once the French were within a few yards the rifles would offer no advantage over the French muskets, but in a close fight Sharpe had every confidence in two of his companions. The French would have lost close to half their force to the deadly rifles and then have to deal with Harper's volley gun and his own brutal sword. It would be a nasty fight, but Sharpe did not fear it. He reckoned such a charge was likely, simply because it was the enemy's simplest solution. Of course the opposing officer might already have dispatched half his force north or southward, unseen to Sharpe, but his instinct rejected the idea. The French would go for the easiest solution and doubtless were waiting for the failing light to make aiming rifles difficult. If Dan Hagman was right, then the French patrol had already lost one man at a range when a musket shot would be a sheer fluke, which meant they must realize they were facing rifles, so waiting for the light to fail made some sense for them.

"You reckon they'll come in a line, Mister Sharpe?" Hagman asked.

"I'm sure they will, Dan."

"Makes it easier for us," Hagman said sourly, "but the buggers don't like lines."

"He'll spread them out if he has any sense."

"If he had any sense," Harper said, "he'd crawl back to his bed. Probably got a warm frow waiting for him. Instead he'll kill his men and probably die himself."

"Why are they waiting, sir?" Lieutenant Love hissed at Sharpe.

"Because they don't want to die," Sharpe said, "and they want the sun to go down."

The western clouds were now rimmed with golden fire, the valley darkening with shadow. Sharpe saw a movement on the far ridge and knew it was a man peering round a rock. He lowered his eye to the rifle and folded up the rear sight. The notch in the sight lined with the nub at the muzzle and both lay over the distant face, but Sharpe kept his finger from the trigger. He doubted the shot would be accurate. Dan Hagman could make the shot, but Dan was a phenomenal marksman. "You don't aim," he had once told Sharpe, "you feel the shot."

And who was the man lined up in the crude sights? Hagman was right, it was probably some farm boy from God knows where, forced by conscription into the French ranks and sent to Spain to be shot at by partisans and terrified by cannon fire. Sharpe lowered the rifle so it rested on the turf and twitched with surprise as Hagman fired again.

"Nineteen left," the old poacher said. He had hit another man on the southernmost end of the French line. Sharpe's target had vanished, ducking behind the rock that sheltered him.

"Well done, Dan," Sharpe called.

"Too easy, Mister Sharpe."

The smoke from Hagman's rifle hung above the valley, drifting slowly toward the stream. Sharpe folded the backsight flat again. He felt annoyed. The enemy officer was being stupid, which offended Sharpe. There was a job to be done and the man was doing it all wrong. That, of course, was to Sharpe's advantage, but like Hagman he could not help feeling pity for the youngsters who would die because of it. The opposing officer had not been completely stupid; he had worked out the route Sharpe must take back to the village and set an ambush in a good place that gave him the high ground, and if it had not been for Hagman's keen eyesight the ambush might well have worked. But now, with his plan foiled, the wretched man did not know what to do, or at least he showed no sign of knowing. Sharpe guessed that the French in Fort Napoleon had spotted the riflemen as they walked the ridge-top to gaze down at the pontoon bridge, and presumably the officer commanding Fort Napoleon had sent a subordinate officer to capture the four strangers, and that officer was now in a quandary. He did not want to retreat to be greeted by his commanding officer's scorn and had no idea how to advance. He seemed to be making no attempt to outflank, had ordered no charge across the stream's valley, and had not even encouraged a musket shot. "He's a rabbit," Sharpe said angrily.

"Who?" Lieutenant Love asked.

"The officer leading them. Doesn't know what he's doing."

"Lieutenant Lapin," Love said happily.

"You know him?" Sharpe asked, astonished.

"*Lapin* is the French for rabbit, sir," Love said, "a masculine noun, though I believe in some regions they use the word *cony*."

"Well, this Lieutenant Lapin is bloody useless," Sharpe growled.

"Rabbits can be cunning little buggers, Mister Sharpe," Hagman said as he primed his rifle again.

"This rabbit's waiting for the light to fade," Sharpe said. The sun must have gone behind the western horizon for the clouds there darkened and their golden rim shrank. There was still a glow in the sky, though behind Sharpe a spreading darkness stained the east. "Soon," he muttered, "and once it's dark we go whether they've attacked or not." He was beginning to expect that *Capitaine* Rabbit was waiting for full darkness so he could withdraw and plead the night as an excuse for losing two men. Three men. Hagman had just shot again.

"Eighteen, Mister Sharpe."

"Leave some for us, Dan," Harper said.

"Plenty to go round," Hagman muttered.

Sharpe glanced to his right and saw the glow of firelight illuminating the distant inner courtyard walls of Fort Napoleon. They must have heard the shots coming from the hills, so had they sent more men? He could see no movement to the east, but any French reinforcements would be hidden by the ridge where *Capitaine* or maybe Lieutenant Rabbit was waiting. General Hill's aide had been certain that each of the two French forts had garrisons of about four to five hundred men, so they could certainly spare more troops, though if the garrison's commander suspected that the outbreak of musket fire in the hills presaged a full attack on his walls he would likely keep the majority of his men behind their battlements. Which meant *Capitaine* Rabbit was all on his own, and faced by three of the best riflemen in the British army, but Sharpe just wished the bugger would make up his mind and move. Sharpe stared across the valley where the shadows were darkening into night. "If he's going to move, he'd best do it soon," he said, "so not long now!"

He used a finger to test how firmly his rifle's flint was held by the doghead. It was a habit he did not like, but he knew he would compulsively test the flint again and again until the fight started. He gazed across the valley at the place he had seen a man and saw he was there again, now just a shape in the fading light. More than a shape, Sharpe could see the man's pale face. He raised the backsight, aimed carefully, held his breath, and pulled the trigger. The face vanished.

"Missed, sir," Lieutenant Love said, "shot went high."

"Bugger," Sharpe said.

"The sun was in your eyes, Mister Sharpe," Hagman said tactfully. Sharpe reversed the rifle and began the awkward process of reloading while prone. It was twilight now, the half-dark half-light prelude to night. There would be a half moon, Sharpe knew, but it had not yet risen and would offer little help till later. "I reckon we start walking now," he called as he clumsily rammed the leather-wrapped bullet down his rifle.

"Now?" Harper sounded surprised.

"They'll follow us on the valley's far side," Sharpe said, "and we just pick them off."

But *Capitaine* Rabbit must have come to a decision at the same time as Sharpe, for he ordered a musket volley that crackled suddenly, obscuring the far crest with thick smoke and spattering musket balls into the rocky knoll where Sharpe sheltered. "Everyone all right?" he called.

"Good as new," Harper said.

"They missed me, Mister Sharpe."

"I'm alive, sir," Love said.

"Then let's go," Sharpe said.

He stood. It seemed a pity to leave the cartridges and ready bullets on the rock, so he scuffed them into the turf with his boot. "Just follow the ridgeline south," he said, and just then *Capitaine* Rabbit charged.

He was not a completely foolish rabbit. He had held back nine of his men, who were now standing on the far ridge and reloading their muskets. The rest leaped down the farther slope, led by *Capitaine* Rabbit, who was waving a saber and shouting them on. "You take the men on the ridge, Dan!" Sharpe shouted, then aimed his rifle down at the stream, waiting for the Frenchmen to leap it. They were dark shapes in the shadowed valley, but he could see the bayonets and the glint of buckles and shako plates. He aimed at the officer, betrayed by his drawn saber, and pulled the trigger just as the man jumped the stream. The gun kicked into his shoulder and his right cheek stung from the flecks of burning powder. The smoke obscured whether or not he had hit the officer, but the shot had felt good. Harper fired as Sharpe bit off a bullet from the next cartridge. He would not bother about the leather patch, but just spit the ball down the barrel and ram the wadding on top. Hagman fired and still the smoke hid Sharpe's view so he ran three paces to his left and saw seven Frenchmen climbing toward him. Rifle to the shoulder, pull back the doghead, aim, and again the rifle kicked back. The Frenchmen, all of whom had fixed bayonets, had instinctively bunched together. "Leave them to me!" Harper shouted and put the volley gun to his right shoulder.

Lieutenant Love fired his pistol and yelped with delight as a Frenchman stumbled.

"If the buggers reach us," Sharpe said to Love, "you run like buggery and take Pat and Dan home."

"Run away?" Love sounded astonished.

"Sometimes it's the best tactic," Sharpe growled, then rammed the rifle and brought the gun to his shoulder. A musket ball ripped past his face, maybe a hand's breadth away. He could see men firing from the far ridge, but the range was far too long for the clumsy French muskets. Six of the seven men were getting nearer and their nervousness was making them bunch even closer together. The officer had vanished and Sharpe could just see the curve of his saber glinting in the stream. The surviving Frenchmen were shouting each other on, then the darkness was split by a gout of flame as the sound of the volley gun bellowed across the valley. The Frenchmen were blasted apart as the seven balls flayed them. Sharpe saw two fall backward, a third was staggering and screaming, then the others were at the summit and Harper was beating at them with the volley gun's butt. Hagman fired again and Sharpe threw his rifle aside and drew his sword.

It was no ordinary sword, or rather it was very ordinary, though not for an infantryman. The sword was a heavy cavalry blade, cheap to produce, long, straight, heavy and clumsy, but Sharpe liked it. In the hands of a strong man it was a butcher's blade, and he slammed the steel into the back of the nearest Frenchman's neck, then lunged into another man's ribs. Harper had beaten one man down and seized the musket of a second man. He was cursing the Frenchman in Gaelic, then more usefully hit him with a massive fist and the man went down. Hagman, a slight man, had sensibly retreated a few paces along the spur and shot one man, then clubbed the last Frenchman in the face with the brass-bound butt of his rifle. That man was staggering, half-stunned, and Hagman drew his sword-bayonet and disemboweled the man with one quick stroke. Not much pity for the enemy there, Sharpe thought.

Seven enemy left, all now standing leaderless on the far ridge and too appalled by what they had seen to even reload and fire their muskets. Sharpe picked up his rifle, took time to wrap a bullet in leather and rammed it down the barrel. "I hate idiots," he snarled. He knelt, aimed the rifle, and fired.

"You missed again," Harper said, amused.

The seven men on the valley's far side turned and ran. Hagman tried a last shot and one of them stumbled, but limped on as Sharpe went down to the stream. The water made a gentle noise as it tumbled over small stones and round the body of a young French officer at whose waist was an empty saber scabbard. "You bloody useless rabbit," Sharpe snarled at him, then knelt in the stream and filleted the dead man's pockets. He found some coins though it was too dark to tell what they were, and a sausage wrapped in paper that he pushed into his cartridge pouch. The night seemed suddenly silent. Three of the four men who had charged up the final slope of the hill were still alive. "What do we do with them, Mister Sharpe?" Hagman asked.

"Make their weapons useless and leave them where they are. And bring me one of their shakos."

They wrenched the dogheads off the French muskets' locks then shattered the stocks by beating them against rocks and threw the broken muskets down beside the four men. "You broke this poor bugger's neck." Harper nudged a dead man with his foot.

"I shot their damned officer too," Sharpe said, proud of his aim in the darkness.

"That was me, Mister Sharpe," Hagman said apologetically. "I know you told me to aim at the buggers on the hill, but I took him first."

"Always shoot the officers first," Harper said, "rule of life that!"

"Oh, surely n—" Lieutenant Love began.

"Home," Sharpe grunted. He kicked a broken musket down the hill and led them south.

Sergeant Latimer was waiting at the edge of the village with the rest of Sharpe's riflemen. "I heard the noise," Latimer said, "and we were coming to help."

"Didn't need help," Harper answered.

Sharpe looked at Latimer in the small moonlight, then at the other men. "You're carrying muskets! Why?"

"El Héroe," Latimer said sheepishly, "he took our rifles."

"The hell he did!"

"Didn't have no choice, Mister Sharpe," Sims said.

"You had rifles and cartridges!"

"Sorry, sir," Latimer said miserably. "He came with all his men. Gave us these," he hefted the musket. "Useless piece of French crap."

"So where are the rifles?"

"In the church, Mister Sharpe," Jack MacNeill said. "And the door's locked."

"You know that?"

"I was watching where they went, Mister Sharpe. You could hear the buggers bolt the door."

"Who has an axe?"

Henderson, a grim-faced rifleman almost as large as Harper,

pointed at the house where they had been billeted. "There's an axe in the house, Mister Sharpe."

"We'll need it. And the rest of you load your pieces of crap. But no shooting without my command. And Pat, load the volley gun." He looked at Latimer. "How many men did the bastard have?"

"Over forty, sir."

Sharpe grunted. "And did he ask about the gold?"

"I said you'd taken it with you, sir."

They waited as Harper reloaded the volley gun, charging all seven barrels with powder, bullets, and wadding. "I need more bullets," he said, "I'm running out."

"How many do you have?"

"After these? Twenty-four." The balls were larger than musket or rifle balls and Harper had been paying a dragoon farrier to cast him more. "I can fire just two or three barrels more?" he suggested. "Or just the center one."

"Give them a full load tonight," Sharpe said vengefully. He had been angry at *Capitaine* Rabbit for leading his men to death, but the anger was now aimed at El Héroe. He might be an ally, but Sharpe would be damned before the bloody man got away with stealing his rifles. "But not yet."

"Not yet?" Harper asked, sounding surprised and disappointed.

"El Héroe will be expecting us to make a fuss," Sharpe said, "and you never do what the enemy expects."

"Enemy now, is he?"

"So long as he has our rifles, yes."

Sharpe led them back to the house. "Any wine?"

"Not even the dog piss they call ale," Harris said.

Sharpe opened the front door and bellowed down the street. "El Héroe! El Héroe! Wake up!"

He had to shout a dozen more times before two men came down the street to the house door. Neither was El Héroe, but evidently his deputies.

"*Qué quieres?*" one of them asked.

"Harris!" Sharpe had understood perfectly, but wanted his knowledge of Spanish to stay hidden. "Can you tell this bugger we need wine?"

Harris hardly needed to translate because the riflemen began chanting, "*Vino! Vino!*"

"*Vino!*" Sharpe snarled at the man. "Now!"

"It'll be more vinegar," Harris grumbled.

The two men, evidently cowed by the harsh shouting, nodded and walked back toward the large house at the village's center that was evidently El Héroe's quarters. Sharpe stilled the noise and stood at the door, waiting. "You really want wine?" Harper asked in a low voice.

"I want El Héroe to think I do," Sharpe said.

"If he gives us wine the boys will drink it."

"That's what it's for, Pat."

"They're coming, Mister Sharpe!" Henderson called from his post at the door.

El Héroe was bringing all or most of his men. Sharpe counted thirty-six *guerrilleros*, all armed, though he could see no rifles, just the long Spanish muskets. Two men were carrying small barrels. "They can have a mug each," Sharpe told Harper, "and tell the buggers to sing."

"Singing there will be, sir," Harper said.

Sharpe waited in the door. El Héroe stopped a pace away. "Captain Sharpe," he said warily.

"My men need wine," Sharpe said.

"I only have the finest wine," El Héroe said grandly, "but you are my allies, so you are welcome to it." He gestured for the two barrels to be brought and Harper eagerly rolled them into the house where Harris tapped the first to a raucous cheer. "I am told," El Héroe said, "that English soldiers are always drunk." He watched scornfully as the riflemen crowded round the barrel to fill their tin mugs.

"And I'm told," Sharpe said, "that all Spaniards are thieves."

"Best thieves in all the world," El Héroe said proudly, "but not fools like you, Captain."

"Like me?"

"You woke the French, yes? We heard firing."

"We fought them."

"So they know you are here. Tomorrow they come for you."

"That would be stupid of them," Sharpe said, "but not as stupid as you."

"Stupid?" El Héroe bristled.

"You stole the rifles," Sharpe said, "but not the ammunition." His men had all kept their cartridge pouches.

"I have ammunition," El Héroe said, though he sounded puzzled.

"You have musket ammunition," Sharpe said, "and it's not the same. You need rifle ammunition and patches for the bullets."

"Patches?" El Héroe asked, still puzzled.

"How do you think the bullets grip the rifling in the barrel?"

Sharpe asked. "If you don't have patches then you've just got expensive muskets."

"Then we make patches," El Héroe said grandly, "we have women who can do that. And you give me your ammunition, Major."

"You can buy it from me," Sharpe said.

"Buy it!" El Héroe sounded astonished.

"I still have your gold. I'll keep it as a down payment and you give me the same again and I'll give you rifle cartridges."

Harper brought Sharpe a tin mug full of wine. "Thanks, Pat." Sharpe took a sip. It was vinegar and he spat it onto the street. "Finest wine?" he asked El Héroe.

"I only have the best wine," El Héroe said. "Good wine makes for good friends, and we should be friends, yes?"

"If we're to fight together, yes," Sharpe said.

"We will fight together and win together. I always win!"

"So does Mister Sharpe," Harper put in.

"Mister Sharpe's famous," Harris offered from the barrel.

"Famous?" El Héroe asked guardedly. "Why?"

"He took an eagle off the French, did Mister Sharpe," MacNeill said proudly.

"I took an eagle too," El Héroe said dismissively.

"You did?" Harper sounded surprised.

"Across the river." El Héroe waved vaguely northward. "An ambush, is that the right word?"

"Ambush, yes."

"We slaughter the French. They fear me!"

"You have the eagle?" Harper asked eagerly.

El Héroe hesitated, then, "It flew away, *sí*?" He laughed.

"That's what eagles do, they fly!" He flapped his hands to imitate wings then waited for Sharpe and his men to laugh.

Sharpe dutifully laughed and saw relief on El Héroe's face. "That was well done," Sharpe said with pretended admiration.

"You will find we are the best fighters in all Spain," El Héroe said.

"I've fought alongside *partidas*," Sharpe said, "and they were all good fighters. Very good!"

There was again a wary look on El Héroe's face. "You have fought with us? Who?"

"La Aguja," Sharpe said.

El Héroe almost spat in derision. "A woman! What does a woman know of battle?"

"She's good," Sharpe said.

"She is woman! War is man's affair."

"La Aguja could run rings round your bloody monkeys," Sharpe said.

El Héroe did not understand or pretended not to. "I have heard talk of La Aguja," he said scornfully, "she married Englishman, yes?"

"She did."

"*Puta*," El Héroe spat the word.

"*Puta?*" Sharpe said, feigning ignorance of the word. Lieutenant Love, who had been hovering just behind Sharpe, stepped forward as if to supply a translation, but Sharpe stopped him with a raised hand.

"She should come here," El Héroe said enthusiastically, "and

I will teach her about Spanish men." He smiled. "And we should be friends, Captain, and you give me rifle cartridges."

"And I keep the gold?"

El Héroe laughed as if Sharpe had made a great joke. "We talk in the morning, Captain. I leave you to enjoy the wine." He turned and walked away.

"He called Miss Teresa a whore?" Harper asked in a dangerous voice.

"He did, Pat."

"He's begging for trouble, so he is."

"He thinks we're going to get drunk, Pat, then he's coming back."

"And when he does?"

"We'll be sober." He stepped into the house. "Drink up, lads."

"It's sour," Harris complained, "and watered down."

"So don't drink it, just pretend to be drunk."

There was a platform in the single-room house; Sharpe assumed it was where the owners had slept. He climbed the ladder and peered out the small window. The church was fifty paces away and guarded by two men, one on either side of the door. El Héroe had walked beyond the small church to the village's largest house, where candlelight glowed from windows. Four men sat at a table beside the front door, their muskets propped against the house wall. They were there to guard El Héroe, just as the two men guarded the church that Sharpe reckoned must have another door, and presumably that was guarded too.

El Héroe now wanted the cartridges and his best chance was to take them from a rabble of drunken soldiers. So why had he watered the wine? Sharpe wondered. Better to have sent good wine, but so far El Héroe had made mistake after mistake, beginning with the musket shot that had bruised Sharpe. He had also lied about the small enclosure beside the bridge, claiming it was garrisoned by two hundred men when at most only thirty or forty could be quartered in its small hutments, and Sharpe reckoned there were probably fewer. That was a question for the morning, tonight he had to retrieve the rifles.

"Pat! Up here!"

Harper joined him and peered through the small window. "Two fellows, no problem."

"They're allies, Pat." Sharpe turned and looked down into the room. "Sing, you buggers!"

"Allies?"

"So no deaths. We sing them a lullaby instead."

"And if they fire at us?"

"Then they're not allies any longer. But the bastard has close to forty men."

Harper grunted. "So what do we do?"

"Confuse them."

The singing was getting louder because Dan Hagman had launched into the song about the colonel's daughter that was ever popular. The men bellowed out the chorus and Sharpe heard Lieutenant Love make a protest at the choice of song, which protest was raucously ignored. "We wait," Sharpe said. "Just make sure none of them get really drunk."

He watched from the window and saw some of El Héroe's men leaving the big house and going to smaller ones along the street. He reckoned they were going to bed. None came to relieve the two sentries guarding the church, both of whom had sat on the shallow steps and were leaning back against the wall. The French, he reckoned, could wipe them out easily. Fifty men from the closest fort could have scoured the village in an hour and so ended the partisan presence at Almaraz. And were more troops on the way? General Hill had talked of an expedition to destroy the pontoon bridge, and that implied that Lord Wellington was planning to advance into Spain and the destruction of the pontoon bridge would prevent French reinforcements from joining his opponents. But suppose the French had worked that out for themselves and had already sent reinforcements to the bridge's garrison? That was not his problem, he decided. He was simply ordered to reconnoiter the forts, but he would be damned if he would do that without rifles to protect his men.

He waited two hours, then calmed the singing into near silence as if his men were falling asleep. He still watched from the window. If El Héroe did plan to steal the cartridges, then now was the time for him to come, but there was no movement in the dark street.

Sharpe went back down the ladder. "MacNeill, Henderson, Elliott! With me. And you too, Pat. Sergeant Latimer? You command the rest. You go out the door and walk that way down the street to the bastard's house," Sharpe pointed in the direction of the big house, "pretend you're drunk and demand more wine."

"*Más vino*," Harris said.

"Just make a lot of noise and fuss," Sharpe said, "but no shooting. They're our allies! If they give you wine, come back here and sing again."

"Can we ask for women?" Latimer asked.

"No you bloody well can't. They'll kill you. Just wine. You got the axe, Joe?"

"I do, Mister Sharpe," Henderson said.

"The rest of you go. Make yourselves a nuisance! You're good at that."

"I'll stay with you, sir?" Lieutenant Love asked.

"Just be silent," Sharpe said. He would rather have left Love in the house, but decided the lanky lieutenant was best under his eye. "And don't cock your pistol."

Sharpe waited as Latimer led the riflemen into the street. Latimer was a decent man, as tall as Sharpe, thin and sensible, but hesitant to impose his authority as if he feared it was insufficient to persuade men to obey him. He was still ashamed that he had allowed El Héroe to take away the rifles, though Sharpe doubted anyone could have done better without provoking a fight that would have ended with dead men on both sides. And now, he thought, he must retrieve the rifles without leaving dead men, or too many dead. "Make a noise, lads!" Sharpe called to them. "*Más vino!*"

They began shouting and Sharpe led his five men out of the cottage's back door. They stumbled past a manure heap and Sharpe led them in the small moonlight the opposite way down the village. Latimer was heading south, Sharpe going north. He stopped once to peer between two of the small houses and saw the guards on the church were now standing and gaping down into the street where his men were bellowing that they were thirsty and wanted wine. Harris was bellowing in Spanish that they wanted good wine, not the goat's piss El Héroe drank. Sharpe grinned and kept going until he reached the end of the village, then he dashed across the road, trusting to the night and his dark green uniform to hide him. He stopped behind the house at the street's far side and peered round its corner to see two more guards at the back door of the church. "We have to get past them," he whispered to Harper.

"Leave it to me and Joe," Harper said.

"No shooting, Pat. It's too close to El Héroe's house."

"No shooting," Harper agreed, and gave his rifle and volley gun to Sharpe. Henderson handed his heavy French musket to Lieutenant Love, hefted the heavy axe he carried, then the two men slid along the backs of the houses, treading softly. The two guards were gazing south, though there was nothing to be seen in the small vegetable gardens that lay at the rear of the houses. The noise and commotion were all in the street and Sharpe thought he heard El Héroe's voice demanding quiet.

"*Más vino, más vino,*" Sharpe's men were chanting.

"*Bien vino!*" Harris bellowed.

Harper dashed from the shadow of the house across a moonlit strip of turf and one of the guards turned and tried to level his musket, but the Irishman threw the muzzle aside with his left hand and delivered a punch with his right. The punch took the Spaniard under the chin and Sharpe guessed it could even have broken the man's neck. Henderson was a pace behind and drove the second man to the ground where he hammered the back of the axe's blade against the man's skull, a blow clearly audible to Sharpe and Love. "Dear Lord God," Love whispered.

Harper gave the first man a kick in the head and then, satisfied, turned toward Sharpe. "They're lullabied," he called softly.

"Wait," Sharpe said to the men beside him. He wanted to see whether the brief commotion at the church's back door had alarmed the pair of sentries at the front of the church, but the raucous shouting of Latimer's men had drowned the noise and the two men stayed out of sight. "Now," Sharpe muttered, and ran to join Harper.

The two men had been guarding a small door. It was locked, though Sharpe could see no keyhole, which meant it was probably bolted from the inside. "Joe?"

"*Más vino! Más vino!*" the shout still echoed down the dark street.

Henderson drew his axe back, ready to slash at the door, but Harper snatched it away from him. "Too noisy, Joe," he said. Instead, he rested the blade against the door's edge and hammered it with his fist so that it sank into the wood. He levered it and the wood partially splintered, allowing him to sink it further until he had the blade well dug in between the door and its frame. Then he levered it again and the door cracked, splintered and burst outward. There was a clatter as a broken bolt fell to the stone floor, but Latimer's men were still chanting loudly.

"Inside, lads."

Sharpe led them into a small dark room, tripped on a stool or chair, and fumbled in his pocket for his firelighter. He opened the tin box, struck the steel with the flint and on the third strike set a scrap of charred linen alight. He blew on it carefully, then Henderson held a candle into the flame and Sharpe snapped the box shut.

There were vestments hanging on a peg and silver vessels on a table. Three other candlesticks stood there and Sharpe lit them all. Harper touched a finger to a pair of chalices then made the sign of the cross. "It's all dusty. Hasn't been used in forever."

"I somehow doubt El Héroe is on chatty terms with God," Sharpe said.

"Because he thinks he is God," Henderson grunted.

"And these," Lieutenant Love reverently lifted one of the silver chalices, "haven't been stolen by the French."

Sharpe lifted the latch of a door that led into the church's chancel and stepped through, rifle in one hand and candle in the other. The altar was to his right, shrouded in shadow through which a great wooden crucifix loomed. To his left the nave of the church looked empty except for a few chairs, but as he stepped down into the nave he saw barrels piled on the north side and, next to them, stacks of muskets. He led his men to the muskets, their hobnailed shoes loud on the stone floor.

"More bloody Frog muskets!" MacNeill said indignantly.

"Captured weapons, Jack," Henderson said.

"And French flints!" Harper said enthusiastically. He had

discovered a wooden box crammed with flints and French flints were always better than the British issue. "Dan'll be happy with these."

"Take them," Sharpe growled, "but where are the rifles?"

The front door of the church, which had not been bolted, suddenly opened and one of the *partidas* who had been guarding the door peered into the church. He gasped, then gave a frightened squeak when Sharpe turned on him with his rifle leveled. The door slammed shut and Sharpe heard the two sentinels running down the street. "This is their armory," he said, waving a hand round the church, "so the bloody rifles must be here."

"They are, Mister Sharpe," Henderson said, "all twelve."

The rifles had been laid on a rough wooden table. Harper picked one up. "They cleaned them!" he exclaimed in wonder, and in the candlelight Sharpe saw that the wooden stock gleamed as if rubbed with oil while the brass furniture all looked glossy bright.

"It's El Héroe," Sharpe said sourly, "always has to look his best. Best wine, best fighters, best horse, and best weapons. He wants to show them off. So bugger him. Pick 'em up, lads, and back to the house."

"Cupid's missing," Harper said.

They found Lieutenant Love, evidently uninterested in the stacks of weapons and powder, kneeling in front of the deep-shadowed altar, his hands clasped and lips moving silently. Sharpe tapped him on the shoulder. "Time to go, Lieutenant."

"Amen," Love replied. The commotion in the main street was dying down, though Sharpe could still hear a few shouts demanding more wine. He stepped through the broken doorway into the darkness beyond, where his eyes were slow to adjust from the small candlelight. The moon had been shrouded by cloud, but suddenly he was aware of men standing just paces away. Four men and the glint of candlelight from within the church reflecting from two bayonets.

"*Señor?*" one of the men asked.

"*Sí,*" Sharpe said.

"*Eres* El Héroe?" the man asked.

His voice was halting, uncertain.

Sharpe was aware of Harper moving up beside him. "*No está aquí,*" Sharpe said.

"*Está en la casa?*"

"*Sí,*" Sharpe said.

The man jerked up a musket, pointing it at Sharpe. "*Quién eres?*" he demanded peremptorily.

"Now, Pat," Sharpe said.

The volley gun fired, sounding like a cannon in the night. A cloud of thick smoke billowed in front of the seven bunched muzzles, the cloud shot through with bright stabs of flame beyond which the seven balls ripped mercilessly into the four men.

Two died instantly, but the two outermost were merely wounded and fell bleeding and moaning under the thick smoke. "Bring a candle!" Sharpe called. "And watch out!" He had seen movement some twenty or thirty paces away and sensed a group of men were running away. He aimed his rifle, then decided it would be a wasted shot.

Henderson brought the candle, shielding the flame from the small wind with his hand. He stood over the four men and stared down. "Bloody hell," he said.

"The good Lord save me!" Love exclaimed.

They were French.

CHAPTER 3

"You are a fool!" El Héroe bellowed at Sharpe. "You disobey orders, you put all our people at danger!" He was spitting with rage. "You are a disgrace!"

Sharpe ignored him. He was using a small knife to ream caked powder residue from the pan of his rifle.

"You will leave," El Héroe said. "I order it. Leave the rifles and the gold here, and go!" He stared belligerently, waiting for Sharpe's answer, and when none came stamped his foot. "That is an order, Major!"

Sharpe blew the loosened scraps from the pan. "I'm going nowhere," he said.

"Sir?" Lieutenant Love leaned forward, evidently attempting to negotiate peace.

"I'm going nowhere!" Sharpe snarled and the lieutenant jumped backward.

Sharpe had called Sergeant Latimer and his men back from their noise-making, distributed the rifles, and listened to the jokes about their cleanliness. Then El Héroe had stormed into

the house with nothing but sound and fury. Sharpe had disobeyed his orders. Sharpe had gone to the old bridge. The
French had seen him. Sharpe had killed Frenchmen, so now
the enemy knew he was here in the hills. "They cannot ignore
that! Tomorrow they come!"

"And just what were the French doing here?" Sharpe demanded.
"Here at the church?" He pulled the trigger to ease the spring
and the new French flint sent a cascade of sparks into the cleaned
and empty pan. Sharpe half smiled as El Héroe twitched in alarm.

"How would I know? Looking for you."

"Then the buggers found me," Sharpe said happily.

"And you kill the French officer who sells me information!"

"Is that who he was?"

"Who else?"

"And he came with other men?" Sharpe asked, "so they all
know he's a traitor?"

"His men not know what he comes for," El Héroe said dismissively. "They think he buys false information from me. But
the French will know you killed him and want revenge.
Tomorrow they come to kill you."

"Then tomorrow we fight them," Sharpe said quietly, but
that only provoked another rant from El Héroe on how Sharpe
was a disgrace, a fool, and a thief. "And you are not even
proper officer!" he finished.

"How so?" Sharpe asked.

"I talk to your men. You were sergeant once, *si*?"

"A bloody good one too," Sharpe said.

"So!" El Héroe spat the word, then paused to gather his
thoughts. "You are not born to command, Major."

"And you are?"

"I have the blood of kings and nobles," El Héroe said grandly. "At dawn we take the road to Truxillo, till the French forget us."

"You mean you run away?" Sharpe asked. He leveled the rifle at El Héroe's stomach. El Héroe must have known it was unloaded, after all Sharpe had just pulled the trigger to provoke a flash in the pan, but he still stepped backward in alarm. "Is that what kings and nobles do?" Sharpe asked. "Run away? Then I'm glad I've got the blood of the gutter in me."

"Why should I die because you are stupid fool? I live to fight on!"

"Then fight tomorrow."

"The French want revenge. They will send many men."

"Then you should stay and kill the buggers."

"I have forty-six men here and it will take two days to assemble more. Tomorrow the French will send two hundred, three hundred men. You will march with us. I order you."

"I'll stay."

"Then you die."

El Héroe left on that dire warning, without taking either the rifles or the gold. Sharpe turned to his men and tapped the French shako he had taken from the men whose ambush he had defeated. "These buggers will be coming tomorrow, lads, so get some sleep."

Lieutenant Love waited till the men had dispersed, then, nervously, turned to Sharpe. "You'll fight against two hundred of the enemy, sir?"

"They'll send two companies," Sharpe guessed, "so a hundred and eighty men at most."

"Even so . . ." Love began.

"We're riflemen, Lieutenant," Sharpe said curtly, "we don't run away."

Sharpe turned the captured shako, cursing because he had not thought to take one from the men he had killed at the church. The one he had taken was heavy, made from boiled leather with a felt lining. It was also old and battered, the blue pom-pom at its crown now little more than bedraggled wisps of wool. Beneath it, on the shako's front, was a diamond-shaped brass plate that bore the number 6. So the 6th Regiment of the Line was part of the pontoon bridge's garrison, and that was worth knowing, though it would have been better had he taken another shako outside the church to see if another French unit was present.

"Only a hundred and eighty men, Mister Sharpe?" Hagman had overheard the conversation with Lieutenant Love. "That's just twelve each. Easy."

There was some uncertain laughter, then Sharpe ordered them to rest, though first he sent Harris, Tongue, and Henderson southward as a picket. He did not expect a French assault on the village in the dark, though he suspected a dawn attack was possible. Oddly, he thought, El Héroe was right. Sharpe had disobeyed orders, not El Héroe's orders, but General Hill's, who had told him to stay concealed until he was ready to report back to the general what he had discovered. Instead he had been spotted, the French had sent men to capture him and he had killed half that force, and now had killed even more. The French would be annoyed, to put it mildly, and that annoyance would turn to outrage when they discovered the death of the officer who had taken the brunt of Harper's volley gun in the dark. But why had that officer been at the church? The man had obviously thought it was safe to approach the village with a small escort, and once there had asked for El Héroe, and the implications of that were troubling. Either El Héroe had told the truth and the Frenchman had been a traitor willing to sell information to the partisans, information that the Frenchman must have known was then sent on to Lord Wellington, or else the French and the so-called partisans had an agreement to live and let live. And that would explain why a French officer had ridden the riverside path so carelessly, because he knew he was in no danger. El Héroe, it seemed possible to Sharpe, had come to an understanding with the French, which meant he had probably sent a man to warn them of Sharpe's reconnaissance to the old bridge.

But why, if that was true, would the French attack in the morning? That was a puzzle. If El Héroe and the French were allied then it suggested the French would leave the village alone, but El Héroe had seemed certain of an attempt at revenge, which suggested that his link to the French was nothing so grand as a full alliance. Besides, it was unthinkable to Sharpe that partisans would befriend the French; the hatred between them was too intense to allow for such an alliance, which only made Sharpe wonder whether El Héroe had truly persuaded an enemy officer to give him information. That thought gave Sharpe a pang of conscience; had he killed a valuable informant? If that was true then he had done a disservice to his own side. He cursed silently. War was supposed to be a simple enough business; just find the enemy and kill him, but what if you did not know who was an enemy and who a friend?

So perhaps El Héroe was right and the French, ignorant of the traitor in their ranks, would assault the village next morning and if El Héroe fled westward then Sharpe would be left alone to protect the few villagers who remained. Good sense told him to retreat with El Héroe, but he was reluctant to just run away with most of his reconnaissance incomplete. He had yet to examine Miravete Castle, nor had he crossed the river, and scuttling away westward would mean he had failed in his orders. Yet staying might mean coping with a determined attack by the French.

Sharpe took a cup of wine from the new supply and went outside the house to where a table and bench stood. He loaded the rifle and propped it against the table as he sat. A nervous Lieutenant Love stooped under the low door to join him. "Sir?"

"Sit down, Lieutenant."

"Are you sure about tomorrow, sir?" Love asked.

"Nowhere near sure. Odds are they won't come."

"El Héroe seemed certain, sir."

"And he's running away," Sharpe said bitterly, "but I'm damned if I will."

"So if they come," Love asked, "we fight?"

Sharpe noted approvingly that Love had used the word "we." "What else can we do?"

"Against two hundred or more, sir?"

"It won't be that many," Sharpe said with a confidence he did not feel. "Maybe two companies?"

"And if it's more, sir?" Love asked nervously.

"If it's four companies we run away, Lieutenant. Sometimes that's the best thing to do." Sharpe recalled Major Hogan's warning against trying to walk on water. It was plain madness to expect his handful of rifles to defeat a large French attack, but at the least he could try. He had never backed down from a fight and he had no wish to slink back to General Hill and confess he had left most of his orders unfulfilled. The sensible course, he thought, was to retreat toward Truxillo and let the French find the village deserted, but there was still a chance that the enemy would do nothing. "We'll see what tomorrow brings," he said, "but one thing is crucial. We can't afford to lose a captive tomorrow. It's shoot, retreat, and shoot again. The damned Frogs can have the village, but they can't have us. Not one of us." Though Sharpe would do everything in his power to keep the damned Frogs out of the village.

Love nodded. "We can't afford to lose a captive because the French don't know we plan an attack on the forts, sir?"

"And our men do know," Sharpe said.

"Was that wise, sir?" Love asked. "I mean, telling them?"

Sharpe turned to look at the lieutenant. "I'm asking my men to risk their lives, Lieutenant," he said patiently. "They deserve to know why. And if they know why they're fighting they'll fight better. They're not cattle to be driven, but men who deserve to be led."

"I see, sir," Love said, sounding dubious. "I'm sure you're right."

"No you're not, but you'll see tomorrow." Sharpe reckoned the French must be alert to the possibility of a raid on the vital river crossing, but so far as he knew they had no confirmation of that. But Sharpe had told his men of Hill's plan to destroy the forts, and if even one of his riflemen was captured by the enemy he doubted that plan would stay secret. "So if we fight tomorrow, Lieutenant, we fight clever."

"Clever, sir?"

Sharpe ignored the question. "And the French," Sharpe said confidently, "won't. They'll be damned fools again. Now get some sleep, Lieutenant."

"You too, sir."

"Before you go." Sharpe checked the lieutenant with a raised hand. "You went with us to the old bridge and that's the track General Hill will have to use to get guns near Fort Napoleon. Is that feasible?"

Love hesitated. "It will be difficult, sir," he said slowly, then brightened, "but we're the Royal Artillery! The difficult is merely a challenge to be overcome!"

"Think about it, Lieutenant," Sharpe said in dismissal. He had his own opinion, but decided to keep it to himself, "and try to sleep. We might be busy tomorrow."

Sharpe also tried to sleep, but was restless. Would the French come? Or would they leave El Héroe's lair untouched? And how would they come, if they came at all? And would Sharpe's fight alert them to a British attempt to destroy their precious bridge? If so, why should he fight at all? Why not just melt into the western countryside and let French suspicions fade? Because it was not in his blood, that was why, and tomorrow, whether it was prudent or not, whether it was two companies or four, Sharpe knew he would fight.

* * *

He woke his men before dawn and listened to their grumbling as they boiled water for tea and readied their rifles, all of the weapons now equipped with fine new French flints. The only signs of life in the village were older women carrying water or children driving goats. Harris spoke to a few of the women and came back to report that El Héroe had left in the night. "He scarpered, Mister Sharpe. Buggered off south, and all his men too."

"So it's just us," Sharpe said, "if they come."

"You reckon they will?"

"They have to," Sharpe said with a certainty he did not feel. "They don't care about El Héroe and his men, because they're useless, but yesterday three riflemen defeated a whole patrol. They need to get rid of us."

He led them north out of the village to a low ridge that overlooked the track coming from the French garrison at Fort Napoleon. Once there he spread his men out to make a line across the ridge from where they could see a half mile ahead to where the path vanished among the low scrubby trees that spread up from the riverbank. The track was narrow, a sheep path, but it was the obvious route for any Frenchmen to follow and once they were out of the trees they would be in easy range of the rifles, while their muskets would be useless. "No one fires until I do," he told them as he walked the long line of men, "and once you start shooting, keep shooting. Officers and sergeants first. Cut the buggers down." He was hiding his uncertainty, trying to sound confident. "Remember! Officers and sergeants first, then thin the other buggers out."

Except the buggers did not come. Sharpe gazed north toward the ridge above the river forts and saw neither man nor beast. The sun rose, bringing warmth, and still no enemy appeared. Harper strolled across to Sharpe. "The bastards aren't very eager, sir."

"Maybe they'll come this evening," Sharpe said.

"Or else they're happy to sit in their forts. That's what I'd do."

"Because you're a lazy bloody Irishman."

"True enough." Harper watched a hawk flying high over-head. The bird slid southward on a small current of air, then suddenly Harper spat. "Jesus, Mary, and Joseph!"

Sharpe turned. Harper had crouched and was gazing fixedly south where the track led away from the village. There were men on the distant skyline, men marching, muskets sloped on shoulders, men marching toward the village.

Sharpe swore. He had forgotten Miravete Castle, which lay beyond the village and guarded the main road to the river. He had supposed the French would send men from Fort Napoleon on the river's bank, but Miravete Castle had to be closer and now there were scores of blue-coated infantry de-scending the track into the valley that lay southwest of the village. "Back to the village," Sharpe shouted, "at the double!"

The French would see him coming, but that had to be endured. They would count his men and see how few they were and that would only increase their confidence. Sharpe could see maybe two companies coming, which together numbered about a hundred and fifty men and those men could see fifteen riflemen running toward the village. They maybe expected to face El Héroe's men as well, but Sharpe doubted that prospect would frighten them. This was a punishment expedition and the French were doubtless anticipating more than revenge. They were eager for food, wine, and women.

He pounded into the village and led his men to the western edge from where he could look down into the valley, where a stream sparkled in the day's new light. A small mist drifted there, fading over the stream that ran almost a half mile away. "A line here!" Sharpe gestured north and south and watched his men find places behind the thorn hedges of the small gardens. They could see the French clearly. They were still far beyond the stream, marching stolidly down the track, which was rough enough to disturb their steps, but they held their formation well enough, marching as if they were on a barrack's square. They were in six files and Sharpe used his telescope to see there were two companies, both of a dozen ranks. A hundred and fifty men, led by an officer on horseback. "Dan!"

"Mister Sharpe?"

"You can take the idiot on the horse, but not till you're sure of him."

"Be a while yet, Mister Sharpe."

"Take your time, Dan."

Hagman sighted the rifle, then rested it, content to let the French get much closer. Sharpe walked behind the line, telling each man to wait until Hagman had killed the French officer before they fired. "They're doing what I expected them to do," he told Harper.

"Marching to death?"

"They never learn. Buggers should be in skirmish order."

"They're still a fair ways off," Harper said. "They'll probably shake out of column once they're over the stream?"

"Could be," Sharpe allowed, but he doubted it. He reckoned these men were not first-rate troops. They were from a battalion put on fortress duty, which meant living behind thick stone walls and watching the main road. Boring duty that dulled a man. At least forty of the approaching Frenchmen should be Voltigeurs, the cunning French skirmishers who would attack ahead of the column, but Sharpe doubted that these men exercised battle tactics. Their job had been to crouch behind battlements and protect the gunners in the castle's bastions. They were second-rate troops led by second-rate officers, but they had already achieved surprise by coming from the castle instead of the river and they would be supremely confident of their numbers.

Sharpe gazed toward the river again, wondering whether the French would be clever and send another company or two from the forts to outflank him, but the land stayed empty. It seemed the troops from Miravete Castle were reckoned to be sufficient, and so they should be. "Except they're facing us," Sharpe said aloud.

"Mister Sharpe?" Henderson had half heard the words.

"I was almost feeling sorry for them, Joe. Bastards have probably never fought riflemen."

Henderson grinned. "There's a lot of them, Mister Sharpe."

"A hundred and fifty, more or less. Call it ten each. All in a day's work, Joe." Sharpe walked on down the line, stopping to crouch beside Dan Hagman. The first rank of Frenchmen splashed into the stream. It was no obstacle, scarcely coming to their ankles. Sharpe held his breath as the last rank came from the water. If the French commander had any sense, he would deploy now by sending his Voltigeurs into a loose skirmish line that would climb to the village first. Forty or fifty Voltigeurs would be a handful for his men, because every shot would have to count and as long as they fought against the skirmishers his riflemen could not pour fire into the bigger target of the close-packed column, but the French did not deploy. They just kept coming. Sharpe trained his telescope on the mounted officer, seeing a mustached face. The man was evidently calling to his men, doubtless promising them an easy victory and lavish plunder. He wore a blue sash across his blue coat. He had been riding in the center of the column, between the two companies, but now spurred his horse to lead the column as it began climbing from the stream. "Buggers will have sopping wet boots," Hagman said, amused, "and they won't like that."

Sharpe gazed at the column. "They don't know we're here," he muttered.

"Probably think we're sleeping, Mister Sharpe."

Sharpe kept his glass on the officer, who had drawn a lightly curved saber that he pointed toward Sharpe. The track rose straight toward the village now, and Sharpe could see the six men in the enemy's front rank laboring for breath as the slope steepened. The mounted officer waved the curved blade toward the crest ahead and shouted again. The column tried to quicken, but lost cohesion and sergeants were bellowing at the troops to hold their files straight. There was a drummer somewhere in those files and Sharpe could just hear the monotonous beats. Then they halted and Sharpe feared the Voltigeurs were being sent ahead, but the halt was merely to dress the ragged ranks. The officer turned his horse to face his men and just then Hagman fired.

It was a very long shot, even for Hagman. The bullet seared down the hill and Sharpe, still looking through the glass, saw the shock on men's faces as the sound of the shot echoed through the valley, then the mounted officer pitched forward until his saddle's pommel checked him, then he slid slowly sideways to fall onto the track.

"Nice one, Dan," Sharpe called, his words drowned as thirteen other rifles fired a ragged fusillade and the whole front file of the column fell. "Keep firing!" Sharpe called and aimed his own rifle a hand's breadth above the column, reckoning the distance would mean his bullet struck into the bloodied and disordered carnage. He fired and automatically dropped the rifle's butt to the ground and fished a new cartridge from his pouch. He moved to his right to escape the cloud of smoke that obscured his view and, as he poured a new powder charge into the barrel, saw that the French had dragged their dead and wounded to the track's edges and were re-forming their ranks. The mounted officer's horse was galloping free, back the way the French had come. Another officer was now yelling at the column, pointing uphill, and the march started again. "Keep hitting them!" Sharpe called.

He hardly dared believe his luck. The French force outnumbered his small squad by at least ten to one, but were so confident, or else so hidebound, that they had not deployed a skirmish line and instead seemed intent on marching in column straight toward his riflemen. A gift from heaven. "Aim carefully!" he called. "And keep shooting!" He rammed a leather-wrapped bullet down the rifle's barrel, stuck the ramrod into the turf beside him, then charged the pan. He brought the rifle to his shoulder and aimed over the open sights at the column's head. Pulled the trigger and fished a new cartridge from his pouch. A paltry scatter of musket balls flew above him. The few French who were in a position to shoot back were all firing high. "Keep hitting them!"

"Shouldn't they be in skirmish order, sir?" Lieutenant Love appeared at Sharpe's side.

"They should, yes."

"Why aren't they?" The lieutenant had his pistol drawn, but had enough sense to know it would be worse than useless at the distance to where the French were being slaughtered.

"Because they're badly trained and worse led," Sharpe said. He rammed another bullet down the rifle's barrel.

The column had stopped. No one there seemed to know what to do. Sharpe used the pause to fish out his telescope and saw that the second officer who had tried to rally the two companies was down. The front of the French was being shredded by rifle bullets and no sooner was it destroyed then the men immediately behind became new targets for the relentless rifle fire. The men in the column's center were panicking, aiming uphill and shooting wildly. A ramrod windmilled through the air, shot from a musket and a sure sign of badly trained troops. Then, at last, Sharpe saw a thin officer gesturing the men of the second company at the rear of the column to spread out. He could see the man shouting and took his eye from the telescope to watch the company scatter across the valley's side to make a loose skirmish line. "Not before time," Sharpe muttered. "Keep those Voltigeurs busy!" he called.

The skirmish line began climbing and Sharpe felt a pulse of apprehension. There were well over fifty men in the skirmish line, each four or five paces from his neighbor, and his fourteen riflemen had to stop them. It would take at least seven or eight minutes for the Voltigeurs to climb the valley side, which gave him time to loose more than two hundred shots, but single men were much harder to kill than troops conveniently packed into ranks, and most of his riflemen were shooting at the remnants of the first company, who were still formed in column on the road. "Ignore the column!" he bellowed. "Kill the skirmishers! And aim carefully!"

The skirmishers were beginning to fight properly, one man kneeling and shooting uphill while his partner reloaded. And the closer they came the more accurate would be their musketry. Sharpe watched the Voltigeurs, saw one fall, but too many rifle bullets were missing. He turned, reckoning that his next position would have to be the houses at the edge of the village where a small crowd of people was gazing anxiously toward him. El Héroe might have fled, but some villagers had stayed behind, and Sharpe had no doubt of their fate if he was forced to retreat beyond the small houses. Damn it, he thought, but he should not have picked this battle. The Voltigeurs were halfway up the slope now, their numbers scarcely diminished by the rifle fire, while the first company, having dragged its dead and wounded to the edges of the track, had resumed its march. He primed his rifle and sought a target down the slope, seeing the thin officer shouting orders as he gestured for the Voltigeurs to spread out further.

Sharpe knelt, brought the rifle's butt to his shoulder, and lined the sights on the officer's pale face, reckoning the bullet would drop to hit his breastbone or belly. He held his breath. Pulled the trigger. The powder in the pan flared, specks stung his right cheek, then the rifle hammered into his shoulder and smoke obscured his view. He ran six paces to his left, looked again, and the man was still shouting and gesturing, then suddenly twisted down as his shako was shot from his head, revealing long fair hair. So another rifleman had fired at the officer. "I want that fair-haired bugger down!" Sharpe shouted. "And keep at them, lads!"

He reloaded. A musket ball clipped the long grass beside him. So they were no longer firing high and the remnant of the column was climbing faster, driven by the hidden drummer. The Voltigeurs were even closer, firing, crouching, reloading, running forward again. "Pat!" Sharpe bellowed to the right of his line. "We'll be pulling back soon!"

"Aye, sir!" Harper called back, then aimed his rifle down the hill and pulled the trigger.

Too many of Sharpe's men were still aiming at the company that had stayed in column and was still approaching, and their bullets tore into the dense formation, which gave the Voltigeurs some respite. Sharpe saw those Voltigeurs fixing bayonets, which meant they were readying for a final charge that must end in his men's slaughter or surrender. He cursed, knowing he had led his men to an ignominious defeat. He took a deep breath, ready to admit the failure and to call his men back, but just then, to his left, from across the shoulder of the hill, a bugle sounded.

The call came again from his left, then to his astonishment he saw a line of horsemen coming fast along the valley's side. More horses spilled over the skyline and were spurred faster. Some of the riders carried lances, most had sabers, and all wore bright red scarves that flapped behind as they galloped. "Keep firing!" Sharpe bellowed.

The Voltigeurs on the right of the French line started running back toward the column, but were too slow. The lances struck, the sabers slashed and the horses kept coming. Sharpe heard a desperate scream as a Voltigeur was lanced in the back, he saw his men's bullets slamming into the column, which was now facing outward with fixed bayonets to make a rally square. The horsemen, Sharpe saw, wore ragged faded uniforms, some yellow, some black. They were partisans who now divided into two streams to gallop either side of the first company and carry their blades to the remaining Voltigeurs, most of whom were now running desperately downhill toward the stream. Which is where they died under the merciless Spanish sabers and lances. "So El Héroe came back?" Harper had joined Sharpe. "Didn't think he had it in him."

"Nor did I," Sharpe said, "but thank God he did, we were about to be beat. Did we lose anyone?"

"Milner got his shako shot off, and the bullet grazed his skull. He'll live, he's got a head made of firebrick."

The bugle sounded again, evidently rallying the horsemen,

most of whom were in the valley's bed where they had finished off the last of the French skirmishers, but a score or more surrounded the column that had formed a ragged rally square and now stood on the road with fixed bayonets. "I'd best take them prisoner," Sharpe said, "unless we want to watch them being butchered. Harris!"

"Mister Sharpe?"

"You speak some Frog, so come here."

"*Bien sûr, monsieur!*" Harris ran to Sharpe, grinning. "That was enjoyable, Mister Sharpe!"

"It was bloody murder," Sharpe said, "but I don't want more slaughter, so you'll tell the bastards to surrender. Come. If El Héroe gives you any trouble, tell him to bugger off."

He slung his rifle and drew his sword. He did not expect to use it, but the sword denoted he was an officer and the sheer size of the blade put fear into most men. He strode down the track. "Tell their officer to meet me," he instructed Harris, who shouted the order at the sullen Frenchmen who were shrinking into an ever-tighter huddle. Sharpe estimated there were about forty or fifty men in the rally square and by now they were surrounded by at least that many partisans who were jeering them. "Quiet!" Sharpe bellowed. "*Silencio!*"

Harris strode toward the frightened men. "*Qui vous commande?*" he demanded, and a thin pale young man with floppy fair hair pushed his way through the front rank. Sharpe recognized him as the man who had deployed the Voltigeurs. Instead of an infantry officer's sword he carried his bullet-riddled shako, and he looked pathetically young, but he had possessed the sense to do what his dead commanding officer should have done, only to be defeated by cavalry, the fatal enemy of all skirmishers.

"*Je commande maintenant*," he said nervously, his eyes on Sharpe's sword.

"*Et tu es?*" Harris snapped.

"*Sous-Lieutenant* Blanchet." He hesitated, looking terrified. "Pierre Blanchet. I belong to the," he hesitated, as if his English was not sufficient, "*trenteneuvième de la ligne*," he added, as if revealing his Christian name would move Sharpe to pity.

"Thirty-ninth regiment of the line," Harris translated.

"Tell him he belongs to me now," Sharpe told Harris.

"But he doesn't," a voice said behind and above Sharpe, "he belongs to me."

He turned, his heart leaping as he looked up. "Hello, Teresa," he said.

"Hello, Richard."

La Aguja had come.

Teresa had met El Héroe earlier that morning. "He was at San Miguel's cave, hiding," she said dismissively, "and ordered me to stay with him."

"Ordered you?"

"He said we would be killed if we came here. He is a coward. *Un cobarde.*" She spat the word, making Sharpe smile. She had brought sixty-three men and had apologized there were not more. "My people are scattered," she had explained, "and I brought what I could."

"It's more than enough," he had assured her.

She wanted to kill all fifty-eight of the French prisoners.

"You know what they do to us?" she asked, before answering her own question. "They kill, mutilate, and rape us. They are not men, they are animals." She had found her own brother tortured and nailed to a cellar wall, and ever since she had fought the French with a fanatical ruthlessness. "Death is too good for them."

"They must live," Sharpe said, "there are rules."

"I spit on your rules. They are my prisoners!"

It was hard to argue with that. Sharpe knew he had miscalculated, that his fifteen rifles could never have defeated both French companies. It had been sheer pride and overconfidence that had persuaded him that he could win, and in the end he had only been saved by Teresa and her partisans. "Right now," he told Teresa, "the French only know about my men and your followers, they don't know General Hill is coming with cannon and thousands of men. And so far every time they've left their forts they've been defeated. So we let them go back to the forts where they'll spread fear of us. The garrisons will be pissing themselves in terror by the time General Hill arrives."

"Better they don't go back at all," Teresa said harshly, "and the garrisons will fear even more because their men just disappeared."

"I can't hold them prisoner," Sharpe said. "I don't have the food for them, and they need surgeons."

"Why hold them prisoner?" Teresa inquired. "Why not just cut their throats?"

"Because if I let you kill them," Sharpe said, "then they'll believe I ordered it and every rifleman ever captured in this war will be executed by the French. There really are rules."

"There should be no rules in war," Teresa said. "War is the absence of law."

"Let them go," Sharpe said, "and in a few days we'll capture them all again."

"Just let them go!" She sounded astonished.

"I want them to spread fear."

Sharpe had already given the French prisoners two handcarts from the village with which they had collected their wounded men from the carnage in the valley. Now all the Frenchmen were in the stables of the large house that El Héroe had occupied, guarded there by Teresa's red-scarved men. The only surviving officer was the young *Sous-Lieutenant* Blanchet, who looked terrified when Teresa ordered him and his surviving men to parade in the stableyard. There was a big stone mounting block in the yard and the prisoners watched in misery as two of Teresa's men destroyed their muskets. A farrier's hammer was used to knock the locks clean off the muskets, then the heavy stocks were cut away with an axe, leaving only the barrels. Harper took the ramrods and bent them one by one, then tossed them contemptuously onto a pile before the useless barrels were given back to the Frenchmen. Lieutenant Blanchet watched silently and only protested when Teresa unbuckled his sword belt. "Be silent," she snarled at him, then tossed his scabbarded sword to one of her followers. "Now," she said in English, "tell them to undress."

Harris grinned. *"Enlevez vous vos vêtements!"* he called.

The prisoners hesitated, but Teresa's men leveled cocked muskets and slowly, unwillingly, they undressed. They were embarrassed because a woman watched them and, while she gloated over them, Sharpe watched her. He marveled, as he always did, at her slim, dark beauty. A hawk's face, he thought, stern and strong, and he wondered whether their daughter would inherit the same good face. His thoughts were interrupted by a protest from *Sous-Lieutenant* Blanchet, who, still in his uniform, marched indignantly toward Sharpe and delivered a harsh sentence in rapid French.

"Tell him to slow down, Harris."

"He's whingeing about being told to strip naked, sir."

Blanchet evidently understood Harris's translation because he launched into another rant, none of which Sharpe understood. Lieutenant Love, attracted by the French lieutenant's anger, came to stand by Sharpe. "He's angry, sir," Love said unnecessarily, "and says it is unseemly of officers to treat their prisoners with such discourtesy. And I must say, sir, he has a point."

Sharpe offered a brutal summation of what Lieutenant Love could do with his point, then pointed at the irate Frenchman. "Tell the bugger that when La Aguja was captured by the French they stripped her naked. She's merely doing what they do."

Blanchet seemed taken aback, looking at Teresa. "La Aguja?" he asked, plainly impressed, then added more urgent words.

"He says he's your prisoner, sir," Love interpreted, "and he doesn't expect an English gentleman to allow this behavior."

"Tell him I'm no gentleman, and add that La Aguja outranks me. And tell him she wanted them all dead and I persuaded her to leave them alive. So what does he want to be? Dead or naked?"

Sharpe was impressed by Blanchet, who had shown courage in objecting to Teresa's orders. He ordered Harris to take the young officer into the house. "He can keep his damned clothes on," he said, "and I'll join you. Give the poor bugger some wine, El Cobarde must have left some here."

"El Cobarde, sir?"

"El Héroe's new name," Sharpe said.

"The coward, that makes sense," Harris said happily and used his rifle butt to steer the Frenchman into the house.

"Should I join you, sir?" Lieutenant Love asked.

"Stay here and watch the prisoners, make sure La Aguja doesn't castrate them."

Love blanched, "Surely she wouldn't . . ."

"Surely she would," Sharpe said, "and I don't blame her."

Love frowned. "Did the French really strip her naked, sir?"

"They did much more than that, Lieutenant. Why do you think she hates them so much?"

Love blushed. He was gazing at Teresa with evident appreciation of her stern beauty. "Poor woman," he murmured.

"She's fine now, got herself a husband."

"She's married, sir?" Love sounded almost disappointed.

"To me, Lieutenant. She's Mrs. Sharpe. Go and introduce yourself. She doesn't bite, much." He followed Harris into the house to discover the rifleman and his captive sitting at the kitchen table sharing a bottle of wine. Blanchet looked nervously at Sharpe and spoke in rapid French.

"He wants to know what we're doing here, sir," Harris translated.

"Tell him we got lost."

"Lost?"

"We were sent to Truxillo to bring some wounded men home and got chased by some bloody dragoons." It was a thin story, but not impossible. The army had retreated through Truxillo some weeks before and wounded men had been left there, though by now those men were either dead or on their way to a French prison camp north of the Pyrenees. But it might put some doubt into the French mind by persuading them that the presence of riflemen in the hills south of the Tagus was pure ill chance and had nothing to do with the pontoon bridge.

"And he wants to know what happens to him now, sir," Harris translated another question.

"He goes back where he came from," Sharpe said, "to Miravete Castle?"

Blanchet nodded, understanding Sharpe's question. "*Oui*," he said. "Miravete *chateau*."

"And he takes his wounded in the handcarts. And tell him he did well."

"Well, sir?"

"I was watching," Sharpe said, "and he was the officer who deployed the second company into a skirmish line. He damn well near beat me. And tell him he can keep his uniform on. And ask him why they didn't attack the village long ago. They must have known El Héroe was here."

Blanchet's reply was long and hesitant, but Harris slowly translated it to reveal that El Héroe and the French garrison did indeed have an understanding. "They leave him alone, sir, and the yellow bastard doesn't attack their forage parties."

"Live and let live, eh?"

"Sounds like it, sir."

Such arrangements were common between the pickets of

both armies. More than once Sharpe had visited a picket line at night to discover his men entertaining their French opposite numbers with tea and tobacco they had exchanged for French brandy. Sharpe had always left them alone, knowing that such fraternization was common. Indeed, he had known Lord Wellington to send friendly messages to opposing pickets warning them to retreat in the face of an impending attack, yet Sharpe had never heard of Spanish partisans coming to an agreement with the French; the hatred between the Spanish and the French was too fierce. "Has El Héroe ever fought them?" he asked.

"He says the bastard attacked their forage parties last year," Harris translated, "then Colonel Aubert arranged a parley."

"Aubert?"

"He commands the forts, sir."

"And what was agreed at that parley?"

Sharpe waited as Harris questioned the young Frenchman. "El Héroe sells them mutton for rations, sir, and they leave him alone."

"That's all?"

"All he'll tell me, sir, unless you want me to put the boot in?"

"No," Sharpe said, "but ask him how many men Aubert commands."

Blanchet refused to answer. "He says he's certain," Harris interpreted, "that you would not betray your country's strength. And he won't either."

"Quite right," Sharpe said, then reached across the table and picked up Blanchet's shako, which had a ragged hole torn just above the tarnished badge. "Thirty-ninth of the line, eh?" He read the number embossed in the badge. "Your whole battalion is here?"

Again Blanchet refused to answer and Sharpe tossed the battered shako back to him. "Keep him out of Teresa's way," he added to Harris, "or she'll make him answer."

"Is that so bad, sir?" Harris asked.

"We do it to them and they start doing it to us. Just let him be."

It was midday before the naked prisoners walked back the way they had come. They were jeered by the partisans, but Sharpe reckoned the Frenchmen were lucky to be alive. He waited until they had climbed the far side of the valley and had disappeared over the skyline before he and Teresa followed, Sharpe mounted on one of her men's horses. "You ride like a sack of grain," Teresa said coldly, still angry that he had insisted on keeping the prisoners alive.

"I'm an infantryman."

"And a father!" she said, suddenly happy.

"How is Antonia?"

"Very well, happy and safe. I think she is a clever girl."

"You can tell?"

"She will be a terror when she grows up!" Teresa laughed.

"Like her mother."

"Only now men will say her mother has gone soft. Letting the prisoners live! And why did you let the officer keep his clothes?"

"Because he's a brave man and a good officer."

"All the more reason to kill him."

The track led southward. They rode slowly, not wanting to catch up with Blanchet and his men, and it was midafternoon before they came to a crossroads. The ruts left by the handcarts showed that Blanchet had turned right, so they followed, finally stopping where the new track crossed a low ridge. Sharpe crawled through long grass to the ridgeline and trained his telescope northward. "Dear God," he said, "that's a bastard."

He was gazing at Miravete Castle, a foursquare stone building perched on a low hillock. He could see cannon muzzles on the castle's top battlement. There was a scatter of stone houses to the castle's east, and he could see that they had been loopholed for defense, but the biggest obstacle was neither the castle nor the houses but a big earthwork the French had thrown up in front of the buildings. It was a great raw bank and its summit was interrupted by cannon embrasures. Sharpe could see the guns' muzzles and reckoned they were the big French twelve-pounders and he imagined them gouting blasts of canister across the open ground. The earth wall was not just a formidable obstacle but it protected the castle and the houses from enemy cannon fire. There was a big French garrison there, and the earthwork with its formidable cannons lay right across the road that General Harris would need to drag his artillery down to the Tagus. "It is a problem?" Teresa asked.

"We need cannon to flatten the forts by the river," Sharpe said, "but to get them there we have to go through the Miravete pass. It could take a week to destroy that castle, and by that time the French will have a small army on the river."

Teresa turned to look back the way they had come. "But the road through El Cobarde's village goes to the river."

"It's a sheep track and the guns won't manage it, or not quickly enough."

"You're saying it can't be done? Guns have wheels, yes?"

"It's not just the guns," Sharpe said, "there are ammunition caissons, supply wagons, a portable forge. Tons of wagons and guns." He sounded gloomy. "And if they can't get past that bastard," he nodded at the castle, "then we'll have to capture the bridge the old-fashioned way," Sharpe paused, "and it will be bloody." He paused again. "I hate sieges."

"General Hill must get the guns through the village!" Teresa said. "We will help."

"Our artillerymen can work miracles," Sharpe said, "but that sheep track won't take the weight of the guns and wagons." He wondered why Hogan had not heard of the strength of Miravete Castle, and supposed that El Héroe had dismissed the French fortress as negligible. "What do you know of El Héroe?" he asked Teresa.

"El Cobarde?" she corrected him. "Nothing except what I saw."

"And what did you see?"

"A man who tells everyone he is a great man, which means he is a small man. He is a coward because he ran away, and he thinks all women will worship him."

"You don't."

"He is handsome," Teresa said grudgingly, "but beneath his good looks is nothing but rottenness. I would rather have my man from the London gutter." She reached out and stroked Sharpe's face. "You need a shave."

"Lost my razor."

"And a haircut, Richard."

"We lost our scissors."

"I have scissors."

"Then you can cut it," Sharpe said as he stared through the glass as Blanchet's naked troops trudged the last few paces to Miravete Castle. He could see a crowd of blue-uniformed men laughing at them from the battlements, but in reality the French had nothing to laugh about. Every force they had sent out in the last two days had been ripped apart and too many men had died. "All the buggers have to do is sit behind their stone walls and that bloody great earth bank," Sharpe said, "and we'll be helpless."

"So you do it the old-fashioned way," Teresa said. "And what is that?"

"It's the way that makes widows and leaves orphans," Sharpe said as he collapsed the glass. "And I reckon we'll be doing it. Let's go back."

"You're frightened?" Teresa said, sounding disappointed.

"Widows and orphans," Sharpe said grimly. "You and Antonia. But we do have one thing on our side."

"What's that?"

"We have rifles," Sharpe said, "and we have riflemen."

Because rifles and riflemen could make the hopeless possible. They rode back.

CHAPTER 4

"I want you to take the Truxillo road," Sharpe told Teresa.

"Tired of me already?"

"Don't be daft. I need to send a messenger to General Hill, and a messenger I trust."

"You should go!" Teresa insisted.

Sharpe shook his head. "We've woken the damned French. They know we're here. If they come to smoke us out, I need to be here. And before I meet General Hill I'm ordered to cross the river and look at the fort on the other bank."

"We can help," Teresa said enthusiastically.

"If I can even get across," Sharpe said dully, then explained that the French had evidently scoured the riverbanks to destroy any boats.

"Of course there'll be boats," Teresa said confidently. "As soon as people knew what the French were doing, they'd have hidden some boats. My men will find some."

"I only need one."

"You'll have one. And besides, you don't want to send a messenger to General Hill before you've crossed the river."

Sharpe conceded the point, and Teresa sent horsemen upriver while Sharpe stayed at the village church that he turned into a small fortress. He wanted a fortress of his own in case the French came in force and the small village church with its thick stone walls was the strongest building available. It was surrounded by open ground, broken only by small gravestones, which gave defenders a killing ground. He used the French crates to make firesteps at each window, then had his men load all the French muskets. "If they come for us," he said, "we fire the rifles and when they get close start using the muskets." There were sufficient muskets for each man to have six, which, fired one after the other, would provide a torrent of lead. There were eight windows to defend; three on both the northern and southern walls and two high windows flanking the door at the western end. The big eastern window above the altar had been bricked up at some point in the church's long history and was now half hidden by a crudely painted wooden screen.

No French force came. Sharpe had put three pickets, each of two men, to watch the approaches to the village, but they saw nothing. Rifleman Henderson led three men to the big house that had been El Héroe's quarters and they returned with sacks of grain, a barrel of salted mutton and three of wine. Henderson also slammed a heavy box onto the church floor. "It was hidden under the kitchen flagstones, Mister Sharpe," he said, "and you'll like it."

Sharpe lifted the lid and whistled in surprise. The box was half filled with coins. He picked up a couple. They were gold and he could see Napoleon's head on both. He tipped one toward a window and saw the words *Napoléon Empereur* inscribed round the margin. Turning them over he saw they were both five-franc pieces. One proclaimed it was issued by the *République Française* and the other, presumably more recent, by the *Empire Français*. "It's a fortune," he said. "I assume you've got a few in your pouch, Joe?"

"Me, Mister Sharpe?" Henderson asked, grinning.

"Keep them safe, Joe."

"God looks after riflemen, Mister Sharpe."

"Let's hope he keeps the Crapauds away."

"After the beating we've given them? The bastards won't dare come near us."

"And if they do?"

"One shot and they'll go right about."

Sharpe left Harris counting the coins. It was indeed a fortune and Sharpe suspected it was payments from the French to ensure El Héroe left them alone. He remembered what Major Hogan had said about El Héroe, that he cared about money, and he took pleasure in imagining El Héroe's fury when he discovered the loss of his French gold. "Why didn't he take the gold with him?" he wondered aloud.

"Too heavy," Harris suggested. "If you're running away you don't want to carry heavy stuff. Besides, he reckoned it was well hid."

Shortly before midday Teresa's men returned to say they had discovered a boat hidden in thick reeds a mile or so upriver. It was big enough, they reckoned, for four or five men.

"Three are enough," Sharpe said. He left Patrick Harper in charge at the church. "If the bastards send a battalion up here then just get out," Sharpe ordered him. "If it's a company you can probably beat them." He hesitated. "I'm sorry, Pat, I'm leaving Lieutenant Love here and he might insist on being in command."

"I can handle Cupid," Harper said firmly.

"But you probably can't handle a full Crapaud battalion."

"If a battalion comes, sir," Harper said, "we'll go west. Find a place to lie low."

"If there is such a place."

"It's like my mother always says, sir, if it's not here it's there."

Sharpe doubted Harper's mother was an expert on infantry tactics, but consoled himself that most of Teresa's partisans would also stay in the church that, with its thick stone walls and plentiful firing positions, would prove a formidable bastion.

Sharpe took Hagman, because the old man had the best eyesight in his company and was also the deadliest rifleman, and Joe Henderson because the big northerner was staunch, reliable, and had assured Sharpe he had grown up with small boats on the River Wear. Lieutenant Love pleaded to accompany Sharpe, who explained to the artilleryman that the danger was from an infantry attack and that he should let Sergeant Harper decide how to counter it. "Besides," he went on, "you've no business on the northern bank. No one's proposing to take guns over the river."

"That's true, sir," Love conceded reluctantly, "and I'll take Sergeant Harper's advice, sir."

"Make sure you do," Sharpe said.

"You think a French attack is likely, sir?" Love asked nervously.

"If I was them, I'd bring a bloody battalion up here, but so far they've showed themselves to be bloody useless, so probably not."

"I'll pray not, sir."

"I'm sure that will help," Sharpe said, then went outside, where Teresa had horses ready. She and one of the men who had discovered the boat led them eastward, only descending to the riverbank when a bend in the Tagus hid them from the French forts beside the pontoon bridge.

The boat was about ten foot long and narrow with a thwart in its center and two clumsy oars in its belly. "It'll do fine," Henderson declared, and heaved the boat from its hiding place into the river.

"Right, get in," Sharpe ordered. "Not you!"

"I'm coming," Teresa insisted, and clambered into the boat and sat on its stern thwart next to Sharpe while Hagman crouched nervously in the bow.

Teresa's man stayed on the southern bank to look after the horses while Henderson rowed across the river. The boat seemed fragile to Sharpe and they had not been afloat more than a minute before water began rising round his boots. "All boats leak," Henderson grunted as he heaved on the oars.

"And sink?" Sharpe asked.

"She dried out, Mister Sharpe," Henderson said, taking a hand from an oar and rapping the boat's hull, "she's been too long out of water. She'll heal up once she's proper wetted."

The current was strong, pushing the boat downstream so fast that Sharpe feared they would be swept round the bend into the view of the French engineers working on the old broken bridge, but Henderson gave the oars some mighty heaves and the craft crunched into the southern bank well short of the bend.

They hauled the boat out of the water and then Sharpe led them uphill through a belt of low trees. They had left their shakos in the boat so their silhouettes on the skyline would not betray them as British troops and, reaching that skyline, Sharpe lay in the sun-warmed grass and used his telescope to gaze at Fort Ragusa.

It was another stone fort on a low steep hill, its battlements equipped with small cannon. Some of the guns faced north up the main road to deter a land attack while others covered the pontoon bridge itself. Between the fort and the bridge was a low bastion, the *tête de pont*, which guarded the northern end of the bridge of boats. He could see infantry and cannon in the low earthwork, which was almost identical to the bastion at the bridge's southern end. He did not see much point in this reconnaissance because, though Fort Ragusa was smaller than Fort Napoleon and would be an easier fort to attack, he did not see any way Hill could get his men across the river short of crossing the Tagus in Portugal, which he doubted was a real choice. He trained the telescope on the fort's high battlements and frowned.

"What?" Teresa asked.

Sharpe gave the glass to Hagman. "Look at those infantrymen on the fort, Dan. Tell me what's on their shakos."

Hagman gazed through the glass. "No idea, Mister Sharpe."

"Not the same as the fellows we shot."

"Nothing like," Hagman agreed, "those are much more fancy."

Sharpe took the glass back and stared again. So far he had discovered troops from the 6th and 39th of the French line; these men's shakos did not have the same diamond-shaped brass badge, but instead had a much larger and more flamboyant brass plate. They were much too far away to read the number on the plaque or even to recognize its shape, but the very fact that they wore a different badge suggested they were from yet another battalion. "There could be three battalions of bloody French infantry here," Sharpe muttered.

"And there are some of them on the old bridge too," Teresa murmured in his ear and Sharpe edged the telescope left and saw a score of men working on the bridge's northern end. They were sawing timbers with long, two-handled saws and the sawn pieces were being carried to the edge of the gaping hole in the bridge's southern arch.

"What the buggers are doing," Henderson said, "is building a wooden arch to replace the old one."

"That'll take weeks," Sharpe said.

"Not so long, sir," Henderson said. "Once they've got the timbers cut it'll go up smartly enough, then they'll lay masonry round the wooden arch. A good engineer could have that bridge repaired in a fortnight."

Sharpe gazed at the shattered bridge's nearer end and saw no men on the closer roadway nor on the bank, which suggested all the repairs were being managed from the northern bank. "Reckon we can get down to the bridge without being seen?" he asked.

"We can," Hagman said confidently.

"You stay here," Sharpe told Teresa, knowing he was wasting his breath, then followed Hagman, who had dropped beneath the skyline and was heading north.

"What are you doing?" Teresa asked Sharpe.

"Slowing the buggers down."

Hagman led them on a long circuit that kept them out of sight of any Frenchman watching from the bridge or from the high battlements of Fort Ragusa. They came to the high road leading from the old bridge and followed it, staying in the low scrubby trees at the highway's edge, until they reached the old bridge itself.

On this northern bank there were no enemy troops at the base of the bridge nor any on the short stub of broken roadway. Sharpe said a prayer of thanks for the enemy's carelessness and lay at the road's edge and gazed across the gap. He could see three officers standing among the men heaving on the huge saws. The men doing the work had discarded their jackets and either worked bare-chested or in shirtsleeves, but the officers had uniforms that looked black. Sharpe stared through the glass and saw that the jackets were a very dark blue with black facings and turnbacks. "Black and blue uniforms," he said.

"It's the dark blue of their artillery, Mister Sharpe," Hagman said.

"The black facings mean they're engineers," Sharpe said. For reasons he did not understand, French engineers were always uniformed as artillerymen. "And I want those three dead." He handed the telescope to Teresa. "You watch them and we shoot them. Dan? Take the officer on the right. Joe? The bugger on the left. The center one is mine."

"Easy shot, Mister Sharpe," Hagman said encouragingly, "two hundred and fifty paces?"

Kill the engineer officers, Sharpe reckoned, and he would certainly delay and maybe even end any effort to repair the bridge. He wriggled up onto the roadway and aimed the rifle across the broken span. Two hundred and fifty yards was nothing for a Baker rifle, and his target was easily recognizable because of the gold braid on his uniform. Hagman was to his right, Henderson to his left, and they were well within sight of the far Frenchmen, who seemed oblivious to their presence. "Dozy bastards," Sharpe muttered. "I'm ready."

"Me too, Mister Sharpe," Hagman said.

"And me," Henderson offered.

"On my order," Sharpe said, "count of three. Fire on one."

He hesitated, reflecting on General Hill's orders that the French were to be undisturbed, that the presence of riflemen in the hills about the river would betray an ambition to attack the pontoon bridge. But, damn it, the French already knew that Sharpe and his men were there, and the whole point of the expedition was to destroy the bridge. But wrecking the pontoon bridge would be useless if the French managed to repair this old bridge. So damn Hill's orders.

"Three," he said.

Three dogheads were dragged back, three good flints were poised above the frizzens that, when struck, would flash open and let the sparks ignite the powder in the rifles' pans.

He had the backsight folded flat and lined the lower notch with the stub of foresight at the barrel's muzzle. He lined them against the far glint of gold braid, then raised the muzzle a fraction so he was aiming just above the distant officer's cocked hat.

"Two."

The barrel wavered slightly. The air, heated by the sun, shimmered above the broken roadway. No wind. He dropped the muzzle to make sure he was still centered on the engineer, saw that he was, and edged it upward a tiny amount, then resisted an urge to make sure his flint was well seated in the doghead.

"One!"

He pulled the trigger. The flint slammed downward and a cascade of sparks flowed from the opening frizzen. A flash in the pan as the powder caught and the slight pause as the fire in the pan found the touchhole and ignited the charge. Then came the bang of the rifle and the brass butt slammed into his shoulder and a burst of smoke made a cloud in front of the muzzle.

"Two down," Teresa said.

"Reload," Sharpe said, though the order was unnecessary because both Hagman and Henderson were already biting the bullets from new cartridges.

"Which two?" Sharpe asked, standing and taking a cartridge from his pouch.

"The center one is alive," Teresa said.

Sharpe swore while Hagman chuckled. "It was a difficult shot, Mister Sharpe."

"Like hell it was." Sharpe rammed the new bullet down the barrel. Hagman had already crossed to the far side of the road where he was kneeling. "I've got him, Mister Sharpe," he said, raising the rifle to his shoulder. "Silly bugger is just standing there with his mouth open."

"Down his gullet, Dan!" Henderson called.

Hagman fired. The shot echoed back from the hills on the river's far side. "Three down," Teresa said happily.

"Bloody idiot," Hagman said derisively, "he just stood there and waited to be killed."

"We'd best get back to the boat," Sharpe said. He reckoned the garrison of Fort Ragusa must send out a patrol to investigate the shots. "And well done, lads. Sorry I missed."

"I reckon your rifle's tired, Mister Sharpe," Hagman said.

"Tired?"

"After a while the barrels get warped," Hagman explained. "I reckon you've had that one a while?"

"Seven years," Sharpe said.

"A Shorncliffe rifle?" Hagman asked, meaning the barracks where the light infantry had trained.

"That's where I got it," Sharpe confirmed.

"They were never the best rifles," Hagman said, "and you tap-load a lot. I'm of a mind that tap-loading tires the barrel, so time to get another rifle, Mister Sharpe."

"I like this one."

"It's served you well, that's a fact." Hagman reloaded his rifle and slung it on his shoulder. There was a spatter of musket fire from the working party on the other end of the bridge, but all the shots went high or else flitted through the trees at the sides of the road. "You've seen all you wanted?" the old poacher asked.

"Enough, Dan," Sharpe said. He supposed General Hill might approve of him creating a disturbance on the northern bank to persuade the French that any expedition to destroy the pontoon bridge might come from the north, from Ciudad Rodrigo, and the death of three engineers would surely lodge that idea in their heads. Though three deaths, however valuable the dead men had been to the French, was nothing compared to the carnage that Sharpe's riflemen and Teresa's partisans had already wreaked on the southern bank. By now, he reflected ruefully, he had well and truly disobeyed Hill's instructions not to poke the wasps' nest, and Colonel Aubert, the commander of the garrison, must surely be sending for reinforcements. And a strengthened French garrison could well be enough to stop Hill's assault. Those gloomy thoughts accompanied him to the boat that Joe Henderson manhandled into the river then clawed them across to the southern bank.

"So what now?" Teresa asked as they splashed onto dry ground.

"We go to find General Hill."

"All of us?"

"Pat Harper will keep the men here," Sharpe said, "and I'll tell him to stay out of trouble."

"My men too?"

"It would help if most of them stayed here. Maybe bring a couple with us to Truxillo? Though I doubt there's any need. There'll be no French on the road."

Sharpe was confident of that. If Marshal Soult, south of the Tagus, sent troops to join Marmont in the north then they would encounter Hill's force somewhere close to Truxillo, which suggested to Sharpe that he and Teresa could ride to that city safely enough. "There might be no French," Teresa pointed out, "but El Cobarde is probably on that road."

Sharpe had forgotten El Héroe. "He'll do nothing," he said curtly.

"You hope."

"The only things he does well are to lie, cheat, and run away."

Patrick Harper reported that all had been quiet at the village since Sharpe left. "We saw a fellow watching us from the hill," he pointed westward, "but he didn't stay long. I'm thinking it was just a shepherd."

"Wrong direction for a Crapaud."

"No sign of them, sir. I think they've learned their lesson."

"And what lesson is that, Patrick?" Teresa asked.

"Don't try and bugger the Rifles," Harper said proudly.

"Let's hope no one tries that with you over the next few days," Sharpe said. "I'm riding to meet General Hill, but I'll be back as soon as I can. Four days? Five? I'll take Lieutenant Love so you'll be in command here."

"God save Ireland!" Harper said wonderingly. "A boy from Donegal in command! Want me to capture the forts, sir?"

"I want you to stay quiet. Keep your pickets awake, but don't poke the wasps' nest. Just wait for my return."

"I wouldn't dream of poking the wasps! But I'll put a picket in El Héroe's house. From the top floor you can see everything."

"And it gives you a chance to search the house thoroughly?"

"The thought never occurred to me, sir," Harper grinned, "but it's a grand idea."

Sharpe reluctantly agreed. "I mean it, Pat, no fight."

"Me, sir? Fight? God save Ireland, I joined the army for food, not for fighting."

"I'll be back as soon as I can."

"Take your time, sir, enjoy Miss Teresa."

Teresa left almost all her men in the village to reinforce Harper's riflemen while she took three as her escort on the Truxillo road. Sharpe and Love were given docile horses to ride. He worried for his men's safety as he clattered southward, but no musket or rifle shots sounded behind him. "There's no need for you to come," he told Teresa.

"And who'll keep you safe if I don't?"

It seemed strange to Sharpe to be riding openly so far behind the French lines. Except for General Hill's force, which he assumed was marching toward Truxillo, the countryside was ruled by the French for at least a hundred miles in every direction, yet he saw no sign of the enemy. They passed through small villages and towns and there was not a blue uniform to be seen. The villagers told of forage parties who came to plunder houses and barns, and those parties, they said, were escorted by hundreds of horsemen to protect the foragers from partisans. "Does that mean El Héroe is actually fighting?" Sharpe asked.

"Not him," Teresa said scathingly. "The partisans here are led by El Sacerdote."

"The priest?"

"He was a priest till the French sacked his church and raped half his parishioners." She thought for a heartbeat. "I suppose he still is a priest because he says Mass for his men, and gives his French prisoners the last rites before he cuts their throats." She smiled. "I like him."

It was evening before Truxillo showed on the southern horizon. The town was built on a hill and loomed above the flat plain. There was an ancient wall circling the buildings, which were dominated by a castle. As they drew closer and as the shadows lengthened across the flat land Sharpe saw red coats on the city wall, and still more guarding the town's northern gate. "The French left weeks ago," Teresa said nonchalantly, "chased out by El Sacerdote's men."

A lieutenant, wearing a red coat with yellow facings, held up a hand as they approached. "*Quién eres?*" His men leveled muskets. They saw a ragged group, mostly wearing the red scarves that many partisans had adopted as a uniform, and Sharpe, in his dark green, looked no smarter than his companions. He was unshaven, his hair was long, and his green jacket was stained.

"I'm here to see General Hill. I assume he's here?" Sharpe spurred his horse forward.

"And you are?" the lieutenant asked.

"Major Sharpe, 95th. General Hill is expecting us."

The lieutenant looked disbelieving, but then caught Sharpe's gaze and straightened. "Of course, sir. The general's in the castillo." He pointed eastward. "Just follow the street inside the wall, sir, you can't miss the place."

They followed the street until they reached another guardpost at the castle's entrance. "It was built by the Moors," Teresa said, "and we chased them out too."

The castle's courtyard was crowded with troops, their muskets stacked about a battery of cannon. Sharpe saw more Scots wearing the yellow facings of the 92nd and others wearing red coats with black facings. "The dirty half hundred," he told Teresa.

"The what?"

"The 50th," Sharpe explained, "hard buggers from Kent." There were men wearing buff facings, the 71st, another Scottish regiment. "I almost feel sorry for the Crapauds," Sharpe said.

"Sorry!" Teresa sounded offended.

"Two Scottish battalions? They're savage fighters."

"Good! And there are more riflemen." She pointed across the courtyard where men in green jackets were making a fire. Sharpe spurred toward them and recognized several. "Sergeant Gerrard!"

"Oh God in his shoddy heaven," the sergeant turned in surprise, "we're all in the shit now."

"How are you, Tom?"

"I was happy till a minute ago, but if you're here? Things must be desperate."

"How many are you?"

"Mustering eighty."

"Who commands?"

"Captain Theobald."

"A good man," Sharpe said approvingly.

"Aye, he is that. I'm guessing he's dining with Daddy."

"Where do I find the general?"

"Through that door," Gerrard pointed, "and upstairs."

"Your men can stable our horses?"

Gerrard looked dubiously at Sharpe's companions. "We can, but I doubt Daddy wants you all at dinner."

"Just me and my wife," Sharpe said, swinging out of the saddle.

The sergeant turned his gaze to Teresa and grinned. "They always said you were lucky, Mister Sharpe."

"I am, Tom, I am." He walked through the riflemen, greeting those he knew, then took Teresa's arm and, beckoning Lieutenant Love to join him, led her through the great door to find a stairway. "He's no fool, General Hill."

"No?"

"He brought more riflemen. Which means we'll win."

"You doubted that?"

Sharpe did not answer, just took the stairs to find two redcoats of the 50th guarding a doorway. "I'm looking for Major Hogan," Sharpe said.

"He's with the general, sir," one of the redcoats answered.

"In there?" Sharpe did not wait for an answer, but just opened the door.

At least a dozen men were in the room, clustered about a table on which maps were spread among the remnants of dinner. They all turned to stare as Sharpe led Teresa and Love inside. Then General Hill took a tentative step toward Sharpe. "Good God!" he said.

"Richard!" That was Major Hogan, sounding equally astonished.

"You're not dead!" Hill added.

"Seems not, sir."

"Well, come in, come in!" Hill gestured.

"I believe you know Lieutenant Love, sir," Sharpe said, then more awkwardly, "and allow me to present my wife." Hill and the other officers stared at Teresa, who wore tight cavalry overalls tucked into tall riding boots. Her short jacket was a discarded rifleman's green coat, belted at her slim waist from which hung a saber, a long knife, and a pistol.

"La Aguja," Hogan said in a loud whisper to Hill.

"Our pleasure, ma'am," Hill said gallantly, offering Teresa a bow. "We heard you were dead also. I am overjoyed that information was wrong."

"I am overjoyed too," Teresa said drily, then smiled at Hogan. "Major," she acknowledged him.

"We heard you were overpowered by the French at Miravete," Hogan explained.

"We killed the French at Miravete," Teresa said vengefully.

"All of them?" Hogan asked.

"At least a company," Sharpe said, "but there's more of the buggers." Hogan cleared his throat meaningfully and Sharpe remembered he was not supposed to offend Hill with any swear words. "A lot more," he added vaguely.

"A lot?" a tall gray-haired man whose elegantly cut red coat had buff facings asked abruptly.

"Colonel Cadogan," Hill introduced the man, "of the seventy-first."

Another Scottish regiment, Sharpe noted, before acknowledging Cadogan's question with an inclination of his head. "My guess, sir, is that they have a full battalion of infantry in the castle and in a pair of stone houses nearby," Sharpe said, "and they've thrown up a big bastard of an earthwork with cannon emplacements to protect the buildings."

"A big earthwork?" Hill asked pointedly, evidently as a second reminder to Sharpe that he disliked vulgarity.

"A very big bastard," Teresa said enthusiastically, "tall as a man with a ditch in front."

"And cannon?" Cadogan asked.

"Half a dozen twelve-pounders," Sharpe said, "and three six-inch howitzers."

"Doubtless all well supplied with canister," Cadogan said sourly.

No one spoke, all of them imagining infantry advancing on a battery of cannon flaying them with canister, the rounds that exploded from the gun's muzzle like duckshot.

"We have cannon too," Hill broke the silence.

"An earthwork," Hogan said flatly. "It'll soak up our fire, sir."

"If we're to take Miravete Castle," Hill said, "it must be done swiftly. In a day." He looked at Sharpe questioningly.

"It will take a week, sir," Sharpe said.

"Colonel Gonzalez disagrees," Cadogan said brusquely.

"Colonel Gonzalez, sir?"

"El Héroe," Hogan explained.

"He's been here, sir?" It was Sharpe's turn to be surprised.

"He was." Hogan looked about the room as if expecting to see El Héroe.

"He was here a moment ago! Why isn't he with us?" Hill demanded, and turned to an aide. "Seek him out, Horace, and ask him to attend us." He looked back to Sharpe. "It was Colonel Gonzalez who informed us of your death. He claims to have witnessed it."

"He also said there were only two companies of French troops in Miravete," Cadogan added.

"Miravete sent two companies against my men, sir," Sharpe said. "And there were plenty more Frenchmen in the castle when their survivors returned."

"Two companies attacked you?" Hill asked.

"Two, sir, and I sent them one back, without their weapons."

"Or uniforms," Teresa added. "Major Sharpe would not permit me to kill the prisoners."

"Of course not!" Hill said.

"And there were plenty of men in the castle when the company returned," Sharpe reiterated. "I suspect it's garrisoned by their thirty-ninth of the line, sir, while the sixth regiment is down at the river. And there seems to be a third battalion in Fort Ragusa, but I couldn't find their number. They were wearing some new fancy shako plate."

"An eagle plate, probably," Hogan said, then, to Hill, who looked puzzled, "they're introducing a new shako plate, sir, a rather ornate eagle badge instead of the old diamond-shaped plate."

Hill frowned as he looked down on the maps, the same maps Sharpe had seen in Badajoz. "I had rather hoped the French would not be aware of your presence, Major Sharpe." He sounded disapproving, "and it seems they were very aware?"

"They were, sir."

"So they're forewarned of our interest," Cadogan said disapprovingly. "And doubtless reinforcing."

Hill sighed. "Two forts, a castle, and the *têtes de pont*." He gazed down at the maps. "And evidence of at least three battalions. I wonder who leads them?"

"A Colonel Aubert, sir," Sharpe said.

"Aubert?" Hill looked at Hogan.

"Never heard of him, sir," Hogan said, "which suggests he's not an outstanding officer."

"That's a blessing," Hill said, "and at least Colonel Gonzalez assures us there's no fortress at the old bridge."

"Oh but there is, sir," Sharpe said, "and they have more cannon there and a small force of infantry. I counted twenty-four muskets, sir, and there are engineers too. But the engineer officers are dead."

"You again?"

"Rifles," Sharpe said shortly.

"Well done, Mister Sharpe," a man in Rifle green said happily. Sharpe recognized Captain Theobald and grinned at him.

"You say there's artillery at the old bridge," Hill asked, "which could enfilade any assault on Fort Napoleon?"

"I could capture that fortlet with a dozen men," Sharpe said.

"You say there are cannon at the bridge encampment?" Colonel Cadogan repeated the general's question testily. "What size?"

"Big, sir," Sharpe said, knowing he was delivering bad news. "Lieutenant Love identified them as twenty-four-pounders."

"Good God," someone muttered.

"Old iron ones," Lieutenant Love added, "I suspect captured from the Spanish."

"God help us," Cadogan whispered.

"And they had three of the old four-pounders there too," Love said brightly.

"I thought they'd stopped using four-pounders," General Hill said.

"They did, sir," Hogan confirmed, "but that doesn't mean they haven't posted a few in strongpoints."

"A useful little gun," Lieutenant Love remarked.

"Useful?" Hill asked.

"Very mobile, sir. They used to move those old fours round a battlefield like chess pieces. Their new six is heavier and harder to move."

"The fours were regimental guns," an older artillery officer said, meaning they were light cannon attached to an infantry battalion. "They were useful pieces, but the infantry complained they didn't make enough noise."

"They did what?" Hill asked in a wondering tone.

"They wanted heavier cannon that would frighten the enemy by their noise alone," the artillery officer explained, "so they replaced the fours with sixes, but they must still have the fours in their depots."

"I'm more concerned about the twenty-fours." Hill was looking at Sharpe again. "They protect the fort at the old bridge?"

"They do, sir, but it's not much of a fort, just a palisade protecting their engineers."

"So they are attempting to repair the old bridge?" Hill asked anxiously.

"They're trying," Sharpe said, "but without engineer officers now."

"How close did you get?" Hill asked.

"We were on the bridge itself, sir, there was some cut stone, but no evidence of masons at work, just a dozen men sawing timbers."

Cadogan bridled at the news. "So you were on the bridge itself? And you weren't discovered?"

"We were discovered, sir," Sharpe said. "I believe we were betrayed, sir."

"Betrayed?" Hill sounded alarmed.

"By your Colonel Gonzalez, sir."

"Oh, surely not!" Hill sounded pained. "And where is El Héroe? He should be here!"

There was no answer to that question. "Why do you say 'betrayed?'" Hogan asked.

"The French knew we were there from the very first, sir. I took two men to the old bridge as soon as I arrived and we were ambushed by the Crapauds that same evening."

"Good Lord," Hill said, "ambushed?"

"A patrol from Fort Napoleon, sir. I think only ten of them survived."

"Out of how many?" Hogan asked, amused.

"Twenty-one," Sharpe said, "and my other suspicion of El Héroe is that when we searched his house we found a hoard of francs in French gold." He deliberately did not specify the amount, suspecting that his riflemen would be helping themselves and he would spare them any sort of official inquiry.

"The hoard doesn't surprise me," a tall man, dressed all in black, said. He had been standing in the shadows and Sharpe had not even seen him, but now recognized the long face and the shrewd eyes. It was El Sacerdote.

"Why do you say that, Padre?" Hill asked respectfully.

"El Héroe," the priest said, "cares only for money. It is his god."

"You carried him our gold?" Hill looked at Sharpe.

"Never gave it to him, sir."

"You brought it back?"

"I left it with my sergeant, sir."

Hogan laughed. "You left Pat Harper with a hundred guineas?"

"They're safe," Sharpe said, hoping he was right and suspecting most of it was already filched.

The door opened and Hill's aide came into the room. "Odd, sir," he said, "but Colonel Gonzalez left a half hour ago with his men."

"Left?" Hill asked.

"At some speed, I'm told, sir. They went north."

"Why?" Hill wanted to know.

"No idea, sir."

"He heard Major Sharpe had arrived," Hogan suggested.

"And he claimed Major Sharpe was dead," Hill went on, "and also claimed you disobeyed his orders, Sharpe."

"I did, sir, but I'm not required to obey Spanish *partidas*."

"Except one," Teresa said pointedly, provoking laughter.

"Colonel Gonzalez," Hill sounded disapproving, "claims you killed the French officer who gave him information."

"I killed at least half a dozen French officers," Sharpe said defiantly, "but I doubt any of them was giving El Héroe any information. If anything, he was giving them information."

"Or selling it," El Sacerdote put in.

"And now the scoundrel has returned to Almaraz," Hill said flatly.

"And taken news of our plans," Cadogan growled, "which doubtless he'll sell to the enemy."

"What plans, may I ask?" Sharpe asked.

Hill looked down at the map. "Presently, Major, our design is to march through the Miravete pass and use the main road to carry the guns down to Fort Napoleon and besiege it. That's what we decided, but that depends on us suppressing the castle swiftly before we march on down to the river, and if you're right then the pass is more heavily defended than we thought."

"It is, sir."

"You approached the pontoon bridge through the Miravete pass?" Hogan asked.

"No, sir, there's a track through the hills to the east of the pass."

"Will the track take cannon?" Hill asked.

"What guns are we taking, sir?"

The tall thin artillery officer, a lieutenant-colonel, answered. "Six five-fives," he said curtly.

"And three nines," a younger artillery officer added nervously, plainly concerned not to offend the older man.

"All formidable pieces," Hill said encouragingly.

"The five-fives," Sharpe asked, "horse or foot, sir?"

"Foot," the older artillery officer said grudgingly.

Which meant that instead of taking the five-and-a-half-inch howitzers of the horse artillery, the gunners would be taking standard artillery howitzers, which were far heavier. Formidable guns, true, but Sharpe flinched at what the gunners would face. "As I remember, sir, the five-fives weigh over two and a half tons each, and the nine-pounders a bit more. It can't be done, sir, not quickly. The slopes are too steep."

"We've managed steep slopes before," the lieutenant-colonel commented curtly.

"Straight up or down, yes, sir," Sharpe said, "but I'm talking about twelve-inch-wide sheep tracks that go across the side of the slope. The guns will be canted sideways."

The tall artilleryman grunted as though to suggest that the ragged rifleman had no idea of his men's abilities. "What do you say, Love?" he demanded. "It was your job to decide on the matter."

Love hesitated. "Major Sharpe is certainly right that it will be difficult to traverse the slopes, sir. It will indeed be difficult, but . . ."

The "but" spurred Major Hogan to clear his throat loudly.

"Major Sharpe," he said very firmly, "has seen more service than any of us. He's fought in Flanders, India, the Galician hills, Portugal, and Spain. I daresay you helped haul the guns to the heights of Gawilghur?"

"I did," Sharpe lied. He had not helped the struggling artillerymen, but he had witnessed the herculean effort the engineers and gunners had made to drag the heavy artillery up an impossibly steep slope.

"Gawilghur," the tall artillery officer said as if the name left a foul taste in his mouth. It was not the first time that Sharpe had detected a dislike of men like himself who had fought in India, a dislike that implied their experience there did not count. He was about to speak, but Hogan answered the artilleryman first.

"I trust Major Sharpe's opinion."

"And Lord Wellington would concur with you, Hogan," Hill said. "His Lordship particularly recommended Major Sharpe to me because of his experience." Sharpe felt himself blushing and gazed down at the map. Hill tapped it with a pencil. "And you're right, Sharpe," Hill went on, "the job would have to be done swiftly." He looked at Lieutenant Love. "You think it can be done swiftly, Lieutenant?"

"No, sir," Love said, blushing.

"Infantry can use the track," Sharpe said.

"You say the track is but a foot wide?" an elderly officer in a red coat asked.

"Yes, sir. It's a sheep track."

"So troops must go single file?"

"No other way to use it, sir."

"Which will be inconvenient," the officer said.

"General Howard is right," Hill put in, "but I daresay it can be done."

"And if it is done," Colonel Cadogan sounded angry, "we'll reach the river, but we'll have no cannon to breach Fort Napoleon's walls!"

"Which leaves only one option," Hill said regretfully, then paused, not liking the next word.

"Escalade," Sharpe said it for him.

"God, I hope not!" Cadogan said. "We'll be enfiladed by those guns at the broken bridge." He looked at the senior artillery officer. "Can the twenty-fours use canister?"

"Roundshot and shell, no canister."

"A small mercy," Hill said.

"It'll be bad enough if we're forced to an escalade," Cadogan said, "but God help us if they have artillery on our flank shooting roundshot and shell. I don't like it."

"Captain Sharpe can take care of those guns," Hogan said carelessly.

"I can," Sharpe said.

"While my men," Cadogan said unhappily, "die on the walls."

"So be glad you have riflemen, sir," Sharpe said.

"You believe in miracles, Richard?" Hogan asked, amused.

"I believe in the Baker rifle," Sharpe said. "And it will get you over those walls."

Escalade, Sharpe was thinking, one of the horrors of war, but it was the only way.

* * *

Major Hogan walked beside Sharpe's horse as he rode toward Truxillo's northern gate. Sharpe, Teresa, and her three men were all riding back to the village where Harper waited in the makeshift fortress, while Lieutenant Love, to Sharpe's relief, was staying with Hill's brigade.

"I suspect," Major Hogan said, "that you don't have much faith in Lieutenant Love's judgment?"

"He's a puppy," Sharpe snarled.

"A clever puppy. He studied mathematics at Cambridge."

"That'll help him get nine-pounders across those hills."

"Be kind to Cupid," Hogan said, amused, "Cupid has been good to you." He nodded toward Teresa. "And I'd rather the two of you waited, Richard."

"And accompanied Hill's force?"

"Exactly. We march tomorrow, so why not wait?"

"I need to rejoin my men," Sharpe said, "and keep an eye on the damned Frogs."

"And El Héroe has already gone," Hogan said meaningfully. "He's at least an hour ahead of you." He looked at Teresa. "Is there another road to Almaraz?"

"Nothing convenient," Teresa answered. She thought for a heartbeat. "We could take the road to Plasencia and follow the river eastward, but it's twice as far. And why would we want to do that?"

"Because El Héroe is almost certainly watching the road between here and Almaraz," Hogan said. He turned and glanced at Teresa's three men. "You're very few and if you're right then he left with at least thirty men."

Sharpe shifted in his saddle. "What does he gain by stopping us?"

"Nothing much," Hogan said, "but that's not why he's watching the road. He's looking out for Hill's men. He needs to count them, count the guns, and take that news to Almaraz. But if he sees you, he'll try and kill you."

"Probably," Sharpe conceded. He thought for a moment. "Why the devil did El Héroe even come here?"

"He came to complain about you, not knowing that you would be coming to Truxillo too, and he came to plead for rifles and gold."

"Which you didn't give him?"

"Of course not," Hogan said shortly. "And he wanted to know why you were sent to him."

"To reconnoiter the bridge, of course."

"Which we also told him. But then we told him how we mean to destroy the pontoon bridge, which surprised him."

"It surprised him to learn we mean to attack Almaraz?"

"It did."

"Then he's an idiot."

"An idiot," Hogan agreed, "and it was idiotic of him to ambush you when you first arrived."

"I still can't think why he did," Sharpe said. "It makes no sense! He said he thought we were French, but if he's on their side, why ambush them? And if he thought we were sending him gold and rifles, why ambush us?"

"Because he thought he was ambushing Spaniards," Hogan said.

"Spaniards!" Sharpe sounded surprised.

"I talked to some of his men and it appears that our hero is having a quarrel with a partisan band centered on Cáceres. It was his fault, he raided their town and took off a score of their horses and some young women and he believed you were those same partisans coming for revenge."

"You mean he's nothing but a bloody bandit?" Sharpe said indignantly.

"But a bandit," Hogan said, "who would love to kill you, and would really enjoy capturing La Aguja."

"Probably," Sharpe said.

"So stay here tonight and march with us tomorrow."

"He will not capture me," Teresa said scornfully. "*Es un pedazo inútil de mierda.*"

"He might be a useless piece of shit," Hogan persevered, "but he has more men."

"The French have more men," Teresa said, "and they try to capture me all the time."

"He'll know by now that you revealed his lies." Hogan turned back to Sharpe.

"So?"

"So he's not happy with you. If he sees you, he's liable to take his revenge."

"He's running for home," Sharpe said, then slapped the stock of his rifle. "If he finds us, he's the one liable to die."

"And that concerns me," Hogan said, "because he's taking news for his French friends, and I rather want him to deliver that news."

"You do?" Teresa asked.

"Before Richard dissuaded the general," Hogan explained,

"the plan was to batter our way through the Miravete pass with our cannon, then go straight on to crack open Fort Napoleon's walls with the artillery. That's the plan El Héroe heard and it's the plan he'll betray. We won't be doing that now, but I want the Frogs to think that's what we'll be doing so they take men out of the forts by the river and cram them into Miravete Castle."

Sharpe laughed. "I thought you were worrying about our lives, and really you're worried about El Héroe's miserable existence?"

Hogan shrugged. "I want him to deliver his news, and what does he want?"

"Us?"

"No! You're just the gravy on his meat. What he wants is to get paid for telling the damned Frogs exactly what's coming toward them. How many men, how many guns, and weight of guns."

"He already knows that!" Teresa said.

"He has a shrewd idea, but he won't know the exact number until he sees the brigade approach. My suspicion is that he's watching the road somewhere and will make his count that he'll then take back to Miravete. And I want him to do that! I want him to see those big nine-pounders because they'll persuade him the plan hasn't changed. And I don't want him seeing you and snatching the chance to capture you."

Sharpe thought for a moment. "He'll make his count close to Miravete."

"Maybe," Hogan said doubtfully.

"The land's flat almost all the way," Sharpe explained. "No nice convenient hills to watch from and escape behind."

"Not till we reach Jaraicejo," Teresa said. "That's where he'll wait, and it's close enough to Miravete that he can send his news quickly."

"And we can ride round Jaraicejo," Sharpe said, stumbling over the pronunciation of the village. "He'll not even see us."

"You're walking on water again, Richard," Hogan said.

"I have to get back quickly, sir," Sharpe insisted. "Pat's a good man, but he'll pick a fight with the whole French army if they piss on him. And besides, I'm now ordered to capture the encampment by the bridge, and I need a few hours to plan that."

"We leave now," Teresa said, "we'll be there by morning."

"And so will El Héroe," Hogan said.

"He won't even see us," Teresa insisted, "and, like Richard, I have left men there."

"They'll be safe," Hogan said.

"Maybe, maybe not. The French know we're in the hills by Miravete, they could send men to search. I want to be there soon!"

"We're going," Sharpe insisted.

"Then take care," Hogan surrendered the argument. "Remember this is all enemy-held territory."

"And dry," Sharpe said.

"Dry, Richard?"

"No water to walk on," Sharpe said, and kicked his heels.

They rode under the arch of Truxillo's north gate and the road stretched before them into the dusk. The moon was almost full, the sky cloudless, and the road looked pale and straight.

Leading to what?

* * *

"Is Major Hogan right?" Teresa asked.

"He usually is," Sharpe said.

"So El Pedazo de Mierda is waiting for us?"

"Not for us," Sharpe said, "he's waiting to count Hill's men and guns."

"But he will see us first."

"Unless we're clever, yes."

"Clever," Teresa repeated scornfully. "How can we be clever if we ride on a road and they are hidden!"

"Aye, but you were right. They won't hide till they're close to home, and they'll hide in the hills. So we just go round them."

"I don't know this country," Teresa said, "I don't know what roads go where."

"But someone does," Sharpe pointed out, "so we find that someone. We'll do that close to Jericho."

"Jaraicejo," Teresa corrected him.

"Besides," Sharpe went on, "the piece of gutless shit thinks Hill is marching tomorrow. El Héroe doesn't expect to see Hill's brigade till tomorrow evening at the earliest. He might have gone home first. He's not expecting anyone tonight."

"Maybe," Teresa conceded.

"Or else he's gone home," Sharpe went on, "and just left a picket to watch the road."

The farther he rode into the gathering night, the more certain Sharpe became that El Héroe would be content with a picket watching the road. He would leave half a dozen trusted men to count the infantry and guns, expecting them to hurry back to him with their findings. He explained his thinking to

Teresa: "Pedazo de Mierda likes his comfort. He's not going to sit in the hills all day and night while he can be at home. He'll just wait for the news then ride to Miravete or Fort Napoleon."

"Which?"

"My guess is Miravete. I'm thinking that's where the French commander is."

Teresa rode in silence for a while. "I don't understand how a Spaniard can fight for the French."

"Money."

"The English have more."

Sharpe shrugged. "Pedazo de Mierda believes the French will win, or he did believe that, which is why he made his bargain with them. He sets up as a guerrilla leader and that keeps the real partisans away from Almaraz. The Frogs pay him for that. Then we came along and he demanded money from us, but I refused to pay him so he's stuck with the Frogs."

"And he lives in comfort while Spain suffers!" she said indignantly.

"Aye, and that worries me."

"That Spain suffers?"

"No, that he lives in comfort. The bastard likes his luxuries, so if I'm right and he is heading home he's going to find Pat Harper and a bunch of riflemen living in his house. They'll have finished his precious wine stores, that's for sure."

"Harper will have set sentries?"

"Aye, Pat's no fool, but he's outnumbered, and the bastard wants those rifles. And he'll want his gold back."

The fear nagged at Sharpe as they rode through the moonlight. He had long learned to put himself in the place of his enemies when he was planning a fight. Knowing what the enemy was likely to do gave a man a huge advantage and Sharpe reckoned he knew what El Héroe planned. He wanted to discover the exact size of General Hill's force and he wanted to get back to his precious house with its lavish furnishings. "He's going to get home," Sharpe said, "and find some manky rifleman fast asleep between his silk sheets."

"Manky?" Teresa asked, not knowing the word.

"Filthy dirty and probably crawling with lice." He grinned. "And it serves the bastard right."

Two of Teresa's men insisted on riding some fifty paces ahead. All three of her men had muskets as well as either lances or sabers. Sharpe's idea was to travel to the village where he had left Harper and then scout it to see whether El Héroe had reoccupied the place, and he feared that any picket left by the Spaniard at Jaraicejo would reach the village faster and warn El Héroe of his approach. "It might be better if we rode round Jericho," he suggested to Teresa, "and get home before El Héroe is warned."

Teresa looked ahead to where the hills rose, their valleys and gullies turned into black shadows by the strong moonlight. "Then we should leave the road soon," she said dubiously. "If we're too close, they'll see us. And a detour will take time."

"Better late than dead."

Teresa grimaced. "There is a village over there," she pointed eastward to where a glimmer of light showed between trees.

"If there's a village there'll be a road toward the Tagus," Sharpe said.

"Or a cattle track."

The two scouts had halted at a crossroads, or more accurately a place where a well-beaten cattle track crossed the main road. There was a stream nearby and the two men were watering their horses while Sharpe dismounted and walked a small way eastward on the track. "It's seen plenty of traffic," he told Teresa.

"Cattle being driven to market," she said.

"It has to lead somewhere. How far are we from Jericho?"

"At least ten miles."

"Then let's make a wide circuit round the damn place."

Teresa was unhappy. "Are we so frightened of the piece of shit?"

"In this moonlight they'll see us from two miles away. By the time we reach the higher hills there could be a company of French infantry waiting to say hello. Besides, I don't want the piece of shit to even know we've returned."

They took the track eastward. Sharpe kept hoping to find another path that would lead north, but they rode for over an hour before they came to a village where such a track existed, and that new one did not lead due north but rather a little east of north. Dogs barked as the horses clattered between the small houses, but no villager dared open a door or shutter to see what horsemen were disturbing their night.

They turned north at the village, now on the smaller track that led toward the dark shadowed hills. "Jaraicejo is over there," Teresa pointed northwest, "and a long way off."

"Then we're probably safe enough."

They rode past an olive grove and, looking eastward, Sharpe saw a thin edge of sword-gray light on the horizon. Dawn was not far off and they had not yet reached the hills. And, for sure, El Héroe would have men watching from those hills, just as he had when Sharpe first arrived on his territory. "We may have to stop and wait another day," he told Teresa.

"We should not have come this way," she said unhappily.

"But we did, and we have to make the best of it."

"We lose a whole day!"

"He'll see us from the hills if we go much farther."

"And he is a coward, he'll run away."

"Or get French help. More likely he'll set an ambush in the hills, and he outguns us."

Sharpe was feeling as frustrated as Teresa. He needed to get back to the village in the hills to discover his men and make sure they were safe, and adding a whole day to the journey was no way to do that. It only increased his men's danger. Hogan had been right, he thought, the best course would have been to accompany Hill's forces, though at best it would still be at least two days before the brigade appeared.

"Now what?" Teresa asked.

They had been riding through a small dark wood and, as they came to the treeline, Sharpe saw a group of houses in a shallow valley ahead. There was a barn behind one of the houses. "We'll rest there," he said. Beyond the hamlet he could see the moonlit track climbing into the foothills.

"We should keep going," Teresa insisted.

Sharpe was tempted. His reason for stopping was to prevent El Héroe's men from seeing them, yet they would show up even better if he waited for dawn. And tomorrow night would be even brighter as the moon neared full. "I want you to wait here with your men," he said, "and I'll go up alone."

"And what good would that do?" Teresa demanded harshly.

"It will make me feel better," Sharpe answered just as curtly, "and I'll go on foot."

"You are a fool, Richard."

"I'll be at the village before sunrise," he said, "and when I know what's happening, I'll come back."

"If you're alive."

"If I'm alive, yes."

"Patrick can look after himself!" she insisted.

"There are at least a thousand Frogs up in those hills," Sharpe said, "and El Héroe's damned men too, and it's my fault Pat is stranded up there. I need to find him."

"Then I come with you!"

Sharpe slid out of the saddle, staggering slightly as he reached the ground. "And we're not going on horseback," he grunted.

"We walk?" Teresa sounded surprised.

"I'm infantry," he said stubbornly, "and besides, two people on horseback are easier to see than two on foot."

Teresa could not argue with that, though she tried. "It must be six or seven miles," she pointed out.

"Maybe four or five," Sharpe said stubbornly, "say two hours' walking. We leave the horses and your men here," he pointed at the barn, "your fellows can bring them up in the morning."

"Two hours?" Teresa asked as she dismounted.

"Three at the most."

"It will be five hours on foot," she grumbled.

"Then we'd best leave now."

Teresa pulled her pair of long-barreled pistols from their saddle holsters, muttered something under her breath, then followed Sharpe.

Into the enemy hills.

CHAPTER 5

The going was easy enough at first as the track climbed gently up a rising gully that was in deep shadow. Small trees clothed much of the slopes, concealing Sharpe and Teresa as they climbed. The sheep track twisted through the trees as it rose toward the summer pastures. Sharpe doubted that El Héroe had put any sentries to watch this track, which was well to the east of the main road. El Héroe might consider himself a great soldier, but so far Sharpe had seen no proof of the man's abilities, and so he made little attempt to be silent or stealthy, but just pushed on into the morning's growing light.

"You think Pat is in danger?" Teresa asked him at one place where the track was just wide enough for them to walk abreast.

"The bastard has over forty men, Pat has thirteen. And he'll be in the bastard's house."

"He will?"

"My lads found gold there, so Pat will hope there's more."

"He can defend the house?"

"Oh, he'll try," Sharpe replied grimly. He had been listening for the sounds of musket or rifle fire and so far had heard nothing, though the fight could be long over by now. "Pat loves a fight. The trouble is that the house has too many windows and doors. He'd be better off in the church."

"He has my men with him," Teresa reminded him, "which gives him enough men to defend the house?"

"Maybe," Sharpe said, "but Pat only knows one way to fight: go straight at the buggers and slaughter them."

"Men say that of you," Teresa said accusingly.

"That's how I end a fight," Sharpe said, "but before that you try and confuse the enemy."

"How?"

"By putting yourself in their place, thinking what the silly buggers will do, and making it impossible for them to do it."

"So what would you do if you were in Pat's place?"

"I'd have pickets well away from the village, and if they said El Cobarde was coming I'd get to the church. It's a small fortress." The church had thick stone walls, high windows, and was surrounded by open ground, while El Héroe's house had too many outbuildings to shelter attackers and too many ground-floor doors and windows.

"Pat will have gone to the church," Teresa insisted.

"If he has any sense, yes, but he probably reckons he can hold the house."

"And maybe he's right?"

"He'll be like a rat trapped in a barrel," Sharpe said. "He might kill a dozen of the bastard's men, but in the end he'll lose."

They had emerged from the small, scrubby trees and were climbing empty grassland. The dawn had lightened the sky, but Sharpe could see no men watching from the surrounding heights. "No flocks up here?" Sharpe asked.

"Not this year," Teresa said. "Take a flock to summer pasture and the French will like as not kill them all."

Sharpe grunted. He assumed the garrison at Miravete must send out forage parties and a flock of sheep would provide enough mutton for a month, and doubtless El Héroe was doing nothing to curb such foraging. Which meant that the garrisons of the three forts were probably well supplied with food that could, anyway, come downriver from the big French supply depots in Talavera. Any real guerrilla force, Sharpe thought, could harass the supply boats on their way downriver, but El Héroe was nothing but hot breath and false words.

He had reached the crest of a saddle and flopped down to rest. Teresa lay beside him, both of them gazing northwest to where the village must lie. He could not see the village, but whispers of smoke beyond the horizon betrayed the early morning cooking fires. "We need to go over there," Sharpe pointed toward the smoke, "and the buggers can see us."

"If they're even looking this way," Teresa said scornfully. "And two people? A man and a woman? How dangerous do we look?"

"And all's quiet," Sharpe said. "We can rest a moment." He hesitated. "And I'm sorry, love."

"Sorry? Why?"

"Dragging you through these hills. It's just that I'm worried about my men."

"And you should be," she conceded. "I left men in the village and I'm worried about them too."

"Probably all safe in their beds," Sharpe said, "and the slimy bastard is tucked up in Jericho."

A flash lit up the dark western sky. "Lightning?" Sharpe said, then a heartbeat later the sound rolled across the hills. It was not thunder and the flash had not been lightning. Instead of a jagged white streak splitting the sky it was a livid effusion of flame blossoming from the ground to the northwest. It lingered briefly then faded, leaving only a great dark and roiling smoke. "An explosion," Sharpe said, "that was black powder!" He was on his feet, rifle in hand. "We have to go!"

"That was the village?"

"Has to be, bugger all else over there."

Then a crackle of musketry came from the northwest. To Sharpe's ear it sounded like a platoon volley, ill timed, and behind it came the distinctive crack of Baker rifles. He swore and kept moving, careless whether he could be seen by any watcher. He reckoned the platoon volley had been fired by El Héroe's men and now his riflemen were shooting back, presumably from the windows of the house. "The bastard had plenty of powder in the church," Sharpe explained as he hurried, "and he must have blown down the gateway of the house."

"You really think Pat is in the house?"

"I know Pat," Sharpe said, "and given a choice he'll take the most comfortable place. I reckon he's in the bastard's house."

The only good news was that the firing continued, which suggested that El Héroe was reluctant to charge through the destroyed gate into the accurate fire of the rifles that punctuated the incessant crackle of musketry. "The bastard's hoping to kill them with musketry," Sharpe said.

"We're a long way away," Teresa said.

"Then we keep going," Sharpe muttered. He reckoned they were at least two miles from where the explosion had lit the skyline, and then another blast flashed red and smoky, followed by the grim sound of the powder exploding. Sharpe swore again. "The bastard must be taking the back wall of the house down."

That was what Sharpe would have done. Fixed the attention of the riflemen on the front of the house by blowing in the gate, and then blasting a hole in the back wall and sending his men through there. In the wake of the second explosion the musket fire seemed to diminish, though the rifle fire kept sounding and after a minute or so the musketry regained its former intensity.

"There are no flames," Teresa said.

"Could be hidden from us." Sharpe was also looking for the glow of a fire started by the second explosion, but no fiery glare showed on the gradually lightening western horizon. He stumbled on the uneven turf. "That bastard will kill them all," he grunted. He reckoned that the second explosion, on the far side of the house, could have started a fire on the ground floor, a fire that would not be visible to him for some moments, but a fire that must surely drive his men from the house into the musket fire that had started to sound even more intense. He cursed uselessly, flinching from the thought that he had betrayed his men by leaving them, that men whom he regarded as closer than brothers were being assailed by flames and musketry, good men dying like rats in a burning barn. He hurried.

He took some hope from the continuing rifle fire that punctuated the musketry, which seemed to diminish again. That suggested good news, that the riflemen, far from fleeing a fire, were keeping a steady fusillade and El Héroe's men were either crouching out of sight or were conserving their ammunition. Sharpe had led Teresa into a fold of the hills so could no longer see if the house was on fire and could only judge the distant battle by its noise, but that was true of most battles. Even on a sunlit day, in the thick of action a man could scarcely see ten yards because of the thick powder smoke, and a soldier learned to read sound as easily as vision.

"What will the French do?" Teresa asked.

"After the hiding we've given them? Nothing. Maybe send a patrol to see what's happening? But they'll probably wait till well after dawn."

Sharpe's breath was shortening as he climbed the fold's farther side. He paused at the top to catch his breath and to let Teresa join him, and as he waited he saw what he feared, the glow of a fire. Yet it was not what he expected. A burning building flamed fiercely, spiraling a plume of sparks and thick smoke high into the sky, while this fire seemed lower, less intense and more widespread, its smoke somehow more gentle. It still seemed like bad news and he imagined the flames creeping nearer and nearer his men. "Not far now," he encouraged Teresa.

"What do we do when we get there?"

"Kill the bastards."

"The two of us?" Teresa asked, sounding amused. "Just like that?"

"Just like that," Sharpe said, not amused at all, "but we have to get there first."

The route to the village was lit by the rising sun that now threw long shadows across a wide grassy pastureland interrupted by ditches and old stone walls. In peaceful times, Sharpe supposed, these high fields would be alive with sheep and goats, but they were empty now and he and Teresa would be very visible if anyone was watching from the village. Yet that seemed unlikely because the northern end of the village was obscured by the widespread fire that plumed its thick cloud of smoke. "It isn't the house burning," Sharpe said, puzzled. "The house is at the other end of the street. It's the church."

"It's the grass round the church," Teresa said.

"So that's where the fight is," Sharpe went on. "Pat did the right thing. Good man." The musketry and rifle fire still sounded, and Sharpe half suspected he heard a rifle bullet whip safely past him. He hurried on. "We need to get closer." He jumped a dry ditch and pushed on as fast as he could, not stopping till he had reached a low wall some three hundred yards from the village's northern end. He crouched behind the wall and trained his telescope toward the church that was half obscured by smoke. "Bugger," he said.

"What?"

"Pat's in the church," he said, "but he's trapped there." He could see the flash of rifles firing from the windows, most of the flashes accompanied by the Baker rifle's distinctive sound. But not all; many of the shots fired from the church were from muskets and Sharpe realized that his precaution of loading all the captured French muskets was paying off.

There could be no other explanation for the heavy fire from the church, which was forcing El Héroe's men to crouch behind the churchyard's wall from where they fired their muskets almost blindly over the top, not caring to expose themselves to the riflemen who were scarce thirty paces away. Every time one of the attackers rose to blast his musket, he became a target for the riflemen and Sharpe could see at least six men lying prone at the low wall's foot. They were not in uniform, which meant they were El Héroe's men. Sharpe handed the telescope to Teresa and laid his rifle on the wall's top. The rifle was loaded, but he had yet to prime the weapon. He lifted the frizzen and poured powder from the horn into the pan, then eased the frizzen back. He pulled the doghead with its new French flint back to full cock, resisted the urge to check the flint's seating, then aimed at one of the attackers. He raised the barrel slightly to allow for the bullet's fall. "If the bastards come for us," he told Teresa, "we run like hell."

"Where?"

"Back the way we came." He pulled the trigger, the doghead snapped forward, the powder in the pan flared bright and a fleck hit his right cheek, and an instant later the charge in the barrel exploded. Smoke gouted across the wall and he could not see whether he had hit his target, not that he cared because he was too busy reloading. He had decided to tap-load, not bothering to wrap each bullet in its leather patch. That would make the rifle inaccurate, but was quicker, and for now he only wanted to scare El Héroe's men into thinking they were being assaulted from the rear.

Teresa helped by firing her pistols at the distant men. It was much too far for the small weapons to do any damage, but the noise was what mattered, and by the time she had fired her second pistol Sharpe was reloaded and fired again. He pulled another cartridge from his pouch and the soft dawn wind shifted the pall of smoke in his front and he saw a tall man standing some paces back from the churchyard wall in a place where he was sheltered from the riflemen in the church by the wall of a house. Sharpe reckoned the fellow was staring toward him, though the man could see little because he was gazing into the rising sun. "Keep firing," he muttered to Teresa and opened the brass lid of the small compartment at the rifle's butt. Took out a patch, wrapped the ball, and rammed it hard down the barrel, grunting with the effort. He laid the rifle back on the wall's coping, primed the pan, and saw the man was still standing. He aimed. The rifle's simple sights were outlined by the grass fire that still burned, though the flames were fading. He raised the barrel slightly. "I hope that's the shithead," he muttered and pulled the trigger. The butt slammed back into his shoulder and the smoke thickened again.

Teresa fired both her pistols at once. The enemy could see the muzzle flashes and powder smoke, so Teresa was moving up and down the wall so her flashes were not always at the same place, hoping to give El Héroe's men the impression that several assailants were behind them. Sharpe tap-loaded again, shuffled five paces to his right, and fired. The tall man he had shot at had vanished, though whether he had been hit Sharpe could not tell.

Men were firing back now, the musket balls mostly going high, though a few smacked into the wall's far side. None came close. The distance was too great for accurate musketry, or indeed for a rifle bullet fired without the leather patch that gave the bullet purchase on the barrel's rifling. "Are the buggers moving?"

"Not yet," Teresa said, firing a pistol. "I want a rifle."

"I'll find you one," he promised and reflected that the likeliest source of a rifle would be the death of one of his men, and that angered him. It was war's fortune to die at the enemy's hand, but to be killed by a traitor was a malign fate. He felt for another cartridge, ripped it open, and poured powder down the barrel. Put the bullet on top and tapped the rifle's butt on the ground to pack the bullet and powder in the weapon's breech. He primed the pan, closed the frizzen, cocked the doghead, stood, and fired. He and Teresa were making a deal of noise and sending bullets fast. An inexperienced enemy, and Sharpe reckoned El Héroe's men were inexperienced, would think there were at least half a dozen men shooting from the wall. What they should do, he thought, was send a dozen men to outflank him, but instead they were merely firing blindly back while Pat Harper's riflemen still struck at them from the church windows.

"There are a lot of them in that house," Teresa said. It was obvious which house she meant, the house in which El Héroe had billeted Sharpe and which stood across the street from the church and was thus outlined against the dying grass fire. Sharpe saw musket flashes from the roof and reckoned the enemy was in the attic and had punched holes through the tiles. More flashes showed at the lower windows. "So the bastards have a fort of their own," he grunted. He took the time to patch another bullet, then aimed at one of the muzzle flashes from the house roof.

At which moment the roof vanished, replaced by a sheet of flame and an explosion of rafters, beams, and tiles. "God save Ireland," Sharpe said, "what have you done, Pat?" He heard screams from the house and in the raw light from the sudden flames that filled the house's four stone walls, saw men running back down the street as if they sought the protection of El Héroe's own larger house. Sharpe fired at them as more rifle fire crackled from the church, and suddenly there were no muskets sounding. "They've run!"

"Cowards," Teresa spat.

Sharpe climbed over the wall. "I'm going to the church."

"Careful, Richard!"

"And you follow me. I'll make sure our men don't shoot at us. Just run like hell when I call you."

He paused to reload his rifle then ran to his right, aiming to circle the northern end of the village. He feared that if he approached from the direction of the burning house he would be mistaken for one of El Héroe's men and shot, so he ran a good way north before heading for the road. Smoke from the burning house drifted southward.

He jumped a ditch onto the earthen road, then slung his rifle and looked toward the church that was standing amidst the gently smoking remnants of the grass fire. Sharpe was in the sunlight, easily visible. He cupped his hands, about to shout, when a voice called from the church. "I see you, Mister Sharpe! You can come in!"

"Dan?"

"It's me, Mister Sharpe!" Hagman called back.

"Teresa will be coming in too! Try not to shoot her!"

"We'll look out for the lass!"

Sharpe walked toward the church. El Héroe's men had vanished down the street, presumably to the large house, leaving the lumpen black shapes of their dead slumped at the foot of the churchyard wall. Sharpe had almost reached that wall when the rear door of the church opened and Pat Harper stepped into the thinning smoke. "That was a grand job we did, sir!" he called. "And thank you for your help."

"I was no bloody help, Pat. You had it under control."

"That I did, sir," Harper said happily, "but you did your wee best, sir."

Sharpe paused to count bodies and saw a dozen sprawled round the churchyard's perimeter. "And did you lose anyone?"

"Sergeant Latimer, sorry, sir."

"Dead?"

"Got one straight between the eyes, sir."

"Poor man. He was married too."

"Four little ones at home as well."

Sharpe sighed, though in truth he was surprised that only one man had been killed, and if he was honest with himself Latimer had not been a good sergeant. He had been too timid and indecisive, but he had still been one of Sharpe's men and for that reason Sharpe vowed to take his revenge on El Héroe. "We'll auction his equipment tomorrow," Sharpe said, "but I want his rifle."

"It's a good one, sir, so you'll have to pay for it."

"Of course I'll pay. I want it for Teresa."

"And the lads are fair flush with money," Harper said, "so the prices will be high."

"Flush? My God!" The exclamation was provoked from Sharpe as he stepped into the church's chancel that was now home to the horses of the men Teresa had left in the village.

"Aye," Harper said, amused, "it fair stinks of horse shit, but I reckon God will forgive us."

"So why are the men flush?" Sharpe asked.

"We made a wee excursion to the bastard's house, sir, I thought he must have had some more money there. Found it under the flagstones in the hallway. I kept your share."

"I thought you might stay in the house," Sharpe admitted.

"My mother gave birth to no fools," Harper said, "God rest her soul, and the bastard's house was too big to defend, and you'd made the church into a fortress. A hundred and eighteen Crapaud muskets, all loaded and ready. I reckoned if the French or El Héroe came we could give them a proper welcome."

"And the explosions?"

"They had those barrels of powder, sir, and Dan found a reel of slow-match. Harris rigged the fuses and I hurled two of the barrels. Pedro threw the last one. He's a good lad." Pedro was one of Teresa's men.

"You did a great job, Pat. Proud of you."

"All in a day's work, sir."

"But I imagine the shithead will be back," Sharpe said, "and maybe the Crapauds too."

"Haven't seen a Frog since you left, sir. Buggers are staying in their forts." Harper turned as the door from the vestry opened. "Miss Teresa! Welcome!"

"The piece of shit is coming back," Teresa said, pointing in the direction of the street, "and waving a white flag."

"Is he now?" Harper hefted his volley gun. "You want to talk to him, sir?"

"He probably doesn't know I'm here, Pat. You be nice to him."

Harper walked to the church's main door, pulled it slightly ajar, and peered out. "A dozen of the bastards," he grunted, "what does he want?"

"His money," Sharpe guessed.

Harper chuckled. "He'll be disappointed, so he will." He jerked his head to one side and Sharpe saw a big wooden box with a broken hasp. He opened it and saw a scatter of gold coins.

"That's your share, sir," Harper said, closing the heavy church door.

"Not much," Sharpe said, "what was your share?"

"A pittance, sir," Harper said with a grin.

Sharpe picked up a couple of the coins. They were again French five-franc coins, each one the equivalent of six months' wages to a rifleman. "How much was in the box, Pat?"

"Just under nine hundred francs, sir, and a few Spanish coins."

"So my share should be about," Sharpe paused, working it out, "about sixty francs, and there's not half that left."

"We shared them with Miss Teresa's men." The partisans Teresa had left in the village were part of the church's garrison and had been firing from the makeshift firesteps. "They're stout lads, sir," Harper said, nodding toward a group of partisans, "not an ounce of fear in one of them!"

Sharpe scooped up the few remaining coins and thought that the French had been paying El Héroe well. He gave the gold to Teresa, and she had no sooner put them in a pouch at her belt than El Héroe's voice called from the street. "Sergeant!"

Harper stiffened, looked at Sharpe, who nodded, causing Harper to pull back the church door a few inches. "I hear you!" he called back.

"Sergeant, I suggest you come from the church."

"We're saying our prayers," Harper shouted back.

"You need to pray! You all die soon."

"Why's that?"

"I was in Truxillo," El Héroe shouted, "and your Major Sharpe was there, with his *puta*."

Teresa growled beside Sharpe and he placed a hand on her arm to still her.

"He was with his lady?" Harper asked. "I'm not surprised. He was always lucky, Major Sharpe was."

"And he is not coming back!"

"Is he not? That's bad news."

"General Hill is angry at him for waking the French. He is ordered to stay in Truxillo, so you are on your own."

"And we're as happy as pigs in clover, so we are," Harper called back.

Sharpe's riflemen and Teresa's partisans had been climbing onto the crates that formed firesteps at the windows and Sharpe gestured at them to stay low. Harper pulled the door half open and crouched beside it, then cocked the volley gun. The weapon's heavy lock clicked loudly and ominously, and the sound plainly carried to El Héroe. "Sergeant!" he called, anxiety clear

157

in his voice. "I suggest you leave the village. I will allow you to go with your weapons, but you will leave everything else here."

"Mister Sharpe told me to stay here," Harper said, "until he gets back."

"He is not coming back! I told you that."

So El Héroe had not seen Sharpe. He must have thought that the firing that came from the higher ground beyond the village was from one of Harper's pickets, and if he had any sense he would have sent men to look for those sentries. Let them look, Sharpe thought.

"Mister Sharpe told me he's coming back," Harper called, "and if he says he's coming back then he will be back. He's an officer of his word."

"So am I," El Héroe said, "and I tell you Major Sharpe is not coming."

"And I was told you're a liar," Harper called.

"He is in trouble! And now General Hill may not come at all because Major Sharpe betrayed himself to the French who are now ready for any attack. You are on your own, Sergeant! And soon the French will come to find what caused the firing this morning."

"We love killing Frenchmen!" Harper retorted. "They're as easy to kill as your monkeys."

"And they will bring cannon!" El Héroe threatened.

Sharpe had crept behind Harper and now looked through the small opening. El Héroe was standing in the gate of the churchyard wall, flanked by a man holding the white flag. Sharpe was tempted to kill him, it was an easy shot for the rifle, but the churchyard wall was lined by El Héroe's men, who could well start the fight again and by now Sharpe's men had only their rifles. The muskets they had used to thicken their fire were mostly unloaded. The rifles would doubtless kill another dozen of El Héroe's men, but Sharpe would also take losses and he already had one man to bury and that was one man too many.

"You must leave, Sergeant!" El Héroe called, evidently emboldened by the lack of response to his previous words, "and you will also leave what you stole from my house."

"His money," Sharpe muttered, amused.

"We stole some wine," Harper called back, "but you probably didn't want it because it tasted like goat's piss. And we took some fine shirts! Thank you for those."

"You took the village's poor box," El Héroe snapped back, "money to help us buy new flocks when the French leave."

"I'll leave you the box," Harper said.

"You will leave the money!" El Héroe almost screamed the words, his agony at losing a fortune obvious.

"I'll do what Mister Sharpe tells me to do," Harper retorted.

"I have told you already! Major Sharpe is not coming back, ever!"

"Then we'll wait for Miss Teresa, La Aguja."

"That *puta*! If that bitch comes, I will share her with my men!"

Sharpe snatched at Teresa's arm, but she was too quick for him. She reached the door and dragged it fully open. She leveled one of her pistols and screamed at El Héroe so fast that Sharpe hardly understood a word, though it was obvious enough she was insulting his manhood and his courage. Then she pulled the trigger. The range was short enough, but pistols were notoriously inaccurate and the ball seared past El Héroe's right ear. He ducked, turned, and fled, pursued by Teresa's curses.

Sharpe pulled her into the church's darkness and kicked the door shut before any of El Héroe's men fired back. "I will kill him," Teresa said.

"Not today," Sharpe said, and turned to Harper. "Start loading muskets, Sergeant, we might need them."

"What's the yellow bastard going to do?"

"For now? He'll go back to his house and lick his wounds, but he will be back. Though he might send to Miravete Castle and ask the Crapauds to help him."

"We could leave?" Harper suggested.

"He's not a complete idiot. He'll have men watching the church. If we go out into the fields, he'll follow us."

"So we wait for the French?"

"If they come," Sharpe said, "though it won't be till late morning. If they come at all." Sharpe thought for a heartbeat. "But the shithead will be back. He wants his money."

He left half his riflemen at their windows to keep watch, while the other half reloaded muskets. Once those weapons were stacked at the windows, he told half his men to sleep while the others kept watch. They could see to the west, north, and south, but there was no window at the church's eastern end where the gaudy altar stood, and it was at that end that Henderson finally heard a noise. "Something's scrabbling there," he whispered to Sharpe.

"Scrabbling, Joe?"

"From up there, Mister Sharpe." Henderson pointed into the shadows of the high-beamed roof. "Listen, sir."

Sharpe listened and heard a low thump, then a scraping sound. He thought the noise came from the high eastern wall. "Buggers are trying to get to the roof," he told Henderson. "Wake the lads."

Sharpe reckoned the thump he had heard was the sound of a ladder being placed at the church's eastern end, which meant El Héroe had devised a plan to get to the high roof and fire down, though to do that he would need to remove some tiles. "Bring me five riflemen," he told Henderson, then waited as the men lined up just in front of the altar. "Quiet, lads," he warned them, then pointed to where the roof joined the stone gable. "Shoot up through the roof tiles," he told them quietly. The muskets could fire faster, but the rifles had more power to shatter through the thick tiles. "Not yet! Listen!"

They listened and heard shuffling noises. El Héroe's men had climbed the ladder and were doing their best to be quiet, but they were also clinging to the steep roof's ridge, which offered their only security from the danger of falling. What El Héroe should have done, Sharpe thought, was have half his men fire from the churchyard's perimeter to cover the noises from the roof, but the fool had not thought that far ahead. A scraping sound suggested that one of the men on the roof's ridge was trying to remove a tile and Sharpe aimed his rifle, guessed where the sound had come from, and pulled the trigger.

The shot shattered a tile and provoked a yelp of alarm. "Pepper them, boys," Sharpe said, and all six rifles fired. As the noise faded inside the smoke-filled church Sharpe heard a body scraping down the steep roof, then a thump as it landed in the churchyard. "Keep at them, lads." He reloaded his own rifle, tap-loading it because accuracy was unnecessary. All they needed to do was keep bullets pouring through the roof's summit. Each shot cascaded broken tile into the church, but the bullets also drove El Héroe's men off the roof in a panicked retreat. At least two of them could not wait their turn at the ladder and preferred to slide down the roof and risk the fall, but after a couple of minutes Sharpe was satisfied they had all gone. "Hold your fire! And well done." He walked to the altar and stared upward, then aimed his rifle and shot at the easternmost tiles of the ridge. "You too, Dan."

It took six shots to clear a large open patch through which the light showed. "If the buggers try using the ladder again," Sharpe told Hagman, "you'll see them and kill them."

"That I will, Mister Sharpe," the old poacher said and squatted by the altar steps gazing upward, which meant the back door that El Héroe had hoped to open into the church was closed.

A half hour later all the muskets were again loaded, the village was quiet, and Sharpe, exhausted, slept.

"Two days," Sharpe said.

He had slept for three or four hours and woken to a silent village. How long, Harper wanted to know, before General Hill arrived? "Two days," Sharpe said again.

"And today's Friday," Harper said, "I think."

"I think so too."

"So late Sunday or early Monday?" Harper looked thoughtful. "The yellow bastard will try to get his money back before then."

"Like as not. It's all he cares about. Without money he's just a bloody deserter from the Spanish army, but with it he can pretend to be a gentleman."

"Gentleman!" Teresa spat. "He's a goat-turd."

"But a dangerous one," Sharpe said, "and he knows you're here."

"So?"

"So think how much the French will pay him if he gives them La Aguja!"

"And like as not they'll give you to the bastard," Pat put in, "and the villagers tell us he's not kind to women. He likes to beat them up a little first."

"I'll cut his *cojones* off," Teresa said, "if he has any."

"I'd rather you didn't get the chance," Sharpe said. "We're leaving."

"Leaving!" Harper sounded surprised.

"Running away?" Teresa asked derisively.

"Choosing a new battlefield," Sharpe said.

"You think the Crapauds will come?" Harper asked.

"I know they'll come!" Sharpe said firmly. "The piece of shit will tell them La Aguja is here, and they won't be able to resist that lure. They want Teresa and they want us, and they'll think we're waiting for them in the church, so they'll bring a cannon to blast the place down."

"That wouldn't be good," Harper said thoughtfully.

"But you told the general that cannons can't be moved in these hills," Teresa objected.

"They can reach this village easily enough," Sharpe explained, "it's the track from here to the river that's the bugger.

Besides, they'll bring a small gun. They have old four-pounders." He turned and looked at Harper. "So we can't stay here."

"Where do we go?" Harper asked.

"The old bridge," Sharpe said.

"They trap us there too," Teresa said.

"Or we trap them," Sharpe countered.

"How?"

"You'll see." He was not entirely sure why he had chosen the old shattered bridge for his refuge, but an instinct had prompted the decision and he was still exploring that instinct. The drawback to the bridge was that it would be easy for the French to use the old main road to bring a cannon to the site, but he remembered from his previous visit that the main road ran for about three hundred paces from the bridge until it tipped over a small ridge, which meant the French would have to bring any cannon to within three hundred yards of the bridge and that was an easy killing distance for rifles. "I hope the buggers do bring a cannon," he said. "Our biggest problem is your horses," he told Teresa. "I can't protect them from Crapaud fire."

"Juan can take them over the hill," she said. Juan was one of her most trusted men.

"And if the Crapauds follow him?"

"I give him permission to run away."

Sharpe laughed. "They'll only follow him if they think you're with them."

"And I stay with you!"

"Probably safest," Sharpe said, "but for the moment we wait here." It went against his instinct to do nothing while an enemy had the time to devise a new assault, but nor did he want to take his men out into the afternoon sunlight and give El Héroe's men a chance to follow. If he did go he doubted he could find a better place than the church to defend, and for the moment his ambition was to keep his remaining men alive and so they would wait and hope that the French did not send a company under the command of an officer who knew his business.

"Are you sure the Crapauds will come?" Harper asked.

"They'll come," Sharpe said, "they might send a patrol first to discover what's happening, but once they know we're cornered they'll send more men and if they've got a lick of sense they'll send a four-pounder with them."

"Should we move now?" Teresa asked.

"Soon," Sharpe said, "but once we're moving we won't be able to see what's coming after us." He turned and stared at the altar. "Pat, I want to see if that ladder's still outside."

The one drawback to the church was that it had no window facing east. There had been one once, the shape of it was clear on the limewashed eastern wall, but it had been bricked up, which meant Sharpe could not see the castle at Miravete nor anyone approaching from the French positions there. He paused at the vestry door. "Anyone see the bastards?" he called to the men watching from the windows.

"Nothing, Mister Sharpe," Hagman answered, nor did any of the others see movement in the village.

"Let's go, Pat," Sharpe said, and went through the vestry and heaved aside the furniture blocking the door. He opened it and was relieved that no musket fired from the churchyard wall. It seemed that El Héroe's men had all gone back to their house. Sharpe darted out, turned the corner, and saw the ladder still propped against the eastern gable, the top of which was flecked dark with bloodstains. "We need it inside the church, Pat."

Harper heaved the ladder over so it crashed down among the graves, then he and Sharpe struggled to carry it through the outer and inner doors. No one shot at them, nor did anyone call an alarm. "We're fighting against choirboys," Sharpe said scornfully. "The buggers aren't even watching us."

Once in the church the ladder was put up against the eastern gable and Sharpe climbed so he was able to push his head through the ragged hole his rifles' bullets had torn in the roof. He laid his telescope on a tile sticky with drying blood and gazed across the valley toward Miravete Castle. It took him a moment to focus the glass, and then he saw what he did not want to see: two companies of blue-coated infantry had just left Miravete and were marching down the track that would lead to the village. "The goat-turd has his reinforcements," Sharpe said. He could see upward of one hundred and fifty men coming toward him and he reckoned they would fight a damn sight better than El Héroe's feeble effort to capture the church. The only good news was that he could see no cannon accompanying the approaching French.

He slid down the ladder, landing with a thump on the tiles. "We're out of here," he growled. He and Harper had retrieved the ladder without interference by leaving through the north door, so that was the route he would take again. "Loaded rifles, lads," he said, "and take a couple of muskets each. Are those barrels wine?"

"Taken from the bastard's house, sir," Harris confirmed.

"Take them, and any food."

This was not what he wanted, but the arrival of the French infantry would make the church a death trap. He handed Sergeant Latimer's rifle and cartridge pouch to Teresa. "The goat-turd," he told her, "will have told the Crapauds that you're here, which is probably why they're coming. They want you."

"They want you too. We go to the bridge?"

"We do," Sharpe said. He was still not sure why he had chosen the bridge, but instinct told him it was the one place where he could win the coming fight. To retreat over the hills was to invite a French pursuit with few if any places to set up a killing defense. Besides, he was ordered to destroy the French encampment at the base of the old bridge and this gave him another chance to examine the defenses. "Let's go!"

He led them at a smart pace down the hill from the village and then up to the ridge where the old road led to the broken bridge. He put Pat Harper at the rear of the small column with orders to watch for any pursuit, but they had gone over half the distance before Harper reported that a pair of horsemen were shadowing them. "Dan? They're yours," Sharpe said.

The horsemen kept a long way off, but Hagman's first shot persuaded them they were too close and both men turned and spurred away, though by now they must have realized where Sharpe was headed.

"If we're on the old bridge," Harper said to Sharpe, "there'll only be two ways out. Either through the Frogs or drop into the river off the broken end."

"A short life and a merry one," Sharpe said.

"God save Ireland!"

"You're too young to die, Pat, trust me." The only response to that was a skeptical grunt. "We just have to hold out for a couple of days," Sharpe explained, "and the Crapauds are going to be nervous of us. Every time they've challenged us we've hammered them hard, so they'll be cautious."

"And we hammer them again?"

"And El Héroe will be no bloody use to them," Sharpe went on. "He'll stay as far away as possible."

Harper nodded. "It's not that I don't trust you, sir," he said, "but the buggers do outnumber us."

"About ten to one, I reckon, but we're the 95th Rifles. I feel sorry for the Crapauds. You still have pistol balls for the volley gun?"

"Enough for three shots, sir. Miss Teresa gave me some of her pistol ammunition."

"You'll only need one shot." Sharpe grinned. "You mark my words, the buggers will run."

It was late afternoon when they reached the shattered bridge. Sharpe led them onto the roadway and to his relief saw that the balks of sawn timber and stacks of cut masonry were still in place. He gestured at the heaps of masonry and stacked timbers that were intended to repair the broken span. "We make those into a barrier at the bridge's end," he explained. "Build it across the roadway between the ends of the parapets, and let's be quick!"

He used his telescope to see that the two French companies were still more than a mile away. They were coming slowly, he suspected because they had been in Miravete's garrison and had not been regularly exercised. So he had a little time, enough he hoped to heap timber and stone into a makeshift wall that would block the broken roadway exactly where the bridge's thick stone parapets ended. His men, seeing what he proposed, and seeing the approaching enemy, worked with alacrity, making a base of thick timbers on which they piled masonry blocks that Harris insisted could form crenellations. "Like an old castle, Mister Sharpe," he said proudly.

"Do it," Sharpe said. "Dan?"

"Mister Sharpe?"

"With me. Elliott! Perkins! Come as well." He led the three riflemen to the crest where he assumed the French would have placed a cannon if they had brought one, and lay on the road staring at the approaching French. "Are the buggers in range?"

"Just coming into range now, Mister Sharpe," Hagman said.

"Then start thinning them out."

"Pleasure, Mister Sharpe."

Sharpe had Elliott and Perkins load rifles for Hagman, each shot carefully wrapped in its leather patch, and Hagman shot them one at a time, his bullets tearing into the front rank of the French. It took ten shots, of which eight struck home, before the officer commanding the French had the sense to order his men out of column and to spread out on either side of the road in loose skirmish order. They kept coming, while behind them El Héroe's men watched from horseback and took good care not to approach within the range of Hagman's rifle.

Sharpe let the enemy's loose skirmish line approach to about two hundred paces before ordering his three men back to the bridge. He had used the time while Hagman shot to examine the enemy with his telescope and had seen no sign of a cannon. He remembered the old French four-pounder, a light cannon that was easily dragged by a dozen infantry-men, and he was surprised the French had not brought one. If rifles were Sharpe's great advantage in this fight, a cannon would have evened the odds; even a small regimental gun could batter down his stout barricade and then shred his position with canister fire. "No cannon, lads," he said as they ran back to the bridge, "so we'll win."

"We always do, Mister Sharpe," Hagman retorted.

Sharpe clambered over the wall, which now stood about four feet high, with the crenellations another foot above that. The enemy had reached the crest and, seeing the wall barring the bridge they stopped and some fired muskets, the shots going high. An officer stood behind one of the French in-fantrymen and rested a telescope on the man's shoulder. "See him, Dan?"

"I have him, Mister Sharpe!" Hagman's rifle fired and the officer staggered backward, his telescope dropping to the road.

"Man the wall," Sharpe told his riflemen, and they lined the makeshift rampart. With Teresa's partisans he had a force of almost fifty men, good men who he knew would prove a formidable defense, but Sharpe reckoned the French must eventually storm the wall. They had the advantage of numbers and, though ill-trained, there would be plenty of brave men among them and, inevitably, some would manage to reach and even cross the wall. "Rifles! Start taking them down."

His men laid their rifle barrels on the wall's top, aimed,

and fired. The enemy had started shooting back, but most of the musket shots went high, with a few cracking into the wall that his men were now calling Fort Sharpe. "Don't tap-load!" Sharpe called to McCann, who was trying to shoot fast rather than accurately. "Make every shot count!"

He went to the wall himself and aimed his rifle at a man on the left of the French line who appeared to be shouting orders. Sharpe fired and immediately started reloading while the smoke from his shot cleared. As he rammed the leather-wrapped bullet down the Baker's barrel he wondered how many shots, either musket or rifle, he had shot in his life. Thousands, he supposed, in Flanders, India, Portugal, and Spain. "And if I live," he said, "I'll add France to that list."

"What?" Teresa asked.

"Nothing, keep shooting."

The loose French line had slowed almost to a halt. They were being hit hard by the riflemen, who knew to take down officers and sergeants first and, increasingly bereft of orders, the men preferred to kneel and fire their muskets, though at three hundred paces they might as well have aimed at the clouds. Some of the French had retreated beyond the skyline to avoid the rifle fire.

"Conscripts," Sharpe said.

"The French?" Teresa was reloading her rifle.

"Youngsters forced into the army." Sharpe leveled his rifle again and looked for any Frenchman giving orders and saw none. He aimed at a man trying to shelter in the shallow road-side ditch and pulled the trigger. "They don't get trained properly, they don't want to be here, and they don't know how to fight."

"They know how to rape, burn, and kill," Teresa said grimly. She pulled the trigger of her new rifle. "And die."

There had to be some officers or sergeants surviving in the French line because Sharpe heard orders being yelled. "Look for the noisy buggers!" he called, and looked himself. He saw no one shouting among the French so aimed at a tall man who had stood to reload his musket. He fired, and felt a fleck of burning powder hit his right eyeball. He blinked it away and bit a new cartridge open.

"Look over here, Mister Sharpe!" Hagman called.

Sharpe ran to the right-hand side of his makeshift wall and saw what had alarmed Hagman. One of the four-pounder cannons from the engineers' encampment beneath the bridge was being hauled up the slope. A dozen men wearing canvas harnesses were dragging the light gun and its limber. The French, perhaps deciding that to drag a four-pounder the long distance from Miravete Castle would be too slow, had summoned one of the small guns from the bridge encampment. The only problem with that was that the main road approached the old bridge by running alongside the river and then turning uphill right beneath the bridge's western side, which meant that the men harnessed to the gun were within musket range and thus were cruelly easy targets for a rifleman. "You know what to do, Dan," Sharpe said, and called for another five men to help Hagman. He joined them, leaning over the parapet to shoot down at the harnessed men. Each harness, Sharpe remembered it was called a bricole, was attached by a drag rope to the axle bosses of the limber, which contained the cannon's ammunition and which, in turn, was yoked to the gun itself. "Stop them!" Sharpe called, and fired down into the harnessed men. Some of Teresa's partisans joined him at the parapet and shot downward, their musket shots sometimes clanging off the barrel of the cannon, which, within seconds of Sharpe opening fire, slowed to a stop. More musket balls clanged off the gun's brass barrel or slammed into the harnessed men who lay bleeding on the road. "Dan, Perkins! Elliott! Make sure no one replaces those bastards in their harnesses. Rest of you, back to the wall!"

The French might have lost any advantage the cannon could have given them, but they were far from giving up. The men on the left of the loose French line were crouching in the long grass. None were aiming or firing muskets, instead they were all fixing bayonets. A quick glance to his left showed that none of the French in the center or on their right were drawing bayonets and slotting them onto muskets, which meant that whoever still commanded the enemy intended two thirds of his force to keep shooting at Fort Sharpe while the left wing charged with bayonets. "Someone there has a lick of sense," he grunted, then stood and walked behind his men, telling them to concentrate their rifle fire on the left of the enemy's line, but to have their loaded muskets ready. "We'll need your toy gun," he told Harper.

"She's ready." Harper patted the volley gun. "You think the buggers are coming?"

"Any minute now." Sharpe touched Teresa's shoulder. "Tell your men to wait till they're really close before firing." There was no point in wasting the partisans' musketry at distant targets.

"I have ten men over the hill," Teresa said, pointing westward, "they might come."

Sharpe knew that ten men had taken the partisans' horses out of sight and, while he did not doubt their bravery, ten horsemen would not save him from the French assault. "We have to fight them off ourselves," he said, and wondered if he would have done better to have stayed in the church. The French still outnumbered him and their commander seemed to know his business. That officer, whoever he was, must be furious. He knew Sharpe had only a handful of men, yet that handful had already hurt him badly and taken his cannon out of the fight. And he knew he would lose still more men as he assaulted the makeshift fort, but he would have most of his men shooting their muskets to keep the riflemen's heads down while his picked troops charged with fixed bayonets. It was not a bad plan, Sharpe conceded, and the French needed to do it quickly before the relentless rifle fire thinned their ranks even more. He glanced at the eastern skyline where Teresa's men might appear, but saw nothing. Not, he thought wryly, that those few men would be of much use except to distract the enemy. At best, he supposed, they would force the French to pause, but their assault would go on. His one chance was to so damage the enemy that they withdrew, but the bastards must know they had him trapped and doomed. He loaded the rifle again and laid it beside Teresa, then drew his long sword. If any of them did manage to cross the wall he would slaughter them. Teresa had her two loaded pistols waiting on the wall's top. "If they get in," she said, tapping one of the pistols, "that one is for me. They won't rape me again."

The enemy's musketry suddenly stopped. He looked right, but the men with bayonets were not stirring. Then he saw a man running behind the enemy's center toward their right wing. "Shoot that bastard!" The man was plainly giving orders and Sharpe knew what that meant. The men who had not fixed bayonets were to hold their fire until the charge began and then fire a volley that would swamp the wall with musket bullets. He heard two rifles fire and saw the running man stumble and fall. He was hit, but still managed to bellow out an order.

"They're coming!" Sharpe shouted, then saw he was wrong. It was not the thirty or forty men at the left of the French line who were coming with their long bayonets, but the whole French line was now running toward him. They were shouting as they ran and the wan sunlight glinted from the long blades at the left of the line.

"Fire!" Sharpe shouted and Teresa's partisans loosed a ragged volley while a dozen of his rifles spat flame and lead toward an enemy who numbered well over a hundred and who were coming to kill him.

Men called him "lucky," but Sharpe's luck seemed to have run out.

CHAPTER 6

Or maybe his luck was holding because, when the leading men of the French charge were about a hundred paces away, a whistle blew. The wounded officer, hit in the leg by a rifle bullet, blew the whistle and every man without a musket fitted with a bayonet stopped and aimed at Sharpe's Fort. "Keep firing!" Sharpe called. Sharpe had known he could never stop a concerted charge by all the French, but it seemed only the men with fixed bayonets were to assault the wall, and that gave him half a chance.

It was not a foolish decision by whoever commanded the enemy. The charge by the thirty or forty men who had fixed bayonets was coming from Sharpe's right, while to his left were a hundred or more men with muskets who would swamp his makeshift fort with lead to cover their comrades' attack. But those muskets were over a hundred paces away, which was still too distant for a smoothbore musket to be accurate, which meant the wounded officer was relying on an overwhelming volume of fire. "Keep firing at the buggers with bayonets!" Sharpe called, and almost immediately the snap sound of the rifles was drowned by a huge volley from the French, but as before most of the shots whipped overhead or else smacked into the stone and timber wall. One ball plucked at Sharpe's left sleeve. "Tap-load," he called. "Save the muskets till they're close, lads."

The charging French, he noticed, were bunching toward their right because that was where the road gave them the best footing, and those men who had already reached the road were stretching their lead over the rest, who were stumbling through the long grass. "We wait till they're real close, Pat," Sharpe called.

"Looking forward to it, sir," came the cheerful Irish reply.

Sharpe sheathed his sword and took his rifle back from Teresa. He reloaded it, taking the time to wrap a ball in its leather patch. He then stared at the closest French and picked out a big man who seemed to be shouting as he ran. He leveled the rifle, lined the sights on a broad blue chest, and pulled the trigger. By the time the smoke had blown clear the big man had vanished, presumably killed.

"To me, now. Both muskets." Sharpe would form a small line at the bridge's center and fire two volleys. He took one of Harper's two muskets. "Your second shot is the volley gun, Pat."

"Indeed it is, sir."

Sharpe tap-loaded his rifle and fired it again, then laid it against the wall. The men charging him were now masking the aim of many of their comrades, which meant that fewer musket balls were being fired at Sharpe's men, and those few were still going high. He reckoned that only about thirty men were charging his position, almost all of them now on the road and all with muskets encumbered by bayonets. He wondered if the muskets were loaded and reckoned most were not.

"Present," he called, not too loudly, and his men raised the French muskets to their shoulders and leveled them. A score of partisans had joined the line and leveled their guns. "Aim low, lads."

"Aim at their balls," Harper called. The kick of the heavy muskets would send the shots higher.

"Wait for it," Sharpe said. He waited, letting the French front rank reach just twenty paces away. "Fire!" He pulled the trigger, there was a pause after the doghead fired the powder in the pan, then the big musket slammed painfully into his shoulder as it fired. "Now ready the second musket," he shouted, "and wait."

The leading men of the French attack were now a bloody writhing mess on the road, obstructing the men behind, some of whom checked, reluctant to keep going until a voice bellowed at them and they stepped over their dead and wounded comrades. They looked young and nervous, and they could see the grim line of partisans and green-jacketed killers waiting with leveled muskets. They shuffled together, seeking companionship, then a voice bellowed, "*Avant!*"

"Fire," Sharpe responded, and a second volley flayed into the hapless conscripts. "Fix swords!" Sharpe called, and his men unslung their rifles and clipped the long sword-bayonets into place. Teresa fired her rifle into the remaining Frenchmen, then Sharpe plucked her shoulder. "Get behind us."

He picked up one of her pistols and shot it at the attackers, but Teresa snatched the second one and ran behind Sharpe's makeshift line. "We just see the buggers off," Sharpe said calmly. His men were tap-loading their rifles and he felt an immense pride in them. He had not ordered them to reload, but they did so anyway. They were trained men, many of them Chosen Men, and they knew their business. A tap-loaded rifle was as inaccurate as any musket, but at the present range that meant nothing. A blind man could hit the demoralized and confused French, and his rifles fired and more French fell, and then the voice shouted "*avant*" again and they came at last, rushing the last few paces and leaping up on the wall.

"Swords," Sharpe bellowed.

The French were inside his fort now, but they were youngsters conscripted unwillingly into their army who were being matched against hardened veterans, and the hardest of those veterans pulled the trigger of the volley gun.

The sound was like a small cannon, the smoke belched in a dense cloud through which seven bullets flensed the center of the French clambering over the wall. Sharpe had a hellish glimpse of men flailing backward and of misted blood streaking outward before the smoke hid the carnage, then he went forward to find survivors. He saw a blue uniform to his right and the big cavalry sword chopped that way to break the man's arm. The man was staggering anyway and Sharpe left him to be finished by another of his men. He was shouting, unaware of what he yelled, looking for the attackers, and he collided with the wall. He turned right, saw another blue uniform, and swung the sword onto the nape of the man's neck. The smoke was thinning and he glanced left and saw that the French who had fired the big volley were now coming toward his fort. And they were coming in overwhelming numbers, while his men were still busy trying to finish off the survivors of the first charge. So this, he thought, was the end, but there were still enemies inside the fort and they were vulnerable, so he kept going, stumbled on a blue-clothed body, and saw another man ahead. The man was clutching his musket against his body and gaping at the fight in front of him where Sharpe's few men were showing the results of hours of practice with their long sword-bayonets.

The man turned and saw Sharpe. He quivered in pure terror and tried to step backward. He was a boy, Sharpe reckoned, maybe eighteen years old, and had no more capability of fighting than he could sprout wings and fly. He still held the musket flat against his body, the bayonet poking above his shako, and he was muttering something wildly. Sharpe drew the big sword back and the boy's gabbling words suddenly became intelligible. *"Maman! Maman!"*

Sharpe pointed the sword back across the wall. "Go," he snarled. The boy quivered and Sharpe reached out with his left hand and pulled the musket from his hands. "Go, you bloody fool." He kicked the boy closer to the wall. "Just go."

The boy scrambled over the wall, losing his shako, and Sharpe threw the musket after him, then saw a man coming from his right. He was furious with himself. Showing mercy in a fight was a quick way to lose it, but he reckoned this fight was already lost and seeing the boy's terror had reminded him of the helpless French officer he had savaged to death in Badajoz. That man had been unable to fight and his death had not contributed one whit to the victory of the night and ever since Sharpe had been haunted by his dying screams. That same savagery was now turned on the man who was lunging a bayonet at him from the right. The bayonet was knocked aside by the heavy sword that Sharpe then punched into the man's face. He hit him with the hilt, which was a disc of steel that drove into the man's nose. It was followed by a kick to his groin and, as the man collapsed in pain, Sharpe used both hands to drive his heavy blade down at the man's spine. No screams this time, just gasps as the dying man writhed at Sharpe's feet.

He turned back to see the remaining French were still coming. "Back to the wall!" he shouted. The French who had crossed the wall were all dead or dying, but so were two of Sharpe's men. Larkin and Elliott were among the bodies. So were half a dozen of Teresa's red-scarved fighters. "Rifles," Sharpe called, "and same again, lads."

Same again, but against twice as many men, and Sharpe was down to a dozen men. The sensible course was to surrender, but Sharpe had seen off one attack and obstinately believed he could defeat this second, more ragged assault.

Then he saw the *guerrilleros* coming from the rear and knew El Héroe's men were joining the French attack. And those men had evidently been reinforced. El Héroe claimed to lead hundreds, though Sharpe had never seen more than forty or so, but it seemed that, for once, the bastard had not been lying because there were at least fifty or sixty horsemen spurring up the road and on the grassland either side. Sharpe reloaded his rifle and looked for El Héroe's garish uniform. If he was to be defeated here then he would at least take that slimy bastard down first. He looked over the rifle's sights and saw no sign of the gaudy jacket. He looked for the distinctive white stallion, but though there were a dozen gray horses among the fast-approaching horsemen, none was El Héroe's mount.

Sharpe fired at a French infantryman, then heard his men cheering. The smoke from his rifle slowly cleared and he saw that the *guerrilleros* were attacking the infantry, who were still in a loose line as they came toward the bridge. They could not defend themselves against the mass of horsemen who rode with lances and sabers. Like Teresa's men they wore red scarves and like her men they pursued the scattered infantry mercilessly. Some muskets fired, but the French were ridden down ruthlessly. Sharpe, his blood-reddened sword low in his hand, could only watch as, for a second time, he was saved by red-scarved partisans massacring his attackers.

"El Sacerdote." Teresa had come to stand beside him.

"It is?"

"I can see him." She pointed. "The black horse. There . . ."

Sharpe saw him then, a black-cloaked figure on a big black horse, wielding a long straight blade. "I thought priests weren't allowed to shed blood?"

"When fighting the devil? Of course they can . . ." She suddenly turned to stare across the wall and leveled her rifle. She pulled the trigger and flinched at the rifle's strong kick and Sharpe, as the smoke blew away, saw she had killed the young man he had spared. The boy was on the ground, his legs twitching. "So where's El Héroe?" he asked.

"The coward ran back to the village," Teresa said scornfully, taking another cartridge from the pouch slung about her neck. "I saw him leave, but he won't stay there. He'll run to the forts."

"No one else will," Sharpe said grimly. El Sacerdote's men had dismounted and were now finishing off the French wounded and searching the bodies for coins. As far as Sharpe could see, not one Frenchman had survived. Some had tried to flee, but the horsemen had pursued them with their nine-foot-long lances and the blue-uniformed bodies lay scattered down the slope to the west of the road. "It's a cruel war," he said.

"They started the cruelty," Teresa said, "and you reap what you sow."

Sharpe turned. "Sergeant!"

"Sir?"

"Sling those bodies into the French wagon park." Sharpe gestured at the French who had died after crossing the wall and who now lay on the bridge's roadway.

"Very good, sir."

"They can bury their own dead," Sharpe said, and went to the bridge parapet and gazed straight down to the enclosure where the pontoon carriages were parked. He counted the carriages and reckoned the French had either moved some or destroyed them because he could only see six of the monstrous wheeled vehicles. A knot of Frenchmen were gazing up at the high bridge, trying to decipher what had caused the fusillades of shots and the powder smoke that drifted wraith-like across the valley. They scattered as the first body was launched over the parapet. It fell and smashed into a carriage. "Just have to search the other buggers before we chuck them, sir," Harper said cheerfully. "That first one had a small fortune. Here, Miss Teresa." He held out a gold-chained pendant in his massive, powder-stained hand. "Not the kind of thing I wear, miss."

"You would look good in it, Patrick." She took the necklace. The pendant was a small egg-shaped ruby, delicately framed with gold. "I shall wear it," she said, and gave the embarrassed Harper a kiss on the cheek.

Sharpe was still staring down into the small encampment at the base of the bridge. Most of the big pontoon carriages had been dragged away, he assumed to the small village of Lugar Nuevo that lay close to Fort Napoleon, and their absence gave far more space inside the small enclosure. There was not only more space, there were also more men. At least fifty French infantrymen were staring back at him and dodging the corpses that came flying from the bridge's high parapet. And not just infantrymen. Sharpe could see the darker blue uniforms of the enemy's artillery and he used the telescope to count the guns protecting the enclosure. There had been five large cannons when he had first visited the bridge, and all were still there, four pointing westward and one northward. Between those monster guns were the puny four-pounders, one of which still lay abandoned a hundred or so paces up the road where Sharpe's riflemen had slaughtered the men hauling it up the slope. The drag ropes lay limp on the blood-soaked road where the corpses were lit by the late afternoon sun. "They've added three of the smaller guns down there, Mister Sharpe." Dan Hagman had come to stand beside him.

"Dear God, you're right," Sharpe said. When he had first seen the encampment there had been four of the small battalion guns, the four-pounders, and now there were seven. And all of the smaller cannon, except for the abandoned one on the road, had a heap of canister rounds piled beside their trails. Four of the small cannon were pointing westward, two northward, and the last still on the road, and all except that abandoned gun had canister piles. No roundshot, just the tin cylinders of canister. "The bastards are reading my mind," he said bitterly. His plan, insofar as he had any plan, was to assault the encampment from the north. He was not worried about the huge black twenty-four-pounder. The French might get off one shot from that before his men were at the embrasure, but he would be lucky to survive blasts of canister from the smaller guns. Sharpe cursed. He had airily promised General Hill that he could capture the place before Colonel Cadogan's infantrymen assaulted Fort Napoleon, but now he saw that would not be nearly as easy as he had thought. Somehow he had to survive the canister rounds. "God damn them," he snarled.

"What?" Teresa asked.

"Too much canister down there," Sharpe said. There were really only two approaches to the encampment and now both were dominated by the small guns that could belch vast loads of canister to flense an attacking force. "It's my fault," he said.

"Yours?"

"We killed their engineers and now they're trying to protect them. There are more infantry and more guns, the bastards."

"Who are bastards?" a grave voice inquired behind Sharpe, who turned to see El Sacerdote, his clerical black clothes damp with enemy blood.

"I have to thank you, Padre," Sharpe said, "you saved us. *Muchas gracias.*"

"On the contrary, I must thank you for drawing the French to a place where they could be so conveniently killed. They are not usually so obliging. May I?" He held a hand toward Sharpe's telescope and Sharpe gave it to the tall priest, who trained the glass on the small village of Lugar Nuevo. The village lay very close to the pontoon bridge's southern end and Sharpe could see a sizable single-masted ship moored at a wooden quay and he guessed it was one of the ships used to bring supplies downriver from Talavera. Those ships would bring food, wine, ammunition, and perhaps reinforcements. "The village is a supply depot, Captain Sharpe," El Sacerdote said in his deep voice. "It's not there to replenish the forts, though it does serve that purpose, but is a place where the French can pile up supplies for any army that crosses the bridge. If the army to the south marches to help the army to the north, they can refresh their powder, ammunition, food, and anything else. If General Hill can destroy Lugar Nuevo's storehouses he will have done Spain a great service."

"I'm sure he will, Padre."

The priest leaned over the parapet and gazed down at the enclosure's defenses. "New cannon?"

"The small four-pounders," Sharpe said.

"Painted black, so they're iron," the priest said, "probably taken from the stores at Lugar Nuevo. They're older guns, but still horribly effective." Most French iron cannon had been replaced by the lighter bronze guns. "And you have to capture this fort?" He pointed down toward the engineers' encampment below the bridge.

"I must," Sharpe said, wondering how in God's name he would get through the storm of canister that would gout from the new guns.

"You must indeed," El Sacerdote said gravely. He gestured westward to the long open slope that lay between the woodlands and the formidable defenses of Fort Napoleon. "Your fellow infantry will come down that slope and that's well within range of the bigger cannons."

"I'm assured the twenty-fours don't use canister," Sharpe said uneasily.

"So they'll use shell and roundshot," the priest said, "and when the attackers reach the fort they'll stop while the ladders are placed. They will make an unmissable target."

"True," Sharpe conceded.

"And you have few men." The priest gestured at Sharpe's handful of riflemen who were still searching the French dead for coins or food.

"Very few," Sharpe said.

"Then perhaps you would do me the honor of allowing some of my men to assist you?" El Sacerdote said, then, without waiting for a response, continued, "I have a score of artillerymen in my ranks and they are forced to fight with musket and lance. It will do them good to man those long guns."

"Man them?" Sharpe asked, not immediately grasping the priest's meaning.

"Hill's men will assault the southern rampart of the fort," El Sacerdote said, "and ignore the eastern wall, because any assault from the east will be within sight and range of the guns across the river." He pointed to Fort Ragusa. "If my men can hammer the eastern wall with roundshot it will distract the defenders on the southern wall."

"It will," Sharpe said enthusiastically.

"Then we shall have the pleasure of killing Frenchmen together," El Sacerdote said. "Probably tomorrow, Captain."

"Tomorrow? General Hill is that close?"

"I rode a half day ahead of him. His army should come tonight. I am, how do you say, scouting for him?"

"I'm damn glad you were, Padre," Sharpe said.

"And now we shall help you assault this battery," he gestured over the parapet, "and together we shall send a mass of Frenchmen to hell." He returned Sharpe's telescope with a polite bow. "I will ride south today," he went on, "to report to General Hill. But first I think it is time for us to explore El Héroe's village."

"He'll have run to the forts," Teresa said caustically.

"The dog returns to its vomit," El Sacerdote said and walked away. He stopped after a few paces and turned back to Sharpe. "I will ride south this evening," he said gravely, "to confer with General Hill. You will want me to convey a message?"

"I'd rather go with you," Sharpe said.

"That would be convenient," El Sacerdote said and offered another slight bow before continuing away.

"You want to go with him?" Teresa asked.

"So far," Sharpe said carefully, "I seem to have disobeyed all General Hill's instructions. He was adamant that he did not want the garrisons disturbed, and I've disturbed them mightily. Now I want to disobey another of his orders."

"Which was?"

"Not to attack the fort here until after his own assault has begun. But if I do that I'll likely fail. A daylight attack will just make us easy targets for the gunners. I want the general's blessing to assault these bastards tonight."

"And you need permission?"

"I do, because if my attack on the encampment alarms the forts, which it will, the bastards will be awake and ready when the general attacks them at dawn. Then, if he fails, I will be blamed."

"But not if he gives you permission?"

"Exactly."

"And if he says no?"

"Then we will attack the encampment at the same time he assaults the forts."

"In daylight."

"Sadly, yes."

"And they have big cannon."

"And canister," Sharpe said, imagining the canister flaying outward in stinking death-clouds of powder smoke.

"Then I will come with you to see the general," Teresa said.

"To protect me?"

"No," Teresa said, smiling, "because General Hill likes women."

"Who doesn't?"

Teresa ignored that. "I can tell by the way he looked at me. He's more likely to say yes to me than to you."

"Then you are coming with me," Sharpe said.

He used the telescope again to stare toward Fort Napoleon and could see four cannon in the fort's high eastern wall that looked toward the old bridge. One of those cannon suddenly fired and Sharpe could see the small dark trace of the cannon ball that was arcing toward him. The French had seen their attack on his makeshift fort fail, had seen their comrades ambushed by El Sacerdote's merciless horsemen, and were now trying to exact revenge. There was an unholy crash as the roundshot struck the stone of the bridge a few feet lower than the parapet. Stone chips flew up as Sharpe stepped back. "Cold barrel," he said, "the next shot will be higher. Time to go."

Sharpe wondered what on earth the French commander was thinking. He had known of the presence of a small group of riflemen in the hills immediately south of the bridge and had sent men to flush them out and each time had been comprehensively beaten, yet still he had sent more men, not one of whom would return. By now he must have learned that General Hill was approaching with a much larger force and that must terrify him. El Héroe had doubtless betrayed what he thought were Hill's plans, so probably Miravete Castle had been reinforced with men and muskets, and the forts either end of the bridge put on full alert, yet Sharpe could see no sign that French numbers had been increased in those forts. The same number of men showed on the ramparts of the bridge forts and the only change from his first visit to the old bridge was the addition of more small four-pounders. He stared obsessively down at the old bridge's fort, wondering how he was to take it even with the help of El Sacerdote's *guerrilleros*. "I need a pair of nine-pounders," he grunted to Harper.

"Aye, that would be a treat. How many of the buggers are down there?"

"I'm guessing a full company of infantry, and a few engineers."

"Gunners too." Harper had borrowed Sharpe's telescope.

"We attack at night?" Teresa asked.

"If General Hill allows it, yes."

"Why would he not?" she asked.

"Because he wants the assault on Fort Napoleon to be a dawn surprise. If we massacre those bastards down there tonight, they'll be wide awake in the forts."

Harper spat over the parapet. "They'll be wide awake anyway. Must be pissing themselves already. They must know Daddy is almost here."

"So General Hill has nothing to lose by letting us attack tonight," Teresa said.

"I'm thinking you and your men should stay up here," Sharpe said.

"I shall stay with you," Teresa protested.

"You're going to be my artillery," he told her. A wicked idea had hatched in his mind and he smiled wolfishly as he pointed to the stacks of masonry that had made his Fort Sharpe possible. "I don't have nine-pounders, but we do have those," he pointed to the remaining pile of stone blocks. "Drop those on the bastards' heads and it will scare them witless."

Harper chuckled, "he's right, Miss Teresa."

"And whoever is up here," Sharpe went on, "has to be clever enough to know when to stop hurling rocks at the bastards. Someone I can trust."

"Why would you stop?" Teresa asked.

"Because we'll be among them," Sharpe said, "and I don't want my skull crushed by a bloody great lump of stone."

Teresa looked stubborn, but evidently relented and called to one of her men to bring a block of masonry that formed one of the crenellations of Fort Sharpe. "*Tíralo a los bastardos*," she ordered him, gesturing over the parapet. The man hurled the heavy block as far from the bridge parapet as he could and they all leaned over to watch it fall. The Frenchmen beneath saw the stone coming and scattered, then the block crashed into one of the pontoon carriages and splinters flew.

"Mary, Mother of God!" Harper said. "It put a hole straight through that wagon bed!" The noise had been awesome, and the blow prompted some of the enemy to snatch up muskets and aim at the faces peering over the parapet.

"Get back," Sharpe said, amused.

"That's as good as a nine-pounder any day," Harper said.

"And as inaccurate, but you can rain stones down on the buggers."

"If you hit one, Miss Teresa, there'll be nothing left of the bastard," Harper said.

"And try to hit the men manning the four-pounders pointing uphill," Sharpe said. "You could shatter a gun wheel with one of those stones."

Teresa, imagining the terror and destruction that the masonry could cause, was now enthusiastic for the task and ordered her men to start piling the blocks beside the parapet above the guns that commanded the southern approach.

"And that's where we'll attack?" Harper asked.

"Better to assault a pair of four-pounders than five," Sharpe said.

"True enough, sir," Harper said.

Sharpe drew the tall Irishman aside. "I'm going to meet Daddy Hill and leaving you in charge, Pat."

"Very good, sir."

"I doubt the bastards will try and dislodge you, but don't provoke them. If you start tossing stones on them, they might call for help from the forts."

"I'll leave them sleeping, sir, so I will."

"But if they try to rescue that four-pounder," Sharpe pointed at the abandoned French cannon halfway up the road, "shoot them."

"And that's not provoking them, sir?"

"That's provoking me, because I want that gun."

"A garden ornament, sir?"

"Just stop them towing it back to their bloody fort."

"They'll not touch it, sir."

"I'll be back before dark," Sharpe said, hoping he was right. "And we'll murder those bastards before dawn."

"If Sir Rowland gives permission," Teresa, who had followed them, said.

"He'll not deny you," Sharpe said. "Not if you're wearing those tight trousers and high boots."

Teresa bridled at that. "I shall wear what I choose," she said stiffly, "and the necklace Patrick gave me. José," she called to one of her men, "my horse."

Harper watched Teresa stride away and chuckled.

"What is it, Sergeant?" Sharpe demanded.

"Oh nothing, sir, really nothing." He still watched Teresa. "But I reckon General Hill will give you anything you want."

What I want, Sharpe thought, is to be away from this damned river and back with the army.

Sharpe, Teresa, and some fifty *guerrilleros* rode back from the bridge. El Sacerdote rode too and insisted they detour for a view of Miravete Castle on its high mound. He used Sharpe's telescope to examine the castle. "I'd say they've reinforced the garrison," he said.

"Looks like it." Sharpe, even without his telescope, could see that the high battlements and the earthwork surrounding the castle were thick with blue uniforms.

"We have woken them up," El Sacerdote said. "Sir Rowland might not be happy."

"He should be," Sharpe said, "there's only one place they can get reinforcements."

"From the forts by the river?"

"Exactly."

A cannon in the earthworks fired, the sound rolling across the valley as the ball thumped into the turf some two hundred paces short of Sharpe. The next shot, Sharpe knew, would have a longer range because the first would have warmed the gun's barrel. "Onward?"

"Onward," El Sacerdote agreed, and spurred his horse back down the slope and so out of sight of the castle.

Twenty minutes later Sharpe saw redcoats on the road. He spurred ahead, trusting to his uniform and the red scarves of the partisans to alert the advancing troops that he was on their side. Those troops had made a two-deep line across the road, but their officer ordered them to ground arms as Sharpe came nearer. Their black facings told Sharpe they were men of the 50th. "Good morning, Captain," he called in greeting. "I'm Major Sharpe, 95th."

"We were warned to expect you, sir."

"We need to see General Hill."

The captain gestured westward. "He's not far behind, sir. Was that French gun aimed at you?"

"He missed," Sharpe said. He turned in the saddle and pointed up the road. "You'd best stop below that skyline, Captain, the bastards have a battery of twelves waiting to greet you."

Sharpe rode on past marching companies and past the first guns hauled by big horses. He found Sir Rowland about a mile back from the vanguard. The general was sitting on his horse at the side of the road, greeting the troops who marched past. "Good to see you, Sharpe," the general hailed him, then touched his cocked hat to Teresa, "and you, ma'am."

Sharpe hid a grin as he watched Sir Rowland's eyes drop down to take in Teresa's leg, then Sir Rowland bowed toward El Sacerdote. "I trust you bring good news, Padre?"

"You face about two hundred fewer enemies, thanks to Major Sharpe."

"Thanks to El Sacerdote and his men," Sharpe put in quickly.

"We heard the firing," the general said. "That was you?"

"I'm afraid so, sir."

"So the rascals are thoroughly awake and expecting us."

"They're awake," Sharpe said.

"But they are expecting an assault on the castle," El Sacerdote put in.

"Which we must capture if we are to move the guns to the river," Hill said.

They had moved farther from the side of the road to allow more companies of redcoats and artillery to pass by. Hill had been joined by a half dozen other officers, all senior to Sharpe and all scowling at his ragged uniform. "You'll not take Miravete by assault, sir," Sharpe said, "but we can send infantry down to the river by a different route."

"Which is not suitable for guns," Hill said unhappily.

"Sadly not, sir."

"Sadly indeed," Hill said, and turned to one of his companions, a gray-haired, thin-faced man who Sharpe remembered from the conference in Truxillo. "Well, Howard, you fancy a dawn assault on the nearest river fort?"

"I'd prefer an assault covered by our artillery, sir."

"We all would," Hill said. He frowned. "Didn't we discuss all this in Truxillo?" The question was a reproof. "We knew then that an infantry assault on the forts would be unsupported by artillery." He was plainly hoping to end the discussion.

"There is more, sir," Sharpe said. He had spoken to General Hill, but General Howard answered. "More bad news?" Howard asked with some asperity. "I suppose we must hear it."

"The fort at the base of the old bridge, sir, has been reinforced. And. I'd like to capture it tonight."

"Reinforced!" Howard sounded indignant. "More guns?"

"They've added more four-pounders to the big twenty-fours on your flank, sir," Sharpe said.

"Those old fours can't reach us," Howard said dismissively.

"But the big guns will hammer us with roundshot and shell," Cadogan grumbled. It was plain that while General Howard was to command the surprise assault on the forts, Cadogan and his Scotsmen would have to make the actual assault alongside the Kentish battalion.

"They won't hammer anyone if I capture the place tonight, sir," Sharpe said.

"How many infantry in that bridge fort?" Hill asked quietly.

"At least a hundred men, sir."

"And you have how many, Major?"

"A dozen, sir."

"You don't have the strength to defeat that many," Hill said, still quietly.

"With my men?" El Sacerdote suggested, "he has more than enough."

"Mine too," Teresa added.

"But only if we attack tonight, sir," Sharpe said.

"If you attack tonight," Howard said unhappily, "then the scoundrels in the two bigger forts will be thoroughly alert and waiting for us." He turned to Hill. "Surprise is our best hope, sir. A night action by Major Sharpe will destroy that surprise."

Hill pondered for a few heartbeats. "Can you wait until General Howard's men mount their assault on the forts, Sharpe?"

"We can, sir, but the gunners manning the twenty-four-pounders at the old bridge will see his men advancing and open fire. I believe our best chance of stopping that is to capture the place tonight."

"There'll be a half moon," Cadogan grunted, "you'll be visible, Sharpe."

"Better a half moon than daylight," Hill suggested.

"I will lose maybe a dozen men in a night attack," Teresa said, "but if I must assault by daylight I will be lucky to have a dozen men left." She leaned down and tugged at the top of her boot. "And a daylight attack," she added, "will open us to the guns of Fort Napoleon."

Hill mused for a moment and Sharpe saw the general was gazing at Teresa. "What time would you attack, Major?" Hill asked.

"In the hours before dawn, sir."

"And you're confident your fellows can capture the place?"

"With La Aguja's help, sir? Very confident."

Hill sighed, then looked at Howard. "I suspect, Howard, that the rascals already know of our presence. Surprise would be an advantage, I agree, but have we already lost it?"

"With that racket Major Sharpe made in the hills, sir? Yes," Cadogan said curtly.

"Then it's spilled milk, and nothing to cry over," Hill said decisively. "Take the bridge fort tonight, Sharpe. Maybe earlier than you suggested so you can send a message telling us that the guns are taken?"

"I will, sir," Sharpe said, wondering what the hell he had just volunteered to do, "and thank you, sir."

El Sacerdote hesitated. "You will advance on the forts through the hills?" he asked General Howard.

"No other way, Padre."

"I will give you a guide," El Sacerdote said, "a local man."

"Grateful to you, Padre," Hill said cheerfully, then turned to Cadogan. "Your rogues will lead the assault, Colonel, so add the Padre's fellow to your leading company."

"Of course, sir," Cadogan replied.

Sharpe tugged at his reins, then remembered his manners. "By your leave, sir?"

"On your way, Sharpe. We'll see you in the morning!"

"You will, sir."

"Ma'am," Hill acknowledged Teresa, who spurred her horse alongside Sharpe's mount.

"So you got what you wanted," she said.

"Not sure I really want it."

"You'd prefer that?" she asked and jerked her head toward a company of the 71st who were carrying four immense ladders. Each ladder looked to be at least thirty paces long and was made from newly split wood that was bright gold in color. The rungs were nailed to the uprights and Sharpe shuddered at the sight. "I've never had to escalade a wall," he said, "and don't want to start now."

"Escalade?" Teresa asked, unfamiliar with the word.

"There are two ways to take a fortress. Batter a bloody great breach with cannon and then storm it, but if you haven't got cannon you put ladders against the wall and climb them. That's an escalade."

"And you've never done it?"

"I'm alive, aren't I? No, love, I almost had to do it in India, but the good Lord opened the city gate instead. Climbing a ladder is a quick way to die. And a ladder that long?" He looked at the nearest soldiers carrying one of the huge ladders.

"One rung breaks and you fall, and even if you manage to cling on, the buggers are dropping stones and roundshot on you." He remembered watching the 74th, another fine Scottish regiment, assaulting Ahmednuggur and seeing them being plucked off their ladders by hurled stones and by musket fire. It had seemed an impossible task until one brave officer, at his third attempt, managed to clamber over the battlements and lay about himself with his claymore. Sharpe shuddered to even remember the man's ordeal.

"The ladders are too long," Teresa said. "The fort's walls aren't that high."

"What did you say, ma'am?" a confident voice called from behind and Sharpe turned to see Colonel Cadogan riding a tall black stallion.

"Your ladders are too long, Colonel," Teresa said.

"You agree, Sharpe?"

"I do, sir."

"So how high are the fort's walls?"

Sharpe thought for a second. "I'd estimate them at forty feet, sir."

"From the ground or from the bottom of the ditch?"

"From the ground, sir."

"We'll see," Cadogan said, then turned to his men. "Well done, lads. Not far now."

The company had reached a tight bend in the road and was having difficulty in maneuvering the long ladders round the sharp curve. "I suppose we can cut the blasted things in half if we have to?" Cadogan wondered aloud.

"How long are they, sir?" Sharpe asked.

"A hundred feet apiece."

"Fifty should be enough," Sharpe said confidently.

"Easier to carry, that's for sure, but . . ." Cadogan paused. "If you're wrong, Sharpe, we'll be stymied. I'll take a look at the fort before I order the ladders shortened. God be with you tonight, Major."

"And with you, sir."

Cadogan spurred on, his men finally managing to carry the ladders round the curve as Sharpe and Teresa cantered past them. A sergeant bellowed at the men to keep silent as the couple rode by and the whistles and catcalls stopped abruptly.

"It's the cavalry trousers and boots," Sharpe said.

"They worked for you," Teresa said accusingly.

"They always do, love, always do."

"*Eres un cerdo*, Richard," she said, not unkindly.

"True," he said, and thought that come an hour or so before dawn the pig must lead a dozen men and a pack of *guerrille-ros* to capture a fort. He kicked his horse uphill. "And there's one good thing about being a pig," he called to Teresa.

"What?"

"Pigs do not climb ladders, love." He touched the hilt of his sword where he had tied a lock of Teresa's hair. "Pigs do not climb ladders," he said again, and rode on.

CHAPTER 7

Clouds had been building in the west all day and as night fell they spread eastward. "It'll be black as Satan's arse," Harper said happily, then looked at Hagman. "You don't need to spoil your good looks, Dan."

Hagman, the old poacher, went on smearing his face with mud. "And if the clouds gape?" he asked. "And the moon shines through?"

"We'll be in shadow," Sharpe said. He would attack immediately to the west of the bridge and the moon, if it was visible, would rise in the east. "At least at first we will be."

"Is that how you were caught poaching?" Harper asked. "With your face all dirtied up?"

"I was caught," Hagman said patiently, "because Lord Cholmondeley set his deer hounds after me. I never could abide hurting a dog, so I scampered up a hornbeam and his whippers-in found me. But His Lordship was right good about it. Arranged for me to volunteer for the army rather than go to jail."

"That was nice of him," Harper said.

"He's a good man," Hagman said firmly, "and he knows me well enough. I taught him how to tickle trout when he was just a lad."

"Pray the clouds stay," Sharpe growled and, like Hagman, scooped up some mud to smear on his face. He had ridden back to the old bridge, which had now been entirely cleared of French corpses by the simple expedient of throwing them from the shattered bridge either into the river or down onto the engineers' encampment. In the last of the daylight he had gazed through his telescope at both Fort Napoleon and the small fort beneath the old bridge, looking for signs of any frantic activity to strengthen the defenses, but all had seemed normal. A dozen men manned the high battlement of Fort Napoleon's tower above which the French flag hung limp on its tall pole, while in the fort below the old bridge the only movement was men hauling the thrown corpses down to the riverbank. Smoke drifted up from the small huts' chimneys. Doubtless the French were cooking their evening meal, yet surely they must know that an overwhelming enemy was just to the south? How could General Hill have brought six thousand troops to this lonely place without being detected? The French must have been told by El Héroe, yet it seemed that dusk must fall on garrisons making no special preparations.

The British, on the other hand, were dividing their forces. General Hill, with the nine-pounder guns, would be moving up the road to attack Miravete Castle just before dawn. That attack was merely a distraction, to convince the French that their attackers were trying to take the castle and so open the road that would allow the nine-pounders to descend into the valley and besiege the river forts. And as the French concentrated on defending Miravete the real assault, under General Howard, was creeping round their left flank to make a daring escalade of Fort Napoleon. By soon after sunrise, Hill hoped, the fort would have fallen and the pontoon bridge doomed, but that hope depended on Sharpe and El Sacerdote taking out the guns that would threaten the right flank of General Howard's infantry assault.

"Will it work, Mister Sharpe?" Hagman asked.

"We'll do our part, Dan," Sharpe said, "but I wouldn't want to be on a ladder."

"Poor boys," Hagman said.

"There's one rule for an escalade," Harper put in.

"What's that?" Sharpe asked.

"Officers go first, sir."

"Do something useful, Sergeant-Major Harper," Sharpe snarled.

"And what would that be, sir?"

"Make sure the rifles don't have flints."

"Thy will be done, sir!"

Sharpe, when he advanced, wanted their movements to be as silent as possible, and more than one night attack had been betrayed by a man stumbling and accidentally discharging a loaded gun.

Sharpe took a final look through the glass, hoping that the last rays of the setting sun would not betray the telescope to the French far beneath him. He watched half a dozen men stacking even more ready ammunition behind the small four-pounders. Most of that ammunition was cylinders of canister. "Harris!"

"Sir?"

"You'll stay here with Teresa. Keep an eye on those two four-pounders facing uphill. The moment you see a portfire alight, start throwing rocks."

"Looking forward to it, sir."

"You're a bloodthirsty bastard, Harris."

"Learned my soldiering from you, Mister Sharpe."

There were at least two hundred stone blocks piled just behind the bridge's parapet and each would strike with the force of roundshot. Sharpe could only imagine the carnage and terror that those falling rocks would cause and, he admitted to himself, he was looking forward to seeing that bombardment. He had asked Teresa's men to move the stones to the bridge's edge so they would be ready. At first some had been stacked on the parapet and Sharpe had forbidden that because an alert man with a telescope in Fort Napoleon could see the masonry, guess its purpose, and send a warning that would ruin the surprise, so now the blocks were being piled just inside the parapet.

"Make sure you wait," Sharpe cautioned Harris. "Wait for either the portfire or for a cannon to fire." The portfire was a stick to which was attached a length of slow-match that was used to fire the cannon. Once lit, the portfire stayed alight until it was either doused or burned entirely away. Most gunners liked to swing the portfire to make the smoldering end glow more brightly and Sharpe expected the French gunners to do the same. Such a small light would be easily visible from the bridge parapet and should precipitate a murderous cascade of masonry. There was always a chance that the portfire might be lit too early, but that was a small risk. Ideally the gun commander would light the match when it was full dark and Sharpe's men were already in position. "Those rocks could shatter a gun wheel," Sharpe said.

"Or turn a gunner into paste," Harris said wolfishly.

El Sacerdote's men would assemble on the hillside above the encampment, but to the west so they could approach on the angle that was not covered by any of the huge twenty-four-pounder siege guns. There was a four-pounder in that angle, but Sharpe suspected the barrage of masonry would dissuade the artillerymen from manning the small cannon. "How will I know when to stop chucking rocks, Mister Sharpe?" Harris asked.

"When I tell you to."

"And that will be?"

"When we reach the embrasure."

"Ah, right," Harris said.

"And don't mess it up, Harris. I don't want my skull crushed by a rock."

"That would be a crying shame, Mister Sharpe."

"It would, Harris, it would. And one last thing, try not to hit the huts."

"The huts, Mister Sharpe?"

"The women are there and they're probably not volunteers."

"Spare the women—got it, Mister Sharpe. Good idea, sir." Harris paused, looking over Sharpe's shoulder. "Company coming, sir."

Sharpe turned to see Major Hogan approaching on horseback. He went to meet him. "Sir!"

"No need for 'sir,'" Hogan said cheerfully. "I just came to see how you were faring." He dismounted and patted his horse's neck. "Sorry I wasn't with you when you met Daddy, but I went with a cavalry patrol to see if any Frog bastards are coming to reinforce the forts."

"And are they?"

"None from the south that we could see. Of course there might be men coming from the north, but we don't have time to worry about that. And General Howard wants to know when you've put the guns here out of action. Think of me as your messenger to take him the good news."

"A very welcome messenger," Sharpe said. He had been worrying how he was to send a message to General Howard. The obvious answer was to send a partisan on horseback, but a nervous sentry could well shoot at a man on horseback whose English was foreign or nonexistent.

"Daddy Hill tells me you're starting tonight's dance?"

"We are."

"And earlier than he'd like?"

"Midnight, probably. Maybe later, but before dawn."

"And how on earth did you persuade him of that?"

"Teresa did."

Hogan looked at Teresa and smiled. "You are a cunning bugger, Richard, and a lucky one."

Hogan walked to the parapet and craned over. He stared for a few seconds, then pulled back. "That's a nasty set of guns waiting for you."

"We have our own artillery, sir."

"You do?" Hogan sounded surprised, then followed Sharpe's gaze to look at the masonry blocks stacked beside the parapet. He smiled. "Cunning, lucky, and very nasty. Won't they be expecting that?"

"I would," Sharpe said, "but what can they do?"

"Umbrellas?" Hogan said.

"All they can do to avoid it," Sharpe went on, "is either get the hell out of the encampment now, or else try to drive me from the bridge."

Hogan took another look over the parapet. "And they seem to be doing neither."

"They haven't thought enough about it," Sharpe said.

"I'm tempted to ride now and tell Howard he needn't worry about those guns," Hogan said, "but I shall do my duty and stay to see the evil deed done."

"Is that why you were sent? To make sure I did my duty?"

"Generals are very touchy beasts, Richard, nervous as hell and needing much reassurance. Except for the peer, of course. But doubtless one day you'll be the same! Enjoy the night! But there is one suggestion?"

"Of course."

"Dropping that masonry is a wondrously vicious idea, Richard. But if you were to approach the fort under a flag of truce I've a mind they might surrender. And while you're down there a demonstration of one falling rock would surely persuade them?"

"Are you ordering me to do that?"

"I would never order you to relinquish a fight, Richard. But think about it. You'll suffer no casualties and still win the fort.

A wise man once said that the best way to win a war is to do it without fighting."

Sharpe thought briefly. "How far is it from here to the French frontier?"

"Oh Lord." Hogan was momentarily surprised by the question. "At a rough guess, Richard, I'd say around four hundred miles?"

"And we have to fight our way through all four hundred to drive the buggers out of Spain. And I want them terrified of facing us. Every time they see a green jacket or a red coat, I want them scared witless."

"I won't argue with that," Hogan said, "but think on it, Richard. Why lose men in an action you can win without bloodshed?"

"I'll think," Sharpe said, and tried to forget the conversation. Yet part of him suspected Hogan had been right, that he could achieve a bloodless capture of the encampment. So why not follow Hogan's advice? Even the most rabid Frenchman would understand the horror that would ensue if half a ton of masonry was tipped onto his position and, given the choice, would capitulate rather than suffer. So why not offer that choice? Because, Sharpe knew, he wanted to tip the stone over the parapet. He wanted to unleash the weapon. Hogan had even offered to negotiate the French surrender himself, but Sharpe had turned him down. He wanted to fight.

"And if they surrender," Teresa said brutally after Sharpe had told her of Hogan's suggestion, "you'll have over a hundred prisoners, and what will you do with them?"

"Keep them quiet," Sharpe said.

"Not while the priest and I are here," she snarled. "They will all die."

"La Aguja is right." El Sacerdote had been listening. "I do not take prisoners, though I do attempt to send them to heaven rather than to hell."

"They deserve hell," Teresa said.

"And those that do," El Sacerdote said calmly, "will go there. The few who might be good men will wait for us in heaven. The choice is not ours, but belongs to God."

Sharpe sighed, knowing he could be facing an argument. "But, Padre, tonight you fight with the British army, and we do believe in taking prisoners. If you massacre them, the bloody French will start treating us the same way. Whatever prisoners we take tonight are mine to deal with."

"We shall respect that," El Sacerdote said to Sharpe's relief. The priest saw Teresa's reaction. "My dear," he said in English, "we must respect Major Sharpe's orders. The French take their British enemies as prisoners and we must not change that."

"They don't take us prisoner," Teresa objected, plucking at her red scarf.

"You are right, my dear," El Sacerdote said sympathetically, "but tonight the final judgment will be left to God, not to us."

Sharpe waited until it was full dark, then led his eleven riflemen out of his makeshift fort and along the road. The clouds had reached the east and they were in their shadow, though there were star-filled gaps where the half moon's light edged the clouds a dull silver. Sharpe knew other men were moving through the night; thousands of men following the sheep tracks over the hills, ready to assemble in the woods above Fort Napoleon, while others were preparing to position the cannon to face Miravete Castle. Colonel Aubert, whoever he was, must know the British were close, but had no idea what a torrent of fire and steel he would face in the dawn.

Sharpe followed the road that first led southward, then looped back north to the riverbank. The big loop was necessary to carry the road from the low ground at the river's edge to the approach to the bridge, which was over a hundred feet higher. It was a gravel road that crunched beneath the riflemen's feet so Sharpe led them onto the grass, yet still thought the noise was loud. He paused where the road turned. "We're going down the road as far as the cannon the bastards abandoned," he said in a loud whisper. "Keep off the road, go softly, and no talking."

"So it's not a garden ornament?" Harper asked quietly.

"Hush, Pat."

They went very slowly. Hagman led, claiming he had the best eyesight, and Sharpe was a pace or two behind the old poacher. The half moon emerged from the clouds after some minutes and bathed the landscape with a silvery light, but by then Sharpe and his men were far enough down the road to be in the shadow cast by the high embankment leading to the bridge. He nevertheless stopped and crouched.

He could hear men above and behind him and knew it was El Sacerdote's partisans following the road before going farther west to the place where they would launch their attack, though Sharpe suspected he and his riflemen would be sufficient if the bombardment of masonry did its job. He tried to imagine the horror of being beneath the falling stones, then wondered if Hogan had been right and he should have offered whoever commanded the French beneath the bridge a chance to surrender.

He started forward again, keeping to the left of the road. There was just enough light for him to see the big box-shape of the abandoned limber, some two hundred paces from the French encampment. He moved toward it, then tripped on one of the bodies of the men who had been dragging the gun uphill. He fell and the stock of his rifle clanged against a tin cup that had been hanging from the dead Frenchman's pack. He froze, sure the noise must have alerted the enemy. He also cursed himself silently. He had demanded stealth and silence from his riflemen, then had caused the loudest noise of the night himself. His men had gone still, and all Sharpe could now hear were mutters from the French defenders and the crackle of a watch fire burning in the encampment. None of the enemy sounded alarmed, so he picked himself up and, using the rifle to feel his way across the dark, corpse-littered ground, made his way to the cannon itself.

"Buggers are asleep." Pat Harper appeared beside Sharpe.

"Don't count on it, Pat."

"We're going to fire this thing?" Harper asked, excitement evident in his whisper.

"If we can. Feel around for the portfire, probably in the limber."

Sharpe had always planned to capture the abandoned four-pounder and use it against its previous owners. The appeal of that idea had been one of the reasons to reject Hogan's suggestion of a negotiated truce. The French had fled from the gun and made no effort to recover the weapon, not even to take away the men killed by his riflemen, and Sharpe had seen how the abandoned gun was more or less pointing straight at the encampment's southern face where the big twenty-four-pounder and its two accompanying four-pounders stood behind their embrasures. He flinched as a slight creak sounded as Harper raised the limber's lid. The limber would contain ammunition and, Sharpe hoped, the tools needed to keep the gun serviceable; the wadhook, sponge, priming wire, reliever, and searcher. He felt along the black-painted barrel and, as he expected, found the vent had a firing tube already installed. He had half expected it because he was certain the French would have loaded the gun before attempting to drag it uphill. Once in position to fire at his men, the gun would have taken a few seconds to load and his riflemen could have turned those few seconds into a massacre of the gunners. It made much more sense to drag the ready-loaded cannon almost into position, turn it, then heave it forward until the barrel just cleared the small rise in the road facing the bridge. One touch of the portfire to the firing tube and the cannon would have lacerated his men and recoiled far enough for it to be reloaded safe from rifle fire. But what, he wondered, had the gunners loaded into the barrel? He drew his sword-bayonet and clipped it onto his rifle, then went to the muzzle and slid the rifle into the cannon. The tip of the bayonet hit whatever was loaded and he moved it carefully to explore the shape. Roundshot. He could feel the curve of the cannon ball.

So the cannon was ready to fire, but loaded with the wrong ammunition. Presumably the French had thought to batter down his wall with their first shot. Sharpe stepped back to the limber. "Can't find a bloody thing, sir," Harper muttered.

"It'll be fine, Pat, there's already a firing tube, we just have to light it. Keep the lads away from the gun."

A canister round was easy to find in the dark, the shape alone giving it away. Sharpe heaved one round from its slot in the limber and carried it to the cannon. He felt along the tin cylinder to find the wooden shoe, the sabot, strapped to its base and put that end into the cannon's barrel before using his rifle's brass butt as the rammer. The canister made a scraping noise as he slid it home, then Sharpe rammed it hard against the waiting roundshot. Loading canister on top of roundshot was common practice, and at two hundred yards would provide a blizzard of musket balls around the heavy cannon ball.

"We're ready," he whispered to Harper, "have the lads put flints in their rifles."

"Let me fire the cannon, sir, please."

"Flints first," Sharpe said, amused at Harper's eagerness. He stooped to the cannon's rear and saw it was pointing more or less where he wanted it; toward where the glow from the French watch fire illuminated the cannons' embrasures. The problem was that the cannon's trail was still attached to the limber. If he detached it the trail would drop to rest on the hillside and the cannon would be aimed much too high and Sharpe had no idea how to change the barrel's elevation. On British cannons there was a big elevating screw beneath the breech, and he could feel something similar beneath the four-pounder. The threads of the screw were as broad as his thumb and thickly greased, but he had no clue how the gadget was turned or even if it could be turned far enough to lower the gun's muzzle. For the first time since coming to the Tagus he wished Lieutenant Love was with him, the lieutenant would know exactly how to aim the gun, but Love had joined the other artillerymen, who would be arriving with General Hill. But how difficult could it be? He wiped the grease from his fingers and decided to leave the cannon attached to the limber; uncoupling it would make too much noise and he doubted he could lower the barrel before the enemy's canister blew them all away. The four-pounder's recoil would smash the limber into splinters, but he only wanted one shot from the gun and leaving it attached to the limber meant it was pointing more or less where he needed it.

There was one last task before he tried to fire the gun. He leaned over to the firing tube that had been inserted into the vent. By touch it seemed to be made of thin metal, presumably filled with finely mealed powder. He pushed it down, feeling the tube's lower end grind into the coarser powder of the charge, then used his powder horn to pour still more powder around the vent. He had little faith in the notoriously bad French gunpowder and wanted some of his own to make certain the gun fired.

"Rifles are loaded, flints in place." Harper came back to Sharpe's side.

"In that case you can fire the bloody cannon," he murmured to Harper, and crouched beside the gun. "Shelter me," he said, and hissed for two more men to crouch with him so their bodies provided a shield that would hide the inevitable light from the enemy down the slope. "I don't know if this will work," he muttered, "but we must try."

He laid his rifle flat, then opened his tinderbox and took out the small crumpled piece of dried linen that was the kindling. He threaded the linen onto the tip of the rifle's sword-bayonet by feel, then struck the flint against the steel just beneath the fragile cloth. "Keep well away from the gun wheel," he muttered to Harper, "just reach over and put the fire on the powder." It took three strikes of the flint for the fire to catch and flare up. "Quickly, Pat! Before the buggers see the light and fire at us. Move to the sides, lads!" Sharpe scrambled away from the gun, frightened that the burning linen would invite an opening volley from the French.

Harper lifted the rifle. The tip of the sword-bayonet was now a small burning mass of linen that the Irishman stretched toward the cannon's breech. The small flames threatened to die, but provided just enough light to see the powder heaped round the vent. "Quickly!" Sharpe hissed. The linen was almost burned through, but then a smoldering patch fell from the bayonet onto the powder.

The powder hissed and crackled, burning bright. Sharpe was about to curse because the gun did not fire and then the fire streaked down the tube and the charge in the barrel exploded. "God save Ireland!" Harper said, though no one could hear him.

Back in Truxillo the young artillery officer had observed that the French had stopped using the four-pounder because it did not make enough noise to scare the enemy. To Sharpe that sounded ridiculous, because the explosion was huge, the noise deafening, loud enough to scare the devil in his lair. His ears rang, but he distinctly heard the clang of canister glancing off the cannon barrels in the French defenses, though he could see nothing of the shot's effect because the ground in front of the cannon was now shrouded in thick pungent smoke. The gun itself had crashed backward and, because the cannon's trail was not resting on the ground but instead was latched to the two-wheeled limber, the gun had shattered the limber, splintering the ammunition chest into fragments. Sharpe's ears were ringing, but he gradually became aware that his men were cheering. "Stop your noise!" he shouted. "And open fire!"

He took his rifle back from an excited Harper, cocked it, then remembered he had not put a flint back in the doghead jaws. His men were snapping shots through the smoke toward the French encampment and Sharpe, as he groped for a flint, feared that the big twenty-four-pounder and its two companion guns would retaliate. "Spread out and lie down!"

His intent was to charge the encampment, but he wanted to be sure the enemy cannons were out of action first and the smoke cloud was reluctant to fade in the still night. Then he heard the screams.

It was the French and, as his hearing returned, he heard the crashes of falling masonry and the screams of men wounded by the heavy blocks of stone. The cannon had been loud, but the noise now was appalling; a succession of thunderous crashes as the blocks hurtled from the parapet. "Fix swords!" Sharpe bellowed as loud as he could. He screwed the doghead down on a new flint then fired his rifle into the chaos that was the French encampment, where a growing fire lit the chaos with a hellish red. The stone blocks were still falling, and one must have hit the watch fire, which momentarily dulled then sprang up with renewed vigor. The fire reached some of the ready ammunition, which exploded, causing a raucous cheer from the men on the bridge. More stones fell, and in the fire's flaring light Sharpe could see Frenchmen scrambling through the gun embrasures to escape the carnage. "Let's go!" he shouted. "Come on!"

He ran down the road, hoping to God that the cannons pointing uphill were out of action. His men pounded behind him. "Harris!" Sharpe bawled. "Enough!"

The stones still fell, looking like flame-touched streaks in the darkness. "Harris!" Pat Harper shouted, his voice echoing back from the huge wall of the bridge's southern approach. "For Christ's sake, stop!"

The stones stopped falling and there was a sudden silence except for the crackle of flames and the cries of the wounded. Sharpe saw men coming from his left and for a heartbeat feared it was reinforcements arriving from Fort Napoleon, then realized it was El Sacerdote's men, shouting as they came. "Come on, lads!" he yelled, and ran through the lingering cannon smoke, toward the encampment.

Bright fire was lighting up the immense cliff-like wall of the bridge's approach and silhouetting men waiting at the crude palisade. A musket fired there, the ball searing high overhead, and Sharpe, aware his rifle was unloaded, slung the weapon on his right shoulder and tugged his long sword free.

The blaze in the encampment was being fed by dull explosions as the flames reached the ready powder bags by the guns. He saw the men manning the palisade suddenly vanish and realized they were running, not from his few men but from the hellish heat and chaos behind them. Some jumped over the earthen bank and sprinted westward toward Fort Napoleon, only to find their way blocked by El Sacerdote's vengeful men. The muzzle of the twenty-four-pounder showed clearly. It was canted slightly so that it was now aimed above the road and marginally to the west. It could still fire, he reckoned, and the sheer blast of the firing could destroy his men, but the gun appeared to have no crewmen. Nor did any of the other cannons, for none fired.

Sharpe was first to the defenses, where he jumped up onto the widest embrasure and saw why the gun was canted. A falling stone had shattered its offside wheel and the whole gun was now resting on the one remaining wheel and an axle boss. He jumped down inside the embrasure and looked for the enemy.

And saw flame-lit horror.

Sharpe had seen nothing like it since the ditch in front of the breach at Badajoz, a ditch filled with the dead and their blood. This was worse. Instead of the dead in mangled piles, the bodies in the encampment were spread out; the details of their deaths all too evident. In the firelight the masonry blocks looked startling white except where they were smeared with blood, their victims looked dark, mere broken men with pulped limbs, broken chests, eviscerated bellies or headless. Some were not dead, but were moving feebly or calling for help. Farther away, close to the two big huts, a huddle of men was shaking in terror. All were armed, yet none raised a musket as Sharpe's riflemen came into the firelight. A boy in infantry uniform, there was no way he could be called a man, was weeping where he had taken shelter beneath the black-painted barrel of a twelve-pounder.

Sharpe edged past the big gun with the broken wheel and stepped into the full light of the fire. It was a burning limber, the flames crackling and spewing sparks high toward the deadly parapet of the bridge. Sharpe carried his sword and, in his dark uniform and with his mud-darkened face and with the flames reflecting from the sword's long blade, he looked to the surviving Frenchmen like a demon come from Satan's pit. The boy beneath the gun gave a despairing cry and shrank from Sharpe, moaning in pain as he shuffled away. Sharpe stepped over a corpse whose head was smashed beyond recognition and whose left hand was roasting in the fire. He kicked the man's arm to free the hand then glared at the men beside the huts. "Who commands here?" he demanded.

El Sacerdote appeared at Sharpe's elbow and repeated the question in French. No one responded for a few heartbeats, so the Spaniard repeated the words, more harshly, and finally a burly man wearing the dark blue of the French artillery, but with the black facings denoting he was an engineer, stepped forward. He spat, and Sharpe instinctively raised his sword, but El Sacerdote put a gentle hand on his arm. "He's been breathing smoke, Captain," he said gently, "let him be."

"Tell him he's a prisoner."

"I think he knows that." El Sacerdote sounded amused, then

had a brief conversation with the Frenchman. "He's a lieutenant in the Engineers, Captain, and by profession a *pontonnier*."

"Pontoon bridge builder?"

"Precisely."

"Tell them to drop their weapons and go to the river's edge." Sharpe turned. "Pat? Take five men and guard the buggers."

"Doing it, sir."

El Sacerdote had turned to the boy sheltering beneath the gun, stooped to him, and spoke in French, but the only response was crying from the lad. "He can join the other prisoners," Sharpe said.

"I don't think he can move," El Sacerdote answered, then put an arm round the boy. He stroked the boy's back. "*D'où venez vous?*" The boy muttered something in answer and the tall priest soothed him by stroking his forehead. "*Quelle paroisse est-ce?*" Again the boy muttered a reply and El Sacerdote went on speaking to him softly. "*Et ta mère est là?*" he asked, comforting the boy with his right hand. "*Votre nom?*" he asked and, when the boy answered and to Sharpe's surprise, the priest drew a long knife from his belt and, still stroking the boy, plunged the blade deep into his chest. The boy gave one startled jerk and then fell back.

"What?" Sharpe asked as the priest stood, cleaned the dagger and pushed it back into its sheath. El Sacerdote smiled and took a small notebook from a pouch with a stub of pencil. He wrote something on a clean page. "The poor boy was doomed. Killing him was the kindest act I could do, but not before he told me his name, where he was from, and which parish. I shall write to the priest of his parish and ask him to tell the boy's mother that her son died bravely and quickly."

"He might have lived!" Sharpe protested.

"With a broken spine? I think not. What would you do to a horse with a broken spine on the battlefield?"

"Kill it quick."

"And why do we treat our animals better than men? Sometimes all a priest can do is to hasten a soul to the next life." He made the sign of the cross. "Now I must look after the other wounded."

"You think the letter will reach France?" Sharpe called after the priest.

"The church has its ways, Major," El Sacerdote said, then knelt beside a man whose legs had been crushed by stones.

Sharpe saw that all the cannons facing westward had firing tubes in their vents. He plucked them out and tossed them into the darkness beyond the palisade. His men, seemingly unmoved by the carnage, were searching the enemy dead for plunder. He saw McCall cut a man's throat with his sword-bayonet and supposed that it was an act of mercy. Hagman was slicing open the tail hems of a blood-drenched blue coat, carefully extracting the small coins that had been concealed there. "Just silver, Mister Sharpe," he said when he noticed Sharpe's gaze, "but it'll buy wine! What do we do with the dead?"

"We have prisoners, Dan, they'll bury their own."

"Toss 'em in the river," Hagman said, "it'll be quicker."

"Maybe that," Sharpe said.

"Just don't toss me into a river, Mister Sharpe," Hagman said with a grin. "I want to be buried proper with my rifle."

"You'll take a shot at the devil, Dan?"

"I'll be in heaven, Mister Sharpe. Parson at home reckons dogs go to heaven and where there are dogs there's good hunting."

"I don't suppose I'll ever find out, Dan."

"Find out what?" an Irish voice intervened.

"Major," Sharpe said, seeing Major Hogan coming into the firelight.

"Find out what, Richard?"

"Whether there's hunting in heaven."

"Fine foxes and superb hounds, I've no doubt. Not that you'll follow them, Richard, but you'll find a lot of brawling in hell. You'll love it." Hogan put an arm round Sharpe's shoulder and drew him toward the river. "Proud of yourself?"

"Not very."

"It was damned effective, I give you that, but maybe unnecessary. I still think they would have surrendered. Did you lose anyone?"

"Not a man."

"They call you lucky, don't they? Do we have any prisoners?"

"Down at the riverbank. Pat's guarding them."

"I want a word with them before I go back to give Howard the good news." Hogan clapped Sharpe on the back, somewhat harder than Sharpe expected. "Well done, Richard!"

Hogan walked on toward the river and Sharpe went to the huts, neither of which had been struck by falling masonry. Light leaked through cracks in the hastily erected wooden walls, then a scream sounded from the hut built against the bridge's vast wall. Sharpe pulled open the door to see that El Sacerdote's partisans were already inside, where they were systematically slaughtering the French who had taken refuge there. "Stop!" he bellowed.

The scream sounded again and Sharpe pushed through the crowd to see a partisan pulling the blanket from a young woman. The blanket was all she wore. She was clinging to it and cowering away from the man assaulting her. Sharpe still had his sword drawn and slid the pointed tip into the man's buttock. The man turned fast, revealing a long knife that he lunged at Sharpe furiously. Sharpe swiped the sword hard to his right, knocking the man's arm away, then punched the disc hilt into the man's face, knocking him backward so he fell onto his victim, bleeding profusely from a shattered nose. Sharpe followed with a brutal kick to the man's groin, then hauled him upright and tossed him aside.

"You should have killed him." Teresa suddenly appeared behind Sharpe. "Maybe I will."

"Go ahead," Sharpe said. The man was curled into a ball, his knife discarded and his hands clasped over his groin. Teresa picked up the knife and tested its point with a thumb, then smiled at the terrified man.

"*Yo soy* La Aguja," she said quietly. The man began crying and pleading for mercy. Teresa spat at him. "*Llévatelo!*" she snarled at his cowed companions, who obediently dragged the man out of the hut. "I am not here to kill Spaniards," she explained to Sharpe, "unless they are traitors." She ordered the rest of the partisans out of the hut. "These poor girls stay here," she said, and Sharpe saw there were four other young women among the score of straw-filled sacks that served as beds. All the girls looked pitifully young, all were terrified, and all dressed only in thin inadequate blankets that they clutched to keep their modesty. "Leave me with them," Teresa said.

Sharpe left her and discovered Joe Henderson outside. "Stand guard on this door, Joe, and no one's to go inside except me or Major Hogan."

"Officer's country, is it, Mister Sharpe?"

"It is."

"It's their brothel?"

"The girls were their prisoners, Joe. It's not exactly like Flo Bailey's at Shorncliffe Barracks."

"I could never afford Flo's prices, Mister Sharpe."

"With the money you've filched so far, Joe, you can afford all of Flo's girls. Just keep everyone out of the hut." Sharpe saw El Sacerdote standing between two of the enormous twenty-four-pounder cannons where he was talking to a dozen of his men. Sharpe pushed his sword home into its metal scabbard and crossed to the tall priest.

"Our target!" El Sacerdote greeted Sharpe, gesturing west-ward toward Fort Napoleon, which loomed on its hill in the light of the half moon.

"Shot will carry that far?" Sharpe asked.

"Easily!" El Sacerdote gazed at the distant fort. "We're look-ing at its western face and I think General Howard will assault the southern face?"

"I'm sure he will. If he assaults the western wall he'll be in easy range of the guns on Fort Ragusa."

"Then we will shoot at the western face. I doubt we'll do much damage, but it should unsettle any Frenchmen on the ramparts."

"I'm afraid I unsettled one of your men."

"I heard. Think nothing of it. You taught him a lesson and I am in your debt." El Sacerdote turned a wolfish face toward the distant fort. "I am tempted to shoot now."

"Don't, Padre. Let's not disturb their sleep any longer."

By now, Sharpe reckoned, the first of the fugitives from his assault on the encampment would have reached Fort Napoleon and their tales of death raining from the sky would be sending tremors of fear through the garrison. They knew by now that a British force was close by and Sharpe doubted that many of the French would get much sleep. Nervousness would keep most awake, while others would be preparing the forts for a siege. Ready ammunition would be piling by the cannons on the fort's ramparts while a barricade would be being built behind the main south-facing entrance in case the British demolished the gate with roundshot then swarmed through the arch with bayonets.

Sharpe climbed onto the nearest embrasure and stared at the distant dark shape of Fort Napoleon. Men would be piling rocks on the ramparts, ready to hurl them down at attackers on their ladders, and those attackers were even now filing across the hills toward the fort. It would be a long night for Howard's men, followed by a bloody fight at sunrise.

He was still staring at the fort when a gun fired from its western rampart. There was a sudden lance of flame, immediately obscured by smoke, and Sharpe waited for the shot to fall. The gun had been fired toward the captured encampment, but Sharpe doubted the shot would reach him. He reckoned twelve-pounders were too heavy to be mounted on the fort's upper battlement and he suspected the heaviest guns practicable on the fort's top fire step would be eight-pounders, still formidable, but smaller and lighter. The barrels would have been taken from their carriage, hoisted to the rampart, and placed on garrison mounts that soaked up much of the recoil.

The sound of the gun arrived before the shot; a flat harsh sound that filled the valley of the Tagus. Sharpe was waiting to hear the roundshot fall, but heard nothing, but then, maybe three hundred yards short of the encampment, there was a fizzing sound and, an instant later, a blaze of firelight.

"Carcass," Major Hogan's voice sounded just behind Sharpe. "The scoundrels want to see what's happened."

The French gunners had fired a carcass, a projectile that looked like canister, but was crammed with turpentine, sulfur, and other inflammables. When the fuse reached the mixture, it burst into flame and would burn for some minutes, lighting up a space some twenty or thirty yards around.

"Buggers could already see what was happening, there was enough fire here," Sharpe grunted, "and there's moonlight."

"But now they're worried we're launching infantry from here." A second carcass landed a little to the left of the first and the two fierce fires showed nothing but empty pasture. "Perhaps the bastards will go back to sleep now," Hogan said, then showed Sharpe a French shako. "You'll see more like this," he said.

Sharpe tilted the hat toward the moonlight and saw that it had an elaborate brass plate; evidently the same kind of plate that had puzzled him when he saw it through his telescope.

The plate had a big French eagle above a space where the numeral 4 was emblazoned. "Another battalion?"

"The Fourth *Étranger*, from Prussia. They mostly garrison Fort Ragusa, but a company was sent here to guard the engineers after you slaughtered three of their officers."

"We're fighting Prussians?" Sharpe sounded surprised.

"Stout troops, Richard, though probably not too enthusiastic about fighting for the French," Hogan said, "but Bonaparte needs troops and he's demanding them from the German states. The buggers will probably change sides if we ask nicely."

The two carcasses burned themselves out and no more shots came from Fort Napoleon's defenders. Hogan took the shako back from Sharpe and prized the plate loose. "I'll head back, Richard, and tell the general he doesn't need to fear anything from his right flank."

"And we stay here?"

"You captured this place, you hold it." He pointed to the second hut, which Sharpe had not explored. "That hovel is filled with French engineers' tools. Hold on to them, Richard."

"I will, sir."

"They're far superior to the tools we're issued, so I want them all."

"You'll have them, sir."

"Then stay here and enjoy the show." Hogan glanced up at the half moon, "I'll guess five hours till dawn. Get some sleep, Richard."

"I'll try, sir," Sharpe said, but knew he would have no rest. El Sacerdote's men were now garrisoning the encampment's perimeter, while Pat Harper with another half dozen riflemen was guarding the forty-six prisoners at the river's edge. Harper had to be relieved so he and his squad could get a couple of hours' sleep and Sharpe now had no other sergeant so he supposed he would supervise the prisoners till dawn. "I'll relieve you in about an hour," he told Harper, "and I'll want to borrow your toy gun."

Harper hefted the seven-barreled gun. "It scares the hell out of them, sir. And they're Germans too, and those boys don't scare easy."

"You and your men can get a couple of hours' sleep," Sharpe went on. "There are straw beds in the hut closest to the bridge."

"Where the wee girls are?"

"They're off limits, Pat."

"Of course they are, sir." Harper paused. "And what do we do at dawn?"

"We watch the poor bastards climb ladders, Pat."

"We're not thinking of climbing them ourselves, are we, sir?"

"I've had no orders, and Major Hogan said we should stay here."

"Praise the good Lord for that, sir. I hate ladders."

"Me too, Pat, me too."

More carcasses were fired from Fort Napoleon, these southward toward the trees that grew thick on the slopes above the fort. The bright flames flared, but betrayed no movement, yet the French were plainly nervous and expecting an attack. So much for surprise, Sharp thought, then touched the hilt of his sword for luck. Pigs don't climb ladders.

CHAPTER 8

"El Héroe?"

"I am ashamed he is a Spaniard."

"Every country has its cowards," Sharpe said.

"He sells those women to the French! They get raped, and he takes French gold." She spat. "If you find him, Richard, he is mine."

"He'll be in Castle Miravete by now," Sharpe guessed, "safe in his bed."

"The girls say he usually goes to Fort Napoleon," she spat the name. "He offered to marry one of the girls, then rejected her. He said she was not worthy to carry his name, then sold her to the French, but only after beating her. He is a pig!"

"He is," Sharpe agreed. He had climbed to the old bridge, from where he was staring westward toward the fort, which was still a dark lump in the river valley. The walls looked ominously high and were dominated by the fort's tower, from which he guessed French officers were watching the moon-touched landscape. Sharpe could see no evidence of British or Portuguese troops in the valley, but he supposed they were still concealed by the low trees that cloaked the valley's southern slopes. He turned and gazed eastward, wondering how far off dawn was.

"And the poor girls aren't allowed clothes," Teresa went on indignantly, "to make it hard for them to escape. And that was the pig's idea, the manky bastard." She paused. "Do we just stay here?" she asked.

"That's what Major Hogan suggested."

"So do we?"

Sharpe nodded toward Fort Napoleon. "If they need help, we'll go there."

"Help?"

"Some poor buggers have to climb the ladders," he explained, "and the bastards on the ramparts will be shooting down at them and dropping roundshot on them and tipping their ladders over. So the best we can do is put a lot of riflemen about two hundred paces from the wall and shoot every French bastard who shows his head. Then our lads have a chance of getting to the top of the ladders."

"General Howard has riflemen already."

"A dozen more won't hurt."

They both fell silent, Sharpe turned again and saw a lightening in the eastern sky, nothing but a gray rim on the horizon. So dawn was close. The moon was low in the west, paler now. The world was silent, except for the sound of the heavy river piling and pouring through the old bridge's great central pier. Sharpe imagined the British soldiers crouched in the wood anticipating what was about to happen. Anticipating and fearing. Those closest to the treeline could see the cannons mounted on Fort Napoleon's high walls and knew that the moment the attack emerged from the wood those cannons would belch fire, smoke, and iron. The cannons would be loaded with canister over roundshot so the long advance would be shredded by an iron hail of death. Ladder carriers would have to carry the long clumsy ladders to the ditch, jump down, and somehow slam their burden up and against the wall while the defenders cut the fuses of shells as short as possible, then tossed them down into the ditch to fill it with screaming shards of exploded iron casings. Other defenders would use axes to hook the ladder tops and cant them sideways as the first brave men climbed the rungs. The marvel, to Sharpe's mind, was that escalades sometimes succeeded. He remembered watching the Scots assail a city wall in India and somehow fighting their way over the ramparts, and every man in the army knew of the miraculous fake assault on Badajoz, where an escalade intended only as a diversion to draw defenders from the breaches had somehow worked and men had scrambled over the massive castle wall to begin the massacre of the city's garrison. He shivered. "Doesn't feel like spring," he said.

"We need rain." El Sacerdote had come to the bridge's top. "The spring pastures are dry."

"All well down there?" Sharpe nodded down toward the captured encampment.

"If you're asking whether the prisoners are alive," El Sacerdote said, amused, "then they are. They have even been given breakfast. One of them swears that relief is on the way."

"You believe him?"

"He seemed certain. He claims Marmont has sent two or three brigades." The priest paused. "Well, to be honest, he wasn't sure whether they were brigades or battalions."

"Brigades," Sharpe said. "He wouldn't send three battalions."

"I agree."

Sharpe gazed at the pontoon bridge. "But whatever they are, if Marmont sent them then they're coming from the north. That'll make an interesting fight."

"My artillerymen are confident they can reach the bridge with the twenty-four-pounders," El Sacerdote said.

If Marmont had sent men then they would need to cross the bridge to join the fight. Sharpe hoped the artillerymen in El Sacerdote's force had not forgotten how to lay a gun, but however good they were, the range was long and the low-lying pontoons made a difficult target. The best way to finish this fight, he knew, was to capture Fort Napoleon and use the defenders' own guns to dominate the bridge. "Not long now."

"May I?" El Sacerdote asked, gesturing at Sharpe's telescope.

"Of course." Sharpe handed over the glass and saw the tall Spaniard train it toward the hills to the south. The sky had perceptibly lightened, though the sun had yet to break the horizon.

"It may be longer than we hoped," El Sacerdote said, handing the telescope back to Sharpe.

Sharpe rested the telescope on Teresa's left shoulder and stooped to the eyepiece. It took him a moment to find what had prompted El Sacerdote's remark and then he saw the long lines of men trailing down the bare hillside toward the thick belt of trees. Some carried the ladders. The figures were indistinct in the night's last darkness, but it was unmistakably a large force of infantry. "That's not good," he muttered.

"What's not good?" Teresa asked.

"The attackers are late," Sharpe said. "They should have been among the trees an hour ago."

"It's a difficult journey for them," El Sacerdote said, "especially on a dark night."

"The sun will be up before they're ready," Sharpe said as he handed the glass to Teresa and offered his shoulder as a rest.

"He's shortened the ladders," Teresa said after a while.

"To quicken the pace," Sharpe suggested. It would have been hard enough following the winding sheep tracks over the hills without maneuvering the hundred-foot-long ladders through the twists, over the crests, and then through the thickets.

"Then we wait," El Sacerdote said calmly.

"So much for surprise," Sharpe said bitterly, knowing the men watching from Fort Napoleon could see the approaching infantry as clearly as he could.

"El Héroe ensured there would be no surprise." El Sacerdote sounded just as bitter. "My hope is that we capture him."

"Not kill him?" Teresa asked.

"Eventually, but after a trial I would like to see him executed as a common criminal. A firing squad or a death in battle gives him the honor of dying like a soldier, and he deserves no honor."

"Tea, sir!" A cheerful Pat Harper appeared on the bridge with a metal pail to which the riflemen had contributed from the tea they all carried in their packs. "There's no milk, sir, and I know you like milk, but it's hot."

"Thanks, Pat." Sharpe dipped his metal mug into the pail and sipped the tea, which had gone lukewarm in the time it had taken Harper to climb from the encampment. "You added brandy?"

"There were ten bottles among the engineers' stores, sir, seemed a pity to waste it."

"Keep them sober, Pat, we might be needed."

"Ah, they won't need us, sir. The lads will be over those walls in ten minutes."

"I hope so," Sharpe said, offering the mug to Teresa. But it would be ten minutes of savagery, he thought, and made worse because the assault must come in daylight rather than in the half-light of dawn. The eastern sky was now brilliant, and the first dazzling glory of the morning sun was showing above the river's valley. "You really reckon those twenty-four-pounders will reach the fort, Padre?"

El Sacerdote stared westward. "Easily."

"It's damn near a mile away!"

"It won't be accurate," El Sacerdote admitted, "but it will reach."

"And French powder is shit," Sharpe observed.

"True enough," El Sacerdote agreed. "So the shot will not have as much power, but it will hit." Not that it mattered, Sharpe thought. Even a twenty-four-pounder hit at nearly a mile's range would have small effect on the fort's walls. Each strike might chip away as much stone as would fill a soup plate, but the noise alone would make the French nervous.

"Buggers are moving, sir." Harper was staring westward.

Sharpe turned and instinctively looked toward the thick

woods, expecting to see the first British infantry show there. The slope was empty and he looked to the fort, then to the river, and saw a score of men crossing the pontoon bridge. The men had come from Fort Napoleon and appeared to be retreating to Fort Ragusa. He leveled his telescope, this time resting it on the bridge's parapet. "Why reinforce Fort Ragusa?" he asked aloud. "Makes no sense."

"They're not," El Sacerdote said.

The Frenchmen had reached the pair of river boats that formed the center of the pontoon bridge and were stooping to the lines that secured the two heavy boats to the lighter pontoons on either side. "They're going to cut the bridge," Sharpe said, astonished. "Why in hell's name do that?"

"In case Fort Napoleon falls," El Sacerdote said. "How will your troops cross to the other bank if there's no bridge?"

"They can't."

"So the French retain Fort Ragusa and General Hill must retire before he's trapped here by General Soult's army and it will take the French two days to restore the bridge."

Sharpe had not really thought beyond the capture of Fort Napoleon, but realized El Sacerdote was right. It would not be enough to capture the larger fort, the smaller northern fort would also have to be assaulted and all the Frenchmen on the river either killed or driven away. If the garrison of Fort Ragusa remained, then they could start repairing the pontoon bridge as soon as Hill left. General Hill would doubtless have destroyed all of the pontoon bridge on the southern side of the river, but he probably dared not stay too long because Marshal Soult would surely be assembling men to overwhelm Hill's forces. If the complete pontoon bridge was to be destroyed then Hill needed to capture the whole bridge, and to do that he needed to assault Fort Ragusa. And if the French broke the bridge by taking away the central portion, that would be impossible and the whole expedition a waste of time, men, and money. It promised to be a much longer and far more desperate day than he had imagined.

A gun firing from Fort Napoleon made him look back. A billow of white powder smoke masked the fort's southern wall, then a shell exploded among the trees, throwing up another cloud of smoke. More guns fired, exploding shells along the treeline where jagged scraps of casing would be killing and wounding the advance companies of British troops who must have been seen from the fort in the day's first slanting light.

The cannonade provoked the British advance. A distant hunting horn sounded and a moment later Sharpe saw redcoats running from the trees, swiftly followed by the ladder parties; each of two men carrying a long clumsy ladder. Riflemen came too, a scatter of them among the redcoats. They had a long way to advance and the French immediately lowered their cannons' muzzles and fired more shell. "It'll be canister soon," Sharpe grunted and almost as he spoke the first canister spread its deadly cone of musket balls and he saw a ladder fall. The riflemen checked and knelt, aimed their guns at the artillerymen on the fort's rampart, and opened fire.

El Sacerdote leaned over the parapet and commanded his gunners to fire. The first two twenty-four-pounders slammed backward as their shots bellowed toward the fort. Both shots fell a hundred paces short, bounced, and crashed harmlessly into the east-facing wall. "The barrels will heat up," El Sacerdote said almost apologetically, "then they will reach the fort." His men were swabbing the barrels with a wet sponge so no burning trace of powder in the barrel ignited the next charge to be rammed down.

All the French cannon on the southern rampart were now firing canister, drenching the long approach with whistling death. "Go on, lads!" Sharpe muttered. "Pat!"

"Sir?"

"Get our lads together, we're going."

"Sir!"

"Assemble by the four-pounder on the road!" Sharpe called after him.

"Richard," Teresa said nervously.

"Stay here, love, and guard the prisoners. Keep them alive."

"What are you doing?"

"They need all the rifles they can get to shoot the buggers on the ramparts."

The first redcoats had reached the steep slope on which the fort was built. They checked there and began firing their muskets up at the ramparts, but the defenders were far above them and protected by the wall's thick parapet. The riflemen were farther back from the fort and higher on the slope and their shots were making the defenders nervous. Sharpe gazed through his telescope and saw a Frenchman heave a shell at the redcoats beneath. He saw the smoke trail from the shell's fuse, then it exploded and two redcoats were hurled aside. More shells were thrown from the fort and still the canister blasted at the advancing men. The huge twenty-four-pounders, manned by El

Sacerdote's partisans, were now crunching their roundshot into the fort's eastern wall, each shot chipping away a small crater. They were doing little damage, but the impacts had persuaded the defenders on that eastern rampart to duck down.

"I'll be fine, love," Sharpe reassured Teresa and gave her his telescope. "You can watch." He kissed her then ran off the bridge and round the road to where the four-pounder gun stood amidst the splintered wreckage of its limber. He waited there as his riflemen assembled; eleven men now.

"Listen, lads," he said, "they need riflemen, so they need us. Our job is just to kill the bastards at the wall's top to give the ladder men a chance to get up. So no tap-loading, don't hurry your shots, aim well, and shoot straight. And loose order, lads, I don't want to lose a bunch of you to their bloody canister. Let's go."

Sharpe led them westward, staying higher on the slope so that he could join the attacking redcoats closer to the trees. That was high enough to lessen the impact of the canister, though he knew he would need to advance into the killing zone for his riflemen to be accurate.

Someone on the east-facing rampart saw the small group of riflemen leave the bridge and a cannon fired at them. Sharpe saw the shot coming, saw the small trace of smoke it left behind as its fuse burned down. The shot landed a couple of hundred paces in front of him, bounced twice, and rolled toward Sharpe. "Bloody fine shot," he said to no one and saw the burning fuse smoking. The French gunner had not cut the fuse short enough and Sharpe scuffed it with his right boot, extinguishing the smoldering fuse.

"Eight-pounder," Harper said.

"Aye, by the look of it, and too bloody accurate. Spread the lads out."

He kept running. El Sacerdote's gunners were still pounding the eastern wall of the fort and that booming fire with its shuddering strikes against the stones was evidently discouraging the French gunners, who did not try a second shot at Sharpe's small party. The defenders on the southern wall, undeterred by the crashes of El Sacerdote's roundshot, were heaving shells down onto the scarp of the fort where the first ladder parties were struggling upward. Other Frenchmen were leaning over the ramparts to fire their muskets, and the cannons on that wall were spraying canister at men still advancing toward the fort. Sharpe checked his men as they reached the treeline from where the redcoats had started their assault and saw the first of those men vanish as they jumped down into the fort's ditch. More and more men leaped down, all disappearing from sight.

"It's a deep ditch," Sharpe said.

"At least it'll be dry," Harper said. The ditch had been hacked out of the hill's summit and any rainwater would settle into the ground beneath. Sharpe wondered if the French had planted sharpened stakes in the ditch. More and more redcoats were leaping down and the French had started to drop shells and roundshot straight down into the ditch that now boiled with smoke from the exploding shells.

"Poor bastards," Sharpe said.

A scattered line of riflemen, some British and some Portuguese, was kneeling some three hundred yards short of the fort and shooting up at the rampart, trying to kill any defender who showed himself. The French gunners had their range and were firing canister, thinning the green-jacketed line with each blast from their guns. The only thing saving the riflemen was their loose line, meaning that the canister was hitting only one or two men with each shot. "We'll join those lads," Sharpe said. "Keep well apart and shoot straight."

He led them down the slope, gesturing for his few men to scatter to his left while he ran toward the right-hand end of the riflemen. His rifle was loaded, but unprimed, so he sank to one knee and used his powder horn to charge the pan, then hauled the doghead back to full cock. He put the rifle to his shoulder and watched the rampart. A man appeared there, a shell held over his head. Another man touched a portfire to the fuse and the first man hurled the shell outward and down into the ditch, then could not resist leaning over to see the result of his effort. Rifle bullets hit the stone crenellations around him, but the man survived and disappeared. "You're mine," Sharpe said to himself. He reckoned the man would be back with another shell and he aimed his sights at the place where the fool had lingered to watch his shell explode.

"Mister Sharpe! Mister Sharpe!" a voice called from his left.

"What is it?" Sharpe kept his eye on his sights, waiting.

"Mister Theobald's wounded. Gone back to the surgeon."

Sharpe glanced to his left and recognized Sergeant Gerrard. A good man, one of the best, but plainly perturbed by the loss of his officer. "Does that leave you in command, Tom?"

"It does, Mister Sharpe. Mister Stokes caught a shell fragment, poor bastard got it in the belly. There's a Portuguese officer, but . . ." Gerrard's voice faltered.

Sharpe sensed Gerrard's reluctance to put his men under Portuguese command, though almost all the Portuguese officers were British and the rifle-armed *Caçadores* knew their business every bit as well as the 95th. "They're good lads, Tom," he said, "they're as good as we are!"

"The boys are fine," Gerrard said, "but their officer? If he's eighteen I'd be surprised and he's a stuck-up little bastard. Thinks he knows it all. He wants us to pull farther back."

That complaint Sharpe did understand. He saw too that the men had retreated some way up the slope, where they were more exposed to the canister fire. "What were Mister Theobald's orders, Tom?"

"Stay here and kill the buggers."

"Then that's what you do, but go forward fifty yards."

"Forward?"

"It'll force the bastards to lower their aim and gunners hate shooting downward. And it'll make our fire more accurate. Do it now. And if the stuck-up little bastard tells you otherwise, tell him you're under my command and he should come talk to me."

"Thanks, Dick!" Gerrard said, then grinned. "Sorry, Mister Sharpe."

"Don't be daft, Tom, we're friends," Sharpe said. "You saw me through Grace's death." He felt tears prick at his eyes as they always did when he remembered Lady Grace. "It was a damn awful time."

"She was special," Gerrard said, then turned and blew three

blasts on a whistle and waved his men forward. Sharpe was already moving. Going forward meant they were lower on the hillside and so could not see as well over the rampart's top, but he reckoned the canister would probably fire high and so spare the riflemen. Besides, going forward would help the accuracy of the Greenjackets. The French gunners could crouch beside the gun while it was fired, but to reload a man had to stand at the muzzle and swab the barrel, then two more men would load the charge and the canister, then ram the shots, and each of those men would be vulnerable to a good rifleman.

Sharpe dropped to a knee again and looked for the gap in the crenellations where his victim would show. "Dan!"

"Mister Sharpe?"

"Can you see the gunners?"

"Not so well, Mister Sharpe."

"Go back up. Take Perkins and Trent with you. They load rifles and you shoot them. Go as far as you need and kill the damn artillerymen." He trusted Hagman's accuracy to shoot from a greater distance and doubted that a group of three men would attract the attention of the French artillerymen.

Hagman ran off, collected the two younger riflemen, and started back up the slope. His shots would thin the gunners, whose only targets now were the riflemen halfway down the slope. The rest of the assaulting force were either in the ditch or else crouched at the base of the hill on which the fort was built. "Get the ladders up," Sharpe muttered, looking back to his sights.

And there the man was, another shell in his hands. He held it over his head and the portfire started the fuse burning. A short fuse, Sharpe knew, and pulled the trigger. He cursed, reckoning he had aimed too low in his haste, but ran a few paces to his left to clear the smoke from his rifle and saw an explosion on the rampart. The man throwing the shell had been hit, fallen backward, and the fuse had reached the powder crammed into the shell. There was a churning cloud of smoke above the wall and Sharpe reckoned a half dozen Frenchmen must have been killed or wounded. He stood to reload his rifle and rammed the leather-wrapped ball down the stubborn barrel. Two guns fired from the rampart and the spray of musket balls went overhead to strike the slope behind where the Greenjackets had been a moment before.

He slotted the ramrod back into its place beneath the barrel, primed the pan, then started walking along the line of riflemen. He was evidently the senior rifleman on the slope and he called to the men as he walked, praising their marksmanship, urging them to load carefully and shoot straight, and assuring them the fort would soon fall. He found Tom Gerrard: "Who are your best shots, Tom?"

"Robertson, Clark, and Milner."

"Send them back up the slope and tell them to pick off the gunners. There's a man of mine up there already."

"Oh, shit!" Gerrard said. "Sorry, Mister Sharpe."

Sharpe saw what had caused the dismay. The first ladder had just been swayed up to clatter against the wall and was at least six feet too short. "There are other ladders, Tom," Sharpe said, "just kill the gunners and keep the rest of the boys shooting."

He walked the rest of the line. "Those poor boys can't get

up the ladders without you!" he called to the men, "so keep killing the bastards!"

A second ladder was heaved into place and again was too short. Sharpe swore and ran back to the right of the line, where his men were firing. The ditch, invisible to Sharpe, was betrayed by the churning clouds of smoke where the French shells landed. The defenders had learned a lesson, which was to avoid poking their heads above the parapet, but just heave the shells over the wall, confident that each missile must land and explode among the crammed assault parties who were trying to put more ladders in place. It would be carnage in the ditch, Sharpe thought. The explosions of the shells were oddly dull, muted perhaps by the deep ditch and by the bodies of the men dying beneath the inadequate ladders. And Sharpe had recommended shortening those ladders. "Pat!"

"Sir?"

"I'm going to take a look. Keep the men firing!"

It was safe enough to run to the fort because the French gunners were having difficulty aiming the cannon low enough, which meant the closer he got the safer he was. A handful of brave Frenchmen exposed themselves long enough to fire muskets and most of them were killed by rifle fire while their musket balls went God knows where. None came near Sharpe, not even when he scrambled up the steep hillside to reach the ditch's edge. There were now five ladders propped against the wall, and all of them were five or six feet too short. Some men had even started climbing them, though God alone knew what they thought they could achieve when they reached the top. A roundshot fell on one of the ladders and plucked two redcoats off the rungs to fall onto the men crowded about the ladder's base. Smoke lingered above the ditch concealing the worst of the slaughter, though the stench of powder and blood was thick in Sharpe's nostrils.

"God save Ireland," Harper said, "but that's nasty."

"What the hell are you doing here?"

"I promised Miss Teresa I'd look after you, sir."

"So we both get killed?"

"Not today, sir," Harper said with his usual blissful optimism. "And those poor bastards will have to retreat," he added, nodding into the red hell of the ditch.

The noise was overpowering. The cannon were still firing from the fort's rampart, though a glance behind assured Sharpe that the canister was still going high. The shells crashed apart in the ditch, where men screamed and shouted, and El Sacerdote's twenty-four-pounder shots were cracking against the fort's eastern face, where French artillerymen were returning fire with eight-pounders. Five miles to the south the British guns had opened fire on Castle Miravete, though that attack was purely a feint and designed to stop men from the castle's garrison coming to the aid of their comrades in Fort Napoleon. And now, to add to the racket, two howitzers had begun firing from Fort Ragusa, lobbing their shells high over the river and above Fort Napoleon to explode on the slope where the riflemen looked for their targets.

"We didn't come this far to run away," Sharpe said. He sensed that the canister fire from the wall's top was slackening and he guessed that the best marksmen among the rifles were finding their targets. But silencing those guns would not cause the fort to fall, only save the lives of a few riflemen, and maybe save the lives of scores of redcoats if they were forced to abandon the assault and retreat through the deadly hail of canister. He looked at the ladders. They had started a hundred feet in length, far too long, and Sharpe had recommended cutting them in half, but now it seemed to him that they had cut each into three pieces, and each one was too short. Nothing to be done about that now unless there were longer ladders back among the trees. He stared into the ditch, where the smoke writhed and where the shells exploded into shrieking fragments of iron. "There might be a way, Pat."

"God save Ireland, sir. Don't even think about it."

"See the ledge?"

"Ledge, sir?"

"I reckon the fort was built before the ditch."

"Makes sense, sir."

"And then they added the ditch, digging it from both sides."

"Ah," Harper said, understanding.

The ladders were reaching upward from the base of the ditch, but Sharpe could see that the ditch had not been dug immediately below the fort's wall, but had left a ledge of rock there, which meant that the wall stood some four or five feet from the inner edge of the ditch. "If we can put a ladder on the ledge, Pat, it could reach."

"Aye, it would."

"Just round the corner," Sharpe said, pointing. He meant the corner where the fort's east wall met the southern wall. It was the southern wall that was under assault, while the eastern wall was only threatened by the captured twenty-four-pounders at the old bridge. That fire was constant and accurate, but those big guns were doing little damage except to frighten the defenders, and Sharpe reckoned most of the French on the ramparts would have crowded to the southern wall to join in the sport of tossing roundshot and shell down into their enemy. "Run back to our lads," Sharpe told Harper. "I want a dozen of them over there," he pointed eastward. "They're to kill any bastard that shows his face on the rampart. I'll get a ladder. Be quick!"

Harper muttered something about Sharpe and insanity, but ran down the slope toward the riflemen, while Sharpe jumped into the ditch. He landed in an area clear of bodies, either wounded or dead, but as he moved westward along the face of the southern wall, he was forced to step on and over dead and dying men. Many had crushed limbs, others had been flayed with shell fragments and lay bleeding and moaning. He thought of the carnage he had inflicted on the French at the old bridge and thought this was payback for the enemy. He was looking for an officer or sergeant and finally saw a slender young man with a drawn sword. "You!" he bellowed, pointing. "Who are you?"

The youngster saw Sharpe's ragged uniform and the rifle slung on his shoulder and looked indignant for a heartbeat, then his mind registered the officer's red sash and the heavy sword at Sharpe's side. "Sir?" he responded nervously.

"Who are you? I'm Major Sharpe, 95th."

The young man stiffened as if standing to attention. "Lieutenant Fitzgerald, sir, 92nd."

"Just who I was looking for," Sharpe said, stepping to one

side as a missile thumped into the ditch a yard to his right. One glance showed it was a roundshot, or else it was a shell that had landed plumb on its fuse, extinguishing the fire. "Assemble a work party," Sharpe ordered, "and get me a ladder to that corner." He pointed behind him.

"Ladders are too short, sir," Fitzgerald said anxiously. He had a Scottish accent.

"Just get me a ladder, Lieutenant, and once you've done that, start taking the wounded out of the ditch. Lay them on the slope where they can't be hit by more shells. We'll sort them out when the fort's taken."

"A ladder, sir?" Fitzgerald asked, bemused.

"And be quick about it! You know how to get something done in this army?"

"Done, sir?"

"Find a good sergeant, give him the order. Quick now!"

Fitzgerald, sensibly, found a sergeant, a big brute of a man named Maclean, who dragged down the closest ladder and detailed four men to carry it to where Sharpe waited. "It'll no reach the top, sir," Maclean warned Sharpe.

"It will, Sergeant. Get it up."

The ladder was heaved up until it lay against the fortress's eastern wall, just two feet from the corner. It was five or six feet too short, but Sharpe clambered up onto the ledge between the ditch and the stonework. "Now heave it up here, Sergeant," he said, tapping the ledge with his foot.

Two big Scotsmen seized the base of the ladder and shoved it upward and Sharpe helped by pulling on the rungs until the ladder was standing inches from the ledge's brink and reaching to within inches of the wall's top. "That's perilously steep, sir," Maclean said, "it'll tip!"

"Two of you are going to hold it steady," Sharpe said, then handed his rifle to the big Scotsman. "Hold on to that for me. I'll collect it from you once we're inside the fort." He drew his sword. "Send men after me, Sergeant."

"I'll be on your heels, sir."

Sharpe edged round the ladder and put his left foot on a rung. God help me, he thought, but this was madness. He had found a way to reach the wall's top, but that was no reason to lead the way. His job was to smother the wall's top with rifle bullets, which would allow the assaulting battalions to climb the ladder, but somehow he had known from the start that he would be doomed to the task. He climbed.

The ladder had been made hastily and the rungs merely hacked out with an axe. They felt fragile. Some moved beneath his weight. The rungs were crudely nailed to the rails, which were equally unfinished, and Sharpe soon found he could not hold the sword and use two hands on the rails, so he paused and pushed his right hand through the guard on his sword's hilt. He had never bothered to replace the sword-knot, a short length of cord or strap that went round the wrist so that if the sword was knocked from his grip he would not lose the weapon. Now the blade hung uncomfortably from his wrist and let him climb faster, though how he would recover the sword for the fight at the head of the ladder he did not know. Just climb, he told himself, because this was the only way to win this fight.

Three brigades of British troops had marched over a hundred miles to destroy the pontoon bridge and all that lay between them and success was one small fortress, and if the fortress could not be taken then the three brigades must march back defeated and the armies of Marmont and Soult could combine to make an overwhelming assault on the smaller British army. Climb this ladder, Sharpe told himself, and the French are properly buggered. His hands were being sliced by splinters from the rails, and a chip of stone, struck from the wall by one of El Sacerdote's shots, stung his right cheek. He climbed. A rung broke, or rather swung down from one nail when the other gave way, and he jarred down onto the rung beneath and only stayed on the ladder by gripping the rails tightly. A bullet struck the stones a foot to his left and he knew it was one of his riflemen shooting low. Or rather he hoped the man was shooting low and not aiming at his back. Sharpe had known of a half dozen unpopular officers declared to be casualties of enemy action when in truth their own men had pulled the triggers. Don't think about it, he told himself, just bloody climb. He climbed.

"Watch above you, sir!" a voice shouted from below and Sharpe thrust his face into the ladder and froze. Something hard and heavy clouted his pack, bounced away, then a shout, almost a scream, sounded close above him and he reckoned a rifle bullet had hit whoever had tried to hurl him from the ladder with a roundshot or stone. He could hear the rifles firing rapidly behind him, hear the bullets striking stone, and one even drove a foot-long splinter from the ladder's right-hand rail. "Keep firing, lads," he muttered and tilted his head back to look beneath his shako's visor and saw he was close to the top. Just bloody climb! He climbed.

The ladder swayed slightly, not left or right, but inward, and the knuckles of his left hand were pressed painfully against the stonework. He began using his hands on the rungs instead of the rails, but the ladder was now so close to the wall that he could not make proper grips. He glanced downward, immediately regretting it, and glimpsed a redcoat behind him and three or four men beyond him, their weight forcing the ladder to bow inward. "Almost there, sir!" a Scottish voice shouted from below.

Easy for you to say, Sharpe thought. His feet could not step properly on the rungs, which, thanks to the ladder's bowing, were now so close to the wall that only his toes in their hobnail boots could get a grip.

It suddenly struck him that he had not heard the French cannons fire for a long time and he reckoned his riflemen, chiefly Dan Hagman, had dropped the gunners. He edged up another rung, daring a quick glance upward to see that he had only two or three feet to go. The ladder stopped about a foot beneath the wall's top and the last few rungs would be the most difficult to negotiate. "First man up is doomed," he remembered a cheerful Scotsman saying to him as they watched the redcoats climb the ladders at Ahmednuggur. The French knew the ladder was here, knew men were climbing it, and could wait beyond the parapet with loaded muskets and fixed bayonets. And all Sharpe had was the sword that hung awkwardly from his wrist. He tried turning his hand to grasp the hilt, but could not turn it far enough. He needed Harper's volley gun, he thought. He needed more sense. He would die here, but at least his death might give the next man on the ladder a chance to scramble over the wall while the enemy was reloading.

Then an explosion not far to his right pummeled his body with a gust of air while shards of jagged iron flew above and below him. One struck his pack while another hit his right hip to give him a sudden sharp pain. He heard shouts from above him and realized that El Sacerdote's gunners were trying to help him by loading the twelve-pounders with shell. And those Spanish gunners were good. A skilled man had cut the shell's fuse to the exact length so the missile neither exploded short of its target nor far beyond it, but had almost blasted Sharpe off the ladder. He twisted his hand again, almost losing the sword, but snatched his arm up just in time. Speed, he thought. That was his best friend now. He had been climbing the last few rungs painfully slowly because the ladder was more or less vertical against the stonework and both footholds and handholds were awkward and precarious. He glanced down and saw redcoats climbing behind him. "Not far now, lads," he grunted, then looked up again. He was headed for one of the embrasures in the wall's top, a space about two feet wide between its merlons. Rifle bullets were hitting those merlons, provoking puffs of stone dust. Sharpe thought of the redcoats who had scaled the walls of the castle at Badajoz, walls three times the height of this one. How the hell had they done it? Not just climbed, but conquered. And what the hell were the French doing above him? He had expected more eight-pounder roundshots to be dropped on him, possibly even a shell with its fuse cut dangerously short, but other than muffled shouts he could sense nothing. Was a man waiting with an axe, ready to chop down as soon as Sharpe's head appeared? Christ, he thought, but he was frightened. Terrified. But the one thing he knew about fear was to fight through it. Courage was not a lack of fear, it was conquering the fear, and to do that he needed a decent foothold on the rungs, a spring upward, and a usable weapon.

Sword first. He had climbed another rung and both feet were now jammed on the same rung, only his toes supporting his weight. His left hand was gripping the ladder's top rung and with his right he rammed the sword down so the flat blade was jammed between the rung he stood on and the stone wall. Gingerly he pulled his hand free of the sword, praying it would not sway and drop, but it stayed fixed and he was able to wrap his right hand round the hilt. He pulled it free. It was usable.

And just then the Frenchman appeared above him, crashing down on his shako and knocking it askew. Sharpe could not spare a hand to adjust the shako that was rammed down over his eyes, but by ramming it upward into the Frenchman he was able to force it backward and up over his forehead. And immediately his face was drenched in blood and he found himself staring into the dead eyes of an enemy. The blood was pouring from the man's mouth that was itself distended into a gaping hole encompassing his cheeks and nose. Sharpe's first reaction was disgust, then he realized the man had been shot from behind, that a musket bullet or shell fragment had entered the base of his skull or at his neck and blown apart its exit wound that was now dripping and seeping more blood. Which meant that a redcoat must be on the southern rampart to fire that shot, or else that a rifleman had fired from the hill to the fort's western side, in which case it was a miraculous shot. The dead man had been clutching a roundshot that presumably he had intended to hurl down on Sharpe, but now his body hid Sharpe. Then the body began to slide backward and Sharpe reckoned the French were hauling the poor man clear of the embrasure.

He seized the man's blue jacket and let the French haul him with the corpse. He raised his right foot and found purchase on another rung just as a twenty-four-pounder shell exploded five or six yards to his right, but above the battlement. It screamed iron fragments down and the men pulling the corpse must have abandoned their rescue efforts because the body went still.

And Sharpe surged upward, flailed with his left foot to find another rung, and threw his right hand over the embrasure, the sword clanging on stone. He dared not let go of the sword to seek a handhold, but instead hauled himself upward by pulling on the dead man's jacket. The corpse slid toward him, then checked, and Sharpe lurched upward, right foot on another rung, and he could see men in blue jackets in disarray in front of him. They were staring across the fort, away from Sharpe, or else crouching to avoid the rifles that still fired from behind and below Sharpe.

He teetered because the corpse had shifted again, threatening to tip Sharpe backward, and he lunged his left hand desperately forward and gripped the corpse's belt. Hauled with all his strength and the belt's buckle must have been trapped against the inner stone ledge of the embrasure because Sharpe surged upward and into the embrasure.

I am dead, he thought. He was on his belly, half on top of a dead man, and there were a dozen Frenchmen in front of him. His sword was still stretched out ahead, but he managed to get his left knee onto the embrasure and pushed himself upright. "Bastards!" he shouted and jumped down onto the fire step.

There was a primal savagery in Richard Sharpe, an urge to fight, to kill, and it had been there since he was a wild child in the stinking alleys of a London slum. It was fed by a well of anger that seethed in him; anger at the bullies of London, anger at the arrogance of supercilious officers, anger at a world that reckoned he was inferior because he had neither education nor the courteous manners of a gentleman. That anger had only one outlet; to fight, and over the years he had become a natural killer, whether with musket, rifle, bayonet, or sword. Every stroke of the sword was fed by anger, and Sharpe did not hear the cheers from behind him, only aware of the enemy who, in his mind, stood for every person who had ever spurned him, mocked him, or looked down on him. And to that anger was added skill, or rather savagery.

The heavy cavalry sword was not a subtle weapon. The blade, forged in Birmingham, was straight, broad and heavy, designed to be wielded by a big man on a heavy horse who could use the sword to slash and thrust. The weight of the blade alone made it dangerous and in battle it served as a club as much as a sword. It was unbalanced, crude and cumbersome, yet Sharpe loved the weapon, mostly because of its weight. He did not have the gentlemanly skills of a swordsman, he did not have a command of the parries and ripostes, the elegant moves that men paid fortunes to learn, but he did have strength. His heavy cavalry sword could batter down an enemy's weapon, could shatter lighter swords or deliver gruesome wounds. It was a blade made for fury, not for finesse, and in battle Sharpe was nothing but fury.

Yet at that moment, almost surrounded by enemies, he did not feel fury, only relief. He had lived! Now all he had to do was survive and win, and so he let his anger loose and began to fight.

CHAPTER 9

He was standing by the embrasure and surrounded on three sides by enemy. Two of them had been hauling back the dead man and they now gaped at Sharpe as though he were a specter from the underworld. Two more were to his right, both in artillery jackets and each carrying an eight-pound roundshot that, Sharpe supposed, had been intended for his skull. To his left were two infantrymen, both with muskets tipped with bayonets.

He started with the infantrymen, rounding on them savagely and sweeping the sword in a haymaking curve that drove both backward. One pulled his trigger and the shot went just wide of Sharpe's waist to strike one of the Frenchmen holding a roundshot. Sharpe lunged with the sword, striking the man who had fired with the sword's tip, which slid off a rib and drove the man farther back. The second man rammed his bayonet forward and Sharpe swayed to his right to avoid it and slammed his sword into the side of the man's neck. He dragged the blade back as blood jetted skyward, then rammed it forward again into the first man's chest. Two down. He turned to his right to discover that the two men who had been hauling the corpse had retreated beyond the two holding roundshot, one of whom was on his knees choking on blood. The second stared at Sharpe, then abruptly dropped the solid shot onto the rampart and backed away. Beyond him Sharpe could see gun crews serving three eight-pounders and at least a dozen corpses, doubtless victims of his riflemen. Little danger that way, he decided, and snarled at the nearest man to go away and the Frenchman, evidently understanding Sharpe's vulgarity, fled. Sharpe turned back to his left, where the rampart made its turn onto the southern wall that was thick with infantry in blue jackets. Except, he saw, a knot of redcoats at the farther end of the rampart. So either the Scots or the Kentish men had reached the rampart. Musket shots came from the French, but Sharpe seemed to have a charmed life as he ran at the nearest men, who leveled their bayonets to receive his charge.

Then the cannon fired behind him, the noise deafening, and the closest three Frenchmen all staggered back, struck by the seven-barreled gun's volley. "That was my last shot!" Harper said, coming to stand beside Sharpe. "Jesus, there's enough of the buggers!"

"What are you doing here?" Sharpe asked.

"Keeping you alive, sir."

One of the men wounded by Harper's pistol balls now rammed his bayonet at the big Irishman. Harper dropped the volley gun, seized the threatening musket just behind the foresight with his left hand and the bayonet's socket with his right. He wrenched the bayonet free by tugging the lock-ing ring toward him, then twisting the socket off the foresight and pulling the weapon free, he reversed the bayonet and rammed it into the man's belly. "You bloody eejit," he said as the man fell.

Sharpe kicked one of the wounded men over the rampart's inner edge down into a courtyard where the French infantry was running toward the back gate of the fort, which led down to the pontoon bridge. "Buggers are running, Pat."

"So they should." Harper had picked up his volley gun and now aimed it at the infantry crammed in the corner of the rampart. The gun was unloaded, but none of the Frenchmen knew that, they just saw a huge man facing them with a ghastly-looking weapon. There was no officer or sergeant among them, no one to give them orders, and they simply fled from the threat. "Christ, but I love this gun," Harper said.

"Keep them running, Pat." Sharpe kicked fallen muskets down to the courtyard and stepped over the wounded men. More riflemen and redcoats had climbed the ladder now. And Sharpe made a line of four Scotsmen and ordered them to advance with fixed bayonets. "Fall in behind them!" he shouted at the men still clambering over the blood-soaked wall. "Pat!"

"Sir?"

"Take men and kill those bloody gunners." He pointed back toward the eastern wall, then stood in the center of the four Scotsmen. "Right, lads, forward! They won't stand."

They turned the corner onto the southern rampart and advanced steadily. A stone staircase led from the rampart to the courtyard and Frenchmen were streaming down the steps to escape the two parties of Scottish and Kentish troops who were closing on the rampart's center. One or two Frenchmen turned to shoot, but each time one of the Scots fired first and the man was hurled backward. "Good shooting," Sharpe said. He had expected a bloody struggle on the rampart, but the French had been so terrified by the success of the assault that they were now abandoning the fort as fast as they could run. The big rear gate had been hauled open and men were streaming over the drawbridge and down the steep slope toward the bridge. There were redcoats there too, and Sharpe guessed that some of the men who had successfully scaled the southern wall had managed to reach the courtyard and open the main gate. The only organized resistance now came from a handful of men who were standing at the top of the short flight of steps that led to the tower's door, and they were still putting up a fight. "Riflemen!" Sharpe called and a half dozen of his men ran toward him. "Pick off those bastards," he pointed down at the men defending the tower.

"They say there's money here," one of the Scotsmen said to Sharpe.

"It'll be in that tower," Sharpe said. "You want to go and find it?"

"Aye, I do."

"Then go, and good luck. And well done!"

The fight on the rampart had ended quickly. Sharpe had expected a more bitter struggle and felt frustrated. Harper had led a dozen men round to the northern rampart, killing gunners on the way and taking others prisoner. The whole rampart was now in British hands. Sharpe walked to join Harper. "Well done, Pat."

"It wasn't a fight, sir. The bastards just turned right about and ran for it." He sounded disappointed.

"It was too easy," Sharpe said, "except for the ladder."

"That wasn't good," Harper agreed. He nodded down to the fight in the courtyard. "Shall we settle that lot, sir?"

"He's doomed," Sharpe said. There was now a lone French officer defending the tower doorway, the steps below him thick with his men's bodies. A redcoat climbed the steps and tried to lunge his bayonet at the single defender, who contemptuously knocked the musket aside with his saber and slashed at the redcoat, cutting open his throat. The man, evidently a Kentishman from the black facings of his coat, sank to join the enemy dead. "Brave bugger," Sharpe said admiringly.

"And a dead one," Harper said as a sergeant of the 50th slowly mounted the steps carrying a half-pike, the ancient weapon carried by men protecting the battalion's colors.

"Poor bastard," Sharpe said, looking at the lone French officer, "he deserves better."

"I'd like one of those spears," Harper said.

"The old poleaxes were better. Heavier. You could do a lot of damage with a poleaxe. I'll buy you one for your next birthday."

"I hope you do, sir."

The sergeant stabbed up with the half-pike, a nine-foot-long spear with a crosspiece behind the long blade. The French officer tried to batter it aside with his saber, but the sergeant had expected the parry and jerked the blade up so the saber went underneath, whereupon the Kentishman dropped the spearhead and lunged it hard up into the officer's belly. It sank to the crosspiece and the sergeant heaved on the pike again to drive its blade clean through the dying Frenchman and pin him to the wooden jamb of the tower's door. There was a cheer and redcoats flooded up the steps to plunder the tower. "God help anyone in there," Harper said.

A sudden flurry of rifle fire made Sharpe turn to see Joe Henderson with the riflemen he had left to shoot down at the tower's defenders now firing upward. A group of Frenchmen had appeared at the tower's summit and some had pointed muskets down into the courtyard that was full of British troops. "Well done, Joe!" Sharpe called. The rifle fire had caused the French to duck down behind the tower's parapet. Above them the tricolor still flew.

Sharpe and Harper were still on the southern rampart, but Sharpe now walked along the eastern fire step past three abandoned cannon to the northern wall. "Mother of God," Harper said, "would you just look at that!"

He was gazing down at the pontoon bridge, which was crammed with fleeing French troops spurred on by redcoats who fired muskets from the fort's southern gateway. The bridge was still intact, the men Sharpe had seen earlier had merely loosened the lashings holding the two boats at the center of the bridge that now bowed westward as the river's current tugged at them. Those men had presumably been sent to prepare the bridge's destruction so the British could not use the pontoons to cross the river, but they had failed to finish their task and now the first of the fugitives from Fort Napoleon had reached Fort Ragusa, where they were being welcomed by the Prussian soldiers at the fort's gate. "We'll be assaulting that next," Sharpe said, nodding toward the smaller fort.

"If we can cross the bridge, sir," Harper said and something in his tone made Sharpe look down to the pontoon bridge.

"The buggers!" he said. In the center of the bridge, where he had seen men working on the lines that lashed the pair of boats to the pontoons on either side, there were now men wielding axes. They were cutting through the remaining lines and, slowly at first, the two boats began drifting westward on the river's current, taking the whole of the northern half of the pontoon bridge with them. Men were still pushing and struggling to cross the southern half of the bridge, which was now crammed with fugitives. For a heartbeat it seemed that the nearer boat was caught up on the pontoons, then it lurched free and both boats drifted clear, breaking the bridge in two and marooning hundreds of men on the pontoons nearest to Fort Napoleon.

Those men still surged forward, ignorant that the bridge was now broken, and their pressure was forcing men off the pontoon's roadway. A few clumsily swam toward the northern shore, but most were being carried downstream, waving for help. Sharpe could see men vanishing beneath the water, carried down by the weight of their equipment. "Poor bastards."

"They were trying to kill us ten minutes ago."

"And now we have to capture that bloody fort without a bridge."

"We'll not manage that," Harper said.

And that was precisely why the French had cut the bridge, even at the expense of the fugitives still trying to reach the northern bank. So long as Fort Ragusa remained in French hands, so long could the pontoon bridge be remade. It might take a month or more, but it would be reconstructed and so link Soult's army to Marmont's forces. General Hill would want to destroy not just the bridge but both forts, and the French had just made that almost impossible.

Harper had wandered to the nearest eight-pounder cannon that was on a garrison mount. "We could encourage more of the bastards to go swimming, sir?" he said, holding up a canister round he had discovered in a box of ready ammunition.

"We've murdered enough of the poor bastards," Sharpe said.

"I thought that was why we were here, sir?"

"They'll become prisoners, Pat."

Harper slid the canister back into the box. "But the gun's loaded, sir," he pointed to the firing tube, "just let me fire it."

"Let it be, Pat."

Sharpe wondered why the guns facing Fort Ragusa had been loaded, then decided the defenders had worried about British infantry going round Fort Napoleon to capture the bridge. And they might well have tried that if the escalade had failed, and then they would have become prey to canister fired from these cannons. Blasts of canister would have scoured the bridge of redcoats and done little harm to the bridge, and the cannon was already pointing down toward the bridge.

"Eight-pounders!" a voice behind Sharpe said enthusiastically. "Useful little pieces." Sharpe turned to see Lieutenant Love hurrying toward him. "Sir! Glad to see you, sir!"

"I'm glad to see you, Lieutenant," Sharpe said as sincerely as he could.

"Eight-pounders!" Love exclaimed again. "Mind if I take a crack with them, sir?"

Sharpe looked at the fugitives trapped on the broken bridge. "They'll all become prisoners, Lieutenant."

"Ah, the quality of mercy! Good for you, sir. But I was thinking of the other fort." Love was stooping to the nearest cannon and began wrenching the elevating screw beneath the breech to raise the muzzle. "Barbara, help me!" he shouted. "I imagine the scoundrels were loaded with canister," he said to no one in particular. "Let's find out!" He jiggled the firing tube in the venthole and, evidently satisfied that its lower end was embedded in a powder charge, looked through the chest beside the gun to find a portfire. He found one and Sharpe offered his tinderbox, but Love used his own to light the slow-match, which began fizzing and spilling small sparks. The lieutenant swung it in a wide circle to make the end glow even brighter. "Nice of you to offer, sir, but my father gave me this tinderbox and it's my tradition that it fires the first gun. Father is a canon, so it seems appropriate!"

"A cannon?" Sharpe asked, puzzled.

"At Wells Cathedral," Love answered absent-mindedly, "probably be a bishop one day!" He lit the portfire, blew on the slow-match to liven the fire, then clasped the pole between his hands and looked heavenward. "And thank you, Barbara, for leaving me a loaded gun. Stand back, sir, and cover your ears. This thing goes bang."

Love touched the portfire to the firing tube and the thing went bang, gouting a thick cloud of smoke that obscured the river. The gun had been charged with canister, which streaked

harmlessly above the fugitives still trapped on the nearer pontoons, but the very sound of the musket balls screaming overhead provoked many to jump into the river to avoid
annihilation. Sharpe, half-deafened by the shot, still heard the
canister balls rattling against Fort Ragusa's high wall.

As the smoke drifted slowly downriver Sharpe saw
Frenchmen on the pontoon bridge throwing their muskets
into the Tagus and returning with raised hands toward the
redcoats massing at Fort Napoleon's southern gate. Lieutenant
Love, meanwhile, had swabbed the cannon's barrel with a
sponge mounted on the butt end of the rammer. He covered
the vent with a cloth pad to stop the escaping air encouraging
a fire in the smoldering remains of the powder charge, then
selected a new bag of powder and a roundshot that he rammed
down the barrel. "I hate using French powder," Love said, "it's
not half as good as ours. Still, it works as often as not." He
used a long metal pricker to pierce the new charge, then found
a firing tube among the paraphernalia the French had left
behind. He slid it down the vent, throwing down the pad of
cloth. "I lack a leather thumbstall," he said to Sharpe, "but
Barbara will preserve us."

"Barbara?" Sharpe asked, bemused.

"Oh, Major Sharpe," Love said, sounding bitterly disappointed. "Saint Barbara is the patron saint of gunners! She
was a noble young lady, a virgin, which is entirely inappro-
priate and somewhat disappointing, and her father, disapproving of her conversion to Christianity, locked her in a
tower. What any of that has anything to do with the science
of artillery is beyond me, yet it is appropriate for gunners

to call on her aid. Do stand aside, sir, the thing will go bang again in a moment."

Someone on Fort Ragusa must have seen what Lieutenant Love was doing on Fort Napoleon's rampart, because suddenly six of their guns opened fire and a roundshot screamed over Sharpe's head while another smacked into the wall just beneath him. "Rifles!" Sharpe yelled. "Here!"

Lieutenant Love stooped at the rear of the cannon that he had reloaded with roundshot and peered along the barrel. "I like it," he said, then stood aside and touched the still-glowing portfire to the new firing tube. The heavy garrison mount seemed to jump into the air, but it still soaked up much of the recoil as the lieutenant's shot screamed over the river to hammer into the northern wall of Fort Ragusa. "A trifle low, Barbara," Love said reprovingly, "but we shall persevere. Major, would you be so kind as to cover the vent with the cloth? Thank you, sir!" Sharpe put the cloth pad back over the vent as the lieutenant dipped the sponge in a bucket of water, then swabbed the barrel. The cloth pad blocked the cannon's vent, thus stopping a draft of air caused by the swabber from igniting unburned powder in the barrel. Sharpe could hear the hissing as scraps of powder were extinguished. "Nothing like a May morning with plenty of Frenchmen to kill," Love said.

"You'll have to batter down that wall to kill many more," Sharpe said, "and eight-pounders won't do the job."

"God hasn't seen fit to supply me with eighteen-pounders, sir," Love said, "but with Barbara's help we humble artillerymen will do our best."

"To do what?"

"To persuade the enemy to flee! Then we can reconnect the bridge and take possession of Fort Ragusa." Love motioned Sharpe to stand aside and touched the portfire to the new firing tube. The cannon fired and a distant clang told of its roundshot striking Fort Ragusa's wall beyond the billow of powder smoke. Lieutenant Love might think he was doing good, but Sharpe reckoned the eight-pounder cannon was doing nothing more than scaring birds.

Sharpe walked to the farther end of the wall so he could stare at the old bridge. He wished he still had his telescope, but even with the naked eye he could just see a group of El Sacerdote's partisans guarding the French prisoners who were dragging their mangled dead down to the river. Most of the priest's men had come to the village of Lugar Nuevo beneath Fort Napoleon, where they were ransacking the French store-houses. Some red-coated officers were there too, doubtless trying to rescue anything useful before the whole village was burned. Already two warehouses were ablaze. "A disaster," an Irish voice said behind him.

Sharpe turned. "Disaster, sir?"

"For the French, Richard!" Major Hogan said, smiling. "We've cut off the only practicable link between Soult and Marmont! Those gentlemen will be most upset."

"We haven't taken Fort Ragusa, sir, and I assume Castle Miravete is still in their hands?"

"It is indeed. Our nine-pounders aren't enough to break down their defenses, but it doesn't signify. We can leave them Miravete, because without the bridge it's guarding nothing.

But to destroy the bridge we do need to take Fort Ragusa, which means we'll have to cross the river somehow." Hogan stared across the wide river at the remaining fort. "God knows how we do it, but do it we must. Another escalade, I fear, and if we do assault the place, I'd rather not see you up another ladder, Richard. You're too valuable to lose and, besides, you're not a *becerro* any longer."

"A *becerro*?"

"A *becerro* is a young fighting bull, Richard."

"You're saying I'm old?"

"Old and experienced, the worst kind of bull to fight." Hogan smiled. "How old are you?"

"No idea. Mother died when I was born and no one else bothered to keep count."

"Really no idea?"

"They tell a horse's age by looking at its teeth," Sharpe said, "and I reckon I'm probably about thirty-five."

"Christ knows how you've lasted that long," Hogan said, then looked down at the burning village, where El Sacerdote's men were still searching storehouses. "No sign of our friend El Héroe, I suppose?"

"I've not seen the bastard."

A cheer sounded behind them and they turned to see that the French tricolor had been lowered from the staff on the tower and replaced by a redcoat's jacket that was too heavy to catch the small wind. "I should have thought to bring a flag," Hogan said ruefully. "Still, that's a grand sight."

"El Héroe might have crossed the river already," Sharpe said equally ruefully.

"He is an expert at running away, so yes." Hogan peered down at the Frenchmen now trudging back across the broken pontoon bridge to their captivity. "There do seem to be some partisans among them. El Héroe's men, I presume."

Sharpe stared down and saw a tangle of men among the fugitives dressed in partisan fashion, some with swathing cloaks and nearly all in the tattered uniforms of the Spanish army. Once off the bridge the defeated men were being driven by redcoats around the fort's western edge, but some of El Sacerdote's men were dragging the Spaniards out from the crowd. "I don't fancy those fellows will live to see another dawn," Hogan said, amused.

The cannon fire from Fort Ragusa had become sporadic and ill-aimed, the gunners reluctant to serve their pieces because of the accurate rifle fire from Fort Napoleon. The range was about five hundred yards, hopeless for muskets, but good practice for the Greenjackets, who were making bets on each shot. "They seem to have plenty of coin to wager?" Hogan suggested.

"Not much out here to spend money on."

"And the hundred guineas you carried here?"

"I'll make inquiries about that."

"I'm sure you will, Richard, I'm sure you will," Hogan paused, "but I do understand that the vicissitudes of war sometimes mean that these things get lost."

"Vicissitudes?"

"Buggerations, Richard."

"Well, I did give some of it to El Héroe," Sharpe said ruefully, "and he's a bugger."

"Ah! So I can report to my masters that you delivered the gold as ordered?"

The gold? Sharpe thought. One guinea only. "I delivered gold, as ordered."

"Perfect," Hogan said happily, "it's from the secret account, anyway, and they're used to buggerations. Ah, I see Cupid is busy!"

Lieutenant Love had recruited half a dozen riflemen to shift a mortar from the eastern ramparts to the northern. Harper was among them, lugging the brutal weapon that plainly had a vast weight because even Harper was straining, but somehow the group managed to turn the corner of the rampart, where Love ordered them to drop the gun. Sharpe and Hogan wandered nearer. "It isn't pretty," Love greeted them, "but with Barbara's help it might get the job done. You don't mind me using a couple of your stout fellows as *matrosses*?"

"*Matrosses*?" Sharpe asked.

"Gunner's assistants," Love said. "I like to think of myself as an efficient gunner, but my efficiency is increased mightily by *matrosses*."

"Pat? Joe! You're Mister Love's mattresses."

"Yes, sir!" Harper snapped, amused.

"Bring me powder and a bomb," Love ordered, pointing to where the mortar's equipment still lay on the eastern battlements. "And Sergeant! No need to bring wedges! I'm not a believer in them."

"He told me his father was a cannon," Harper said to Sharpe as he went past, "mad as a whisky priest!"

Lieutenant Love was using a handspike to adjust the mortar so it was aimed directly at Fort Ragusa. "There will be joy in heaven if this works," he said enthusiastically. He drew a knife from his belt and slit open an eight-pounder powder bag, then tipped some into the mortar's mouth. He evidently decided he had poured too much because he scooped a handful out and tossed it over the rampart. A French round-shot hit the rampart close by with a deafening crack, but the lieutenant seemed oblivious to it. "I do believe this is one of their new pattern mortars," he remarked to Sharpe, "and rather subtly designed. A Gomer mortar, I do believe! The old de Vallières were crude, but this is a thing of beauty." He found a firing tube that was part of the eight-pounder's equipment and rammed it into the mortar's vent before breaking off the tube's top. "Ah, the bomb! Well done that *matrosse*! Pop it in, Sergeant, there's a good fellow. No! Wait! Set it on the rampart."

The bomb was ten inches in diameter, a sullen black ball of iron that Sharpe knew was crammed with gunpowder. A fuse projected at one side and the lieutenant, having taken another look at Fort Ragusa to judge the distance, took his knife and sliced off two inches of the quick-fuse. "Now pop it in, Sergeant, but make sure the fuse is pointing toward the side of the barrel so the fire has an easy job to reach it. Careful now, don't scrape the fuse on the barrel! That's it! Just drop it, it won't go bang. Splendid! Now fetch another bomb in case this one doesn't work."

"Yes, sir," Harper said then rolled his eyes at Sharpe as he went to fetch the second bomb.

"You think it might not work, Lieutenant?" Hogan asked.

"Barbara moves in mysterious ways, her slaughter to perform," Love said, "and it might fly too far, or it may fall too short, or the fuse may not ignite." He peered into the mortar's chamber. "But this baby seems well seated in its cradle. Of course I didn't use wedges, but I have never subscribed to the notion of using wedges to allow the fire to lap around the bomb, so to speak. I believe it guarantees the fuse's ignition, but it also disperses the force of the initial explosion, thus causing the projectile to fall short. But with Barbara's help this might well be perfect, despite the weapon's French manufacture and the employment of French powder."

"You want British powder?" Sharpe asked.

"Oh, sir, that would be a joy! But alas, the powder wagon is at Miravete Castle."

"Dan!" Sharpe shouted, "collect half a dozen horns, bring 'em here!"

"Right away, Mister Sharpe!"

"Horns?" Lieutenant Love asked.

Sharpe unbuckled his powder horn and tossed it to Love. "Best British gunpowder, Lieutenant, and more coming."

"Barbara answers prayer!" Love exclaimed. He used the spring-loaded catch on the horn's nozzle to eject a pinch of the powder onto one palm, then rubbed it with a finger. "Splendid!" he exclaimed. "I could not be more joyful!" He tossed the pinch onto the mortar bomb. "Fly well," he said to the bomb, "and wreak havoc among our enemies. I would stand back, gentlemen," he said to Sharpe and Hogan. "And Sergeant? Good man, put the bomb down and stay two paces away. With Barbara's help, this first baby might suffice." Love took the portfire he had used to fire the cannon and swung it in the air to freshen the burning tip, and then, when satisfied, he raised his eyes to the cloudless sky. "Barbara!" he called. "Lend your power to this bomb's flight! Smite our enemies with your wrath!" He leaned forward and touched the portfire to the firing tube. "Amen!"

There was a brief hiss as sparks and smoke vented from the firing tube, then an immense crack as the powder charge in the mortar exploded. Smoke enveloped the rampart, but as it cleared in the small wind Sharpe could see the smoke trail of the bomb's fuse arcing over the river. He could even see the bomb itself and it seemed to him that it would overfly Fort Ragusa altogether. It was spinning wildly, which meant the fuse's smoke trail was a whirl in the air.

"Fall!" Lieutenant Love ordered the bomb, "fall!!"

It fell, but beyond the fort, presumably on the main road. It exploded almost as soon as it vanished from sight and another immense cloud of smoke billowed beyond Fort Ragusa.

"Damn," Lieutenant Love said lightly, "Babs can be a stubborn bitch at times. No doubt that's why she kept her virginity, silly woman."

"Maybe wedges for the next bomb?" Hogan suggested.

"Do you know what you're talking about?" Sharpe asked softly.

"Of course not," Hogan said, and then, louder, "and perhaps elevate the barrel, Lieutenant?"

"I like the standard forty-five degrees," Love said, "it makes the mathematics easy. I suspect the answer is less powder."

He used the cannon's sponge to clear the hot detritus from the mortar's belly. Sharpe's riflemen were harassing the gunners on Fort Ragusa's southern rampart and the cannons' rate of fire had dropped significantly. At least those gunners were not using mortars to drop bombs into Fort Napoleon's courtyard, and Sharpe glanced down to see that Teresa had come from the old bridge and her men were now helping haul El Héroe's followers from among the surrendering French. Those men would die, Sharpe knew, and he had no sympathy for them. They were *anfrancesados*, supporters of the French, and while the French prisoners would be transported to captivity in England, the Spaniards would have their throats cut.

"Right, Sergeant," Love's voice drew Sharpe back to the rampart, "second bomb. I've cut the fuse, just lift it in."

"You're using British powder?" Sharpe asked.

"And not very much," Love responded, "its efficiency is splendid. Because of the saltpeter, of course. We import first-rate saltpeter from India and the French are forced to scrape it from the walls of cesspits, poor devils. What a ghastly job that must be! Wading waist-deep in shit to scrape mineral deposits off the walls. Still, they are French, so they possibly don't notice. Well done, Sergeant! You make a fine *matrosse*!"

Harper muttered something under his breath, then, "Another bomb, sir?"

"You think it will be third time lucky? Fie on you, Sergeant, for your lack of faith. Barbara will be rightfully ashamed of her first effort and will doubtless guide this bomb to bring perdition upon our enemies."

Sharpe looked over the parapet. The pontoon bridge was empty now except for a scatter of French corpses who had been shot from the southern bank. Two redcoats were gingerly crossing the bridge. "Engineers, I expect," Hogan said, but he had hardly uttered the words when a small cannon in the far *tête de pont* bastion fired a canister round. It was very long range for canister fired by a small cannon, but one of the musket balls hurled one of the two redcoats back in a spray of blood.

"Rifles!" Sharpe called. "Punish those bastards."

"That was stupid of them." Hogan nodded down to the two men, one lying dead, the other scuttling back to Fort Napoleon. "We won't be able to destroy the whole bridge till we've taken that bastard of a place over there." He nodded at Fort Ragusa and the much smaller *tête de pont*.

"Cut the cables on this bank?" Sharpe suggested.

"And the pontoons drift downriver and become stranded, and therefore could be rescued. Whereupon it takes their engineers two days to put it back into operation. No, we have to destroy the whole thing, we're told they have no other pontoon train in Spain, so we must turn this one into splinters."

"Stand clear, gentlemen," Love commanded, and Sharpe saw that a new firing tube jutted from the mortar's vent. "Now, Barbara," Love exclaimed in a loud voice, "I have given you good English powder, milled in God's own country, and I expect you to drop this baby smack in the middle of the foe! See to it, woman!"

"Not how I was raised to address the saints," Hogan said mildly, then watched as Love put the portfire to the firing tube.

Another brief hiss and a puff of smoke, then the sharp crack of the powder charge exploding, and again Sharpe saw the fuse's smoke trail arcing over the river. "Better, I do believe," Hogan murmured.

To Sharpe it seemed that this second bomb was going higher and he assumed it would also fly farther, but then it curved and the smoke trail etched a fast downward fall.

"Please, Barbara!" Love cried aloud.

And the bomb disappeared behind the nearer rampart of Fort Ragusa. "He did it!" Hogan exclaimed. The bomb had dropped straight into the inner courtyard of Fort Ragusa. For a few heartbeats nothing happened, then the bomb exploded and almost instantly the noise of that explosion was swallowed by another and even bigger eruption, the noise of which hammered Sharpe's ears. The smaller fort's walls now acted like a giant mortar, blasting smoke, fire, and objects high into the sky.

"God in his heaven!" Harper murmured. "Well done, sir!"

"The enemy is confounded!" Love said happily. He was applauding himself and dancing from one foot to the other. "We have smitten him!"

Scraps of scorched timber, broken masonry, and human bodies were falling into the river and onto the outskirts of the fort, where a fire was now raging. The gunners, those who survived, were fleeing the ramparts, presumably for another stairway like the one inside Fort Napoleon. Other men were scrambling from the fort's southern gate and fleeing eastward on the riverbank, where they were joined by the score of soldiers who had been manning the *tête de pont*.

"I do believe you hit a magazine, Lieutenant!" Hogan said approvingly.

"Oh Babs!" Love looked up to the smoke-smeared heavens. "You glorious bitch!"

"Cruel bitch," Hogan said under his breath. He stared down at the two lengths of broken pontoons, both bending down-river. "Now we just have to destroy those," he murmured, "and we're done here."

Hogan set off down the stairs while Sharpe stayed on the ramparts. He was bone tired. Lieutenant Love, justly proud of his achievement, was endlessly trying to describe how what he called the trajectory of the missile was subject to mathe-matical formulae, while Harper was earnestly begging the lieutenant to let him fire another bomb. "Bugger the sums, sir, I can make it tragic for them, please!"

"There's no need for a further shot, Sergeant, the blessed Barbara has given us victory." Smoke still churned from the courtyard of Fort Ragusa, and Sharpe suspected the scene inside the smaller fort was scorched carnage.

Sharpe moved away from the mortar, wandering to the southeastern corner of the fort, where he leaned through the embrasure to see that the ladder he had climbed was still there. The wood of the crudely hacked rungs looked white in the sunlight, except halfway down where a great splash of blood had discolored the timber. He suddenly felt sick, not because of the blood but at the memory of how the ladder had bowed into the wall. Someone had once told him he had as many lives as a basketful of cats, but one of those lives had just been spent on that ladder. He straightened up to find Dan Hagman beside him, holding out his rifle. "One of the boys from the horrible half hundred asked me to give it to you, Mister Sharpe."

"Thanks, Dan."

"And the Scottish colonel sent this to you." Dan held out a dark green bottle. "He says to tell you thank you, and he's sorry the bottle's already opened, but he was thirsty."

"Me too." Sharpe took a swig and almost choked. He had expected wine, but it was a pungent brandy. "Help yourself, Dan."

"I already did, Mister Sharpe, but thank you."

"No, thank you, Dan." Sharpe toed a French corpse with a boot. "You kept those buggers off me."

"I snaffled a couple, Mister Sharpe." Hagman looked away to gaze down into the courtyard. "That poor bastard is still alive!" Hagman added in astonishment.

"Which one?"

"The officer at the tower door."

It was the man who had been pinned to the tower's doorway by a Kentish sergeant's half-pike. Sharpe had thought the man must be dead, but he was moving slowly, trying to drag the pike free of the wood behind him. A British officer, seeing the man, leaped up the steps and unceremoniously dragged the pike free of both door and officer. He threw the bloodied pike down onto the steps, then efficiently ordered a stretcher fashioned from two muskets threaded through the sleeves of two red jackets, and the Frenchman was carried away to wherever the surgeons waited. "He was a brave man," Sharpe said.

"But not long for this world," Hagman said, "not with nine inches of steel through his guts."

A rumble of artillery sounded. At first Sharpe thought it was distant thunder, then realized it was the artillery duel at Castle Miravete, which evidently still held out against General Hill's field guns. Not that that distant fight meant anything now. The pontoon bridge was doomed, which meant Miravete's garrison had nothing left to guard.

"And we're over the river!" Hagman said happily, and Sharpe saw that the redcoats had discovered a pair of small boats, maybe from the stores in Lugar Nuevo, and were ferrying men to the northern bank. "We'll be finished here soon," Sharpe said. He supposed he should go down to the courtyard and see whether any of the senior officers had orders for his men, but he felt too tired. He sat on the rampart, his back against a merlon, and took another swig of the brandy.

"We'll go back to the army?" Hagman asked.

"For sure, Dan."

"Then what?"

"Buggered if I know, but some time or other we have to leave Portugal and march into Spain." And that, he thought, was what the last few days had achieved. Now Lord Wellington could invade Spain either north or south of the Tagus, and the French would be hard put to combine their armies against him. "I could go to sleep here," he said.

"Why don't you, Mister Sharpe?" Hagman said. "You've done enough for one day."

But any thought of sleep was wiped away by the sound of an explosion that brought Sharpe to his feet. A second explosion followed, then two more as a vast cloud of dirty smoke appeared above the river. Harper was cheering. More explosions sounded and Sharpe ran to the northern rampart, where he saw that the pontoons were being destroyed one by one. Powder kegs had been put in each hull, then connected by quick-match, and each explosion blasted timber high into the air. "If Major Hogan's right," Sharpe said, "that's the only French pontoon bridge in Spain."

"Major Hogan is always right!" an Irish voice said, and Sharpe turned to see Hogan beaming a few paces away. "It's a grand sight, is it not? And the southern half will go soon. They're just laying the quick-match now. Then we'll blow down as much of the forts as we can, and off we go!"

"Not before I kill El Héroe," Sharpe said vengefully.

"That piece of shit will be long gone," Hogan said ruefully. "He's good at running away. Your Teresa is still looking for him, but I reckon he crossed the bridge before they broke it and either he's dead in Fort Ragusa's courtyard or he's ten miles beyond by now and still running."

"I looked for him on the bridge," Sharpe said, "but didn't see him."

A sudden cheer went up from the crowded courtyard of Fort Napoleon and Sharpe supposed it was prompted by the destruction of the pontoon bridge, then Harper touched his elbow. "Sir," the Irishman said quietly.

Sharpe turned to look down. The courtyard had been filled by redcoats, but now they were all pushing backward to clear a space in the courtyard's center. He saw Teresa at one edge of the cleared area and realized the men were cheering her, then he saw why. Opposite her on the steps coming from the tower were three men. They stopped at the top, where the bloodied half-pike lay abandoned. Two of the men wore the partisans' red scarves and they were holding a third man between them.

It was El Héroe.

CHAPTER 10

Teresa began screaming insults at El Héroe. "You married a formidable woman!" Major Hogan said, amused.

"Then God help the poor bastard," Harper sounded equally amused.

"That's Mrs. Sharpe?" Lieutenant Love asked nervously.

"Aye," Sharpe said, "and she's not happy." He did not sound amused.

Teresa was still screaming insults at El Héroe. She was speaking in rapid Spanish, but amongst the vituperations Sharpe understood that she was questioning his manhood and accusing him of treason. Most of her red-coated audience did not understand a word, but they cheered her fury. "She'll not fight him, surely?" Love asked.

"She'll kill him," Sharpe said, "she's not a very forgiving woman." He drew his heavy sword, tempted to go down to the courtyard, but he knew that would take time not only to negotiate the steep stairs, but also to bull his way through the thick crowd, and by the time he reached her either Teresa or El Héroe would already be dead. "Dan!" he called.

"Mister Sharpe." Hagman ran to his side.

"Teresa's about to fight that piece of rat shit. She ought to win, but just in case . . ."

"I'll finish him, Mister Sharpe," Hagman said and primed his rifle. "Would you be wanting me to kill him now?"

"Teresa will never forgive you. She wants him herself."

"Then we'd best give the lass a chance, Mister Sharpe."

Teresa was now challenging El Héroe to fight her. "Or are you too much of a coward?" She was screaming in English now, Sharpe supposed to encourage her audience who were chanting, "Fight, Fight!"

"You call yourself a hero!" Teresa screamed, "but you were hiding in a bread oven! You can't hide now and you have a choice!" The crowd had silenced to hear her and Teresa was still speaking English. "You have a choice, you piece of manky shit," Teresa screamed, "you either fight me or my husband. He's up there!" She pointed to Sharpe who, surprised, touched his sword hilt to his mouth and used it to blow a kiss down to her.

El Héroe looked up and saw Sharpe, who realized this was the first that El Héroe had learned of his marriage to Teresa. For some reason the knowledge angered El Héroe, who tore his arm from one of the men holding him and pointed at Teresa. "*Puta!*" he shouted at her.

"Let him go!" Teresa ordered the two men, and they stood aside, leaving El Héroe alone on the flight of steps. He was still dressed in his yellow Spanish dragoon uniform that was crossed by two white sashes. He had his gold-hilted saber scabbarded at his side, and now drew it. The curved blade reflected a stab of bright sunlight as he flourished it.

"Too curved," Sharpe said. "I'll bet he doesn't know how to use it."

"He'll just slash it, Mister Sharpe," Hagman said in warning, "and if he catches her, he'll slice her in half. But I can kill him first."

"Let her be, Dan. She'll never forgive me if you put a ball in his brain."

Some British officers were trying to establish order in the courtyard. Colonel Cadogan was bellowing for there to be silence, but was being ignored. He crossed to Teresa and spoke to her, but Sharpe saw the anger on her face as she replied. Cadogan was doubtless trying to stop the fight, but Teresa's response was to draw her long-bladed knife from its scabbard. The knife, narrow-bladed and wickedly sharp, was her favorite weapon and had given her the nickname La Aguja, the needle.

Cadogan stepped back, seemingly resigned to the inevitable, and Teresa walked to the center of the open space ringed by excited redcoats. To Sharpe she looked slim, small and vulnerable. "I should go down," he said.

"You'll not get there in time." Hogan touched Sharpe's arm to check him.

"The lass will gut him, sir," Harper said, "she's quick as lightning."

"Don't worry, Mister Sharpe," Hagman said, "I'll put a ball through one of his eyes if he gets lucky."

El Héroe must have known he was a dead man, because if Teresa failed to kill him then the vengeful crowd of redcoats would surely tear him to pieces. They may not know who he was, or what he had done, but the redcoats saw a swaggering man in officer's uniform who was faced by a woman and they knew where their sympathies lay. They had mostly fallen silent, but cheered again when Teresa spat the word "coward" at El Héroe.

Teresa was standing still, but the insult spurred El Héroe forward. He was plainly nervous, he knew of La Aguja's reputation, and her evident lack of fear was unsettling, but he must have reassured himself that he was better armed, much taller and stronger, and surely capable of teaching La Aguja a lesson.

Then Teresa turned her back on him. "Colonel!" she held the knife upright as if she was saluting Cadogan as she spoke to him. "If he wins, you let him go free, yes?"

"Madame . . ." Cadogan began, then faltered, unsure what to say.

"If you let him go free, Colonel," Teresa went on, "my husband will hunt him down and kill him." She paused and Cadogan, somewhat nervously, nodded abruptly. Teresa swept the knife down and turned to face El Héroe again. "If you win, coward, you can run away."

"Why's she doing that?" Hogan asked, puzzled.

"She's giving him hope," Sharpe said. "Right now, he knows he's a doomed man, so she's giving the bastard something to fight for."

"But why?" Lieutenant Love asked.

"Because he'll fight better," Sharpe said. "She doesn't want an easy victory, she wants to humiliate the bastard."

Hogan chuckled. "I do love that girl."

"The bastard should have attacked while her back was turned," Harper said.

"She expected that," Sharpe said, "which is why she held the knife upright."

"Using it as a mirror, Mister Sharpe?" Hagman asked.

"She knows what she's doing, Dan." Sharpe prayed he was right. He had seen her kill before, but had never seen her in such a formal setting, one against one in a fight in which skill would win. Teresa had hatred and confidence to match against El Héroe's desperation to live and, Sharpe was sure, an equally desperate need to demonstrate his superiority. But fear was checking that need and he simply stood and watched Teresa.

"Come on, you gutless turd," she spat, "time to die!"

The chant of "Fight! Fight!" had started up again and El Héroe, unable to endure the mocking jeers, hefted the saber.

And attacked.

El Héroe attacked as Sharpe had expected. Wildly.

He ran at Teresa and swung the saber in a wild slashing cut that was powerful enough to slice her head from her body.

Except she ducked.

The blade missed the top of her head by two fingers' breadth; she stood, stepped forward, and slashed the knife at El Héroe's right arm that was now across his body.

"She should have skewered him," Hogan said regretfully.

"She's taunting him," Sharpe said.

The swift knife cut had slashed through the yellow sleeve to give his forearm a wound that Sharpe suspected had cut to the bone, but would not slow him down, merely enrage him.

Teresa skipped back as El Héroe backswung the saber as wildly as before. She watched it pass, moved a swift pace to her right, and sliced the knife again, this time cutting El Héroe's upper left arm, again a trivial wound, but which stained the yellow sleeve with blood.

"She'll bleed him to death with a thousand cuts!" Harper said happily.

"She's fast, Mister Sharpe," Hagman said, still aiming his rifle at El Héroe.

"She's showing off," Hogan sounded disapproving.

"Wearing him out," Sharpe said, "so she can finish him fast."

The crowd was cheering her on, urging her to slaughter the bastard, and jeering at every savage saber cut that El Héroe gave. He was again swinging the saber savagely and Teresa retreated in front of the attacks, always stepping to her right to avoid backing into the onlookers and not offering any counterattacks, but always avoiding the hissing blade. She had begun the fight with her back to the fort's main gate that led north and had now retreated a quarter of the way round the courtyard, and still she went backward, still circling the make-shift arena and dodging each massive slash. Sharpe could see her talking to El Héroe, though he could not hear her voice over the jeers of the watching redcoats. He knew she would be mocking him, insulting him, goading him to keep giving his useless attacks.

"She'll have to close on him soon," Hogan said, sounding worried, "and he's a lot taller and heavier than she is."

"Makes him an easier target, Mister Hogan," Hagman said.

"Then shoot him now!"

"Don't," Sharpe said. "Oh, God!"

His exclamation came because El Héroe, realizing that his

sweeping cuts were achieving nothing, had lunged with the saber instead, but he had forgotten the blade's curve and the point of the weapon slid to the left of Teresa's waist. The belly of the saber touched the red sash she wore round her waist but lacked the force to slice into it, and Teresa was already moving again, stepping to her right, but El Héroe, perhaps encouraged that his weapon had at last touched her, lunged again. This time Teresa skipped backward until she had opened a space between herself and her opponent. She stopped, close now to the steps leading up to the tower. Again she taunted El Héroe, then, just before he leaped at her, she tossed the knife from her right hand to her left and stepped toward him.

The change of hands surprised El Héroe, who backed away, and Teresa followed up by slicing the knife toward his face, driving El Héroe even farther back. He seemed to have forgotten he carried a saber because he made no parry or counterstroke, but just stepped backward again, whereupon Teresa tossed the knife back to her right hand and threw it.

She threw the blade straight at El Héroe's face and he twisted desperately away and stumbled, falling to one knee. The knife had missed him by inches and skittered across the paving stones to come to rest beside a Scottish sergeant, who picked it up and went as if to throw it back to Teresa.

But Teresa had turned and ran to the tower steps. El Héroe shouted in apparent victory. He could see she was unarmed and he still had the saber. He got to his feet and strutted toward the tower. Now, he knew, she could not dodge or skip away, she had nowhere to go unless she dragged the tower door open. He was cursing her as he stalked closer.

"Now, Mister Sharpe?" Hagman asked.

"No, Dan, she's won."

"Dear Lord, preserve her!" Love prayed.

"She's a cunning lass," Harper said approvingly, because Teresa had seized hold of the pike's shaft that had pinned the French officer to the wooden jamb of the tower's door. Till now El Héroe's weapon had outranged her, its blade far longer than her knife, but now she held a nine-foot pike with a blade discolored by congealed blood, and El Héroe, seeing the danger, stopped. Teresa came down the steps slowly, leveling the pike at his belly.

"You knew she was going for the pike, Richard?" Hogan asked.

"It's what I'd have done," Sharpe said, then touched Hagman's shoulder. "It's all right, Dan, you can relax."

"Pity, Mister Sharpe, I was looking forward to killing the bugger." Hagman rested the rifle and, with practiced skill, pulled the trigger and eased the doghead down safely.

"Have you ever faced lancers, Richard?" Hogan asked, nodding down toward Teresa, who was holding the pike leveled at her enemy.

"I have."

"Nasty things," Hogan said.

"The trick," Sharpe said, "is to get past the blade, then the bugger holding the shaft is easy meat." There was a double click as Hagman recocked the rifle. "Hold it, Dan."

"Holding it, Mister Sharpe."

Hagman had cocked the rifle because it seemed that El Héroe had worked out the trick for himself, because he used his saber to knock the pike's blade to one side and then leaped forward, safely past the narrow blade and with his saber swinging back in another haymaking slash aimed at Teresa's head.

"God! She's fast!" Hogan breathed. "How did she do that?"

Teresa had evidently anticipated the move because, with lightning speed, she had kept the pike swinging round until its butt end faced El Héroe. And the pike's butt was fitted with a small spike, an inch of metal designed to help the pikeman ram the weapon into the ground if he was facing cavalry. She ducked beneath the wild saber stroke and rammed the spike forward to hit El Héroe in the chest. She hit hard, hard enough Sharpe thought to have broken one of El Héroe's ribs, and the blow stopped the Spaniard short and elicited a gasp of pain. Teresa jabbed the pike's butt again and El Héroe stepped back, saber low now, and obviously hurt.

Teresa also retreated, far enough to let her swing the pike back so that its blade again faced El Héroe. Then she stepped forward, jabbing the blade toward her enemy, who flinched as he raised his saber to knock the pike aside. "Broken rib?" Hogan suggested.

"Aye, she's hurt him," Harper said happily.

Another jab of the pike, and this time El Héroe managed to hit the saber against the pike's shaft, but Teresa had seen the parry coming and held the pike so rigidly that the saber's light blade scarcely moved the heavier pike. She jerked it up and lunged, striking El Héroe's sword arm just beneath the shoulder. He squealed as she pulled the blade downward, starting more blood to stain the yellow sleeve. "She's weakening his arm," Harper said approvingly.

"He hasn't got long," Hogan said happily.

"She'll make him suffer first," Sharpe said.

"Surely not?" Love spoke softly.

"She hates him," Sharpe said, "and she should. He'll not die easy."

Teresa had found a rhythm with the heavy pike that jabbed again and again. She did not drive the long narrow blade home, but contented herself with breaking El Héroe's skin until his bright yellow uniform was dotted with bloodstains on his arms, chest, and thighs, none of the wounds disabling him, but each enraging and humiliating him. And each starting a huge cheer from the watching redcoats. El Héroe was close to tears and constantly tried to swat the pike away, and each swing of the saber plainly hurt him as his chest muscles pulled against the broken rib.

Then, at last, a massive swipe of the saber managed to knock the pike aside so unexpectedly that it flew from Teresa's grip to clatter on the paving stones. "Oh, my dear Lord!" Love gasped.

"No, Dan!" Sharpe said, seeing Hagman raise his rifle and brace for the shot. "Don't shoot."

"Shoot, man!" Hogan ordered.

"No, Dan! No!"

Hagman lowered the rifle. Teresa had dropped to one knee and El Héroe, seeing his opportunity, sprang forward with the saber raised for a final death-dealing blow. He bellowed in triumph, ignoring the searing pain in his chest as he began the fatal downward stroke, but then the bellow turned into a terrifying scream. The saber flew from his hand, he clutched at his crotch with both hands, and screamed again.

"There's always a second knife," Sharpe explained calmly. "She keeps it up her left sleeve."

"God save Ireland," Harper said, "but she's a grand lass."

"Vicious too," Hogan added.

Teresa had dropped almost to the ground before striking upward and now she rolled to one side, got to her feet, and walked round her screaming victim, whose thighs were sheeted with blood.

Hagman laughed. "Right in his goolies!"

El Héroe was crouched, still clutching his crotch and still wailing. "Don't hold them, you eejit!" Harper bellowed. "Count them!"

"Poor bastard," Hogan murmured, then Teresa kicked the wailing man in the arse, toppling him to the stones where the blood spread. Then she raised the smaller knife in her right hand and bowed to Sharpe, who blew her another kiss. The redcoats were cheering wildly as El Héroe bled to death in the courtyard's center.

"Did she do what I think she did?" Lieutenant Love had gone pale.

"She did," Sharpe said, "and she gouged the blade too."

"So die traitors," Hogan said. "Now let's finish what we came to do."

Separate Soult and Marmont, by destroying a bridge.

* * *

Sharpe went down to the courtyard, where El Héroe's corpse lay in a fly-ridden pool of blood. The courtyard was still crowded, though men were giving the corpse a wide berth. General Hill had arrived, his face beaming and, seeing Sharpe, he beckoned him. "I am told we owe you thanks, Major Sharpe."

"Every man involved deserves thanks, sir."

"True, true! And Fort Ragusa is ours too?"

"Thanks to Lieutenant Love, sir."

"Cupid strikes, eh?" Hill asked with a smile. "I'll make sure he gets credit, but General Howard and Colonel Cadogan tell me you were the first man over the rampart here?"

"I'm sure two of the colonel's men got there before me, sir."

Hill nodded. "A nasty business, escalade," he said, then glanced at the corpse. "And I'm told your wife put on quite a show!"

"He was a traitor, sir, and got his deserts."

Teresa, seeing Sharpe with Hill and his aides, had hung back, but now the general beckoned her forward. He bowed to her. "Madame!" he said. "I am told you disposed of El Héroe?"

"He was a Spaniard," Teresa said coldly, "so it was a Spaniard's duty to kill him."

"I thank you for it," Hill said, bowing again. "With allies like you, I cannot see how we can lose this war!" Which, Sharpe thought, was a generous comment from a man who at first had not wanted Teresa's help. Then Hill looked past Sharpe and his face brightened. "What do you bring me, Captain?" he asked happily.

A captain of the Highlanders was carrying two French eagles, the proud standards of every French regiment. Each eagle had a flag attached. "I'd like to claim they were taken in battle, sir," the captain said, "but in truth they were being stored in the tower."

"They were taken in battle," Hill said loudly enough to be heard by every man in the courtyard, "by exceedingly brave men!"

That prompted a loud cheer from the redcoats, many of whom were clutching bottles plundered from the fort's storerooms. Hill touched the fringed flags of both eagles, as if he could scarcely believe they were real, then looked at Hogan. "And the pontoon bridge?"

"Half is destroyed, and the other half should be firewood soon, sir." Even as Hogan spoke the explosions began on the northern bank as pontoon after pontoon was gutted by powder kegs. Smoke blossomed above the fort's ramparts.

"And what do we do about this?" General Hill gestured at the fort's high walls. "If we leave it the scoundrels will just move back in, and presumably make another bridge?"

"We'll knock down enough of the walls to make the forts useless," Hogan said, "and they'll have to bring pontoons from France or make new ones here if they want a crossing, and El Sacerdote has burned their timber framework at the old bridge."

"Then I'd say our work is done!" Hill said happily and then, much louder, "Very well done!" Then the general stiffened as a screech sounded from the tower, where a redcoat's jacket hung from the flagstaff. "Oh good G . . ." General Hill began irritably, stopping abruptly before he uttered a blasphemy. "Good gracious! Someone's murdering a cat!"

A piper of the 71st had climbed the tower and had begun playing. The Scottish soldiers in the courtyard cheered. "Back to Portugal, sir?" General Howard asked.

"Tomorrow, I think. Let's make sure there's nothing here the scoundrels can salvage first."

El Héroe's corpse was carried to the river and tossed in, joining the scorched fragments of the bridge to float downstream. More captured French powder was ferried over the Tagus to where redcoats used sledgehammers and picks to make cavities in the walls of Fort Ragusa. The powder kegs were crammed into the holes and exploded to raucous cheers. The French cannon and mortars that survived the demolition were spiked. A small group of French soldiers, survivors of the day, watched from a hill half a mile away, doubtless flinching when the fort collapsed in a cloud of powder and smoke dust.

Sharpe and Teresa walked back over the hills to see that the French garrison in Castle Miravete was still under the fire of a battery of British nine-pounders. "Now you assault them?" Teresa asked, seeing the damage the British guns had wreaked in the earthern berm that protected the fortress. They had done good work because at least two of the big French twelve-pounders were out of action, and the gunners at the rest were being harried by riflemen of the King's German Legion.

"No need," Sharpe said, "they're only here to protect the pontoon bridge. Once we've gone they'll go too." He looked northward, over the low hills, to see the great plume of smoke drifting slowly westward on the breeze. "We've won, love," he said, "and you killed the bastard."

"I did it too quickly," Teresa said. "I wanted him to suffer."

"Good Christ!" Sharpe said. "He suffered. He's still screaming on his way to hell!"

"I was frightened you'd have one of your men shoot him before I killed him," Teresa said, watching as a British shell exploded against the wall of Miravete Castle.

"Never crossed my mind," Sharpe said.

"You are a bad liar," Teresa said. She put her arm through Sharpe's. "So back to Portugal?"

"For a few weeks."

"Just a few weeks?"

"We just unlocked the door to Spain, love," Sharpe said, "and we'll be going through it. All the way to France."

"And I go with you," Teresa said, "all the way."

"And we'll win," Sharpe said, "because the sorry bastards don't have rifles, and we do."

HISTORICAL NOTE

Major-General Sir Rowland "Daddy" Hill's raid on Almaraz in the spring of 1812 was one of the great British successes in the Peninsular War. It followed the hard fighting that had succeeded in capturing the two great frontier fortresses, Ciudad Rodrigo and Badajoz, that barred any British advance into Spain. With those cities captured, the one great danger facing a British invasion of French-held Spain was the possibility of the French combining the armies of Soult and Marmont to oppose Wellington's army. The River Tagus divided those two formidable armies and Wellington's solution to his problem of keeping them separated was as ingenious as it was daring. He would make the Tagus impassable.

There were bridges at Toledo, Almaraz, and Alcántara, and the latter two would have provided easy communication between Marmont in the north and Soult to the south of the river. The bridge at Alcántara, closest to Portugal, had been built by the Romans and destroyed early in the war. It was denied to the French by British occupying forces, who could use the bridge thanks to an ingenious device that enabled a sliding timber drawbridge to cross the broken span. The Roman bridge at Toledo was available to the French, but was so far inland that it would impose an enormous delay in marching time. The danger was the bridge at Almaraz, which would offer a swift link between the southern and northern armies of the French. That link was broken in the early years of the war, when the Spanish destroyed the northern span, but the French had replaced the shattered bridge with a pontoon bridge a little downriver.

That bridge of boats was guarded by Forts Napoleon and Ragusa, and by two *têtes de pont*, or bastions. The *têtes de pont* blocked the immediate entrances to the bridge, while the forts, close by, commanded the approaches to the pontoon bridge. A third fort, Miravete Castle with its outlying works, blocked the road to the bridge in the southern hills above the river. All three forts were formidably strong and garrisoned by around 1,500 French troops. Against them Hill led about 7,000 men, mostly British, but reinforced with a fine Portuguese brigade and some troops from the King's German Legion.

Hill's force reached the Miravete pass at dawn on May 17. The initial plan had been to batter the Miravete fort with artillery, storm it, and then use the main road to carry the heavy artillery down to the river, where Fort Napoleon could be similarly attacked, but a reconnaissance of the fort suggested that the Miravete position would be difficult to subdue and the time taken to open the road would give the enemy time to reinforce the two forts guarding the pontoon bridge. An alternative plan was swiftly adopted. One part of Hill's force would besiege

Miravete Castle to keep it busy and to suggest that its capture was the prime objective of the British, and meanwhile General Howard would lead a formidable force through the hills and descend on Fort Napoleon, which would have to be captured by escalade.

That alternative plan also had problems. The sheep track through the hills was more treacherous than expected, the ladders were too long to be carried easily through the twisting path through the trees, and when dawn came on the 18th a substantial part of Howard's force had still to arrive. Howard nevertheless decided to attack with the 50th and part of the 71st and ordered them forward. The ladder carriers, now carrying much shortened ladders, went first and were met with cannon and musket fire from Fort Napoleon's defenders, who had been aware that the attack was coming. Nevertheless the ladders were successfully carried into the fort's ditch and swung up against the ramparts, only to discover that the ladders, having been shortened to make their journey through the thickets easier, were now too short. The attackers were trapped in the fort's ditch, where they could be assailed by roundshot and shells simply dropped from the high rampart.

Yet the fort had a weakness; the distance between the foot of the walls and the lip of the ditch. That distance should have been no more than a foot, but at Fort Napoleon that berm was about a yard wide, and the attackers realized that by propping the ladders on the berm, rather than planting them in the ditch's base, they would reach the full height of the wall. Captain Candless of the 50th was supposed to be the first man to scale a ladder and jump down among the defenders. He died, but other men now succeeded in climbing the ladders and routing the French. They would have been much helped by the accurate rifle fire of the British 95th and the Portuguese riflemen who could pick off defenders visible above the ramparts.

French resistance in Fort Napoleon collapsed when the high rampart fell. The commander of the fort tried to rally his men, but was mortally wounded when a sergeant of the 50th ran him through with a pike. Most of the garrison fled, and the only place to find safety was to cross the bridge and join the defenders of Fort Ragusa.

The bridge was thus crowded with French fugitives and their British pursuers when the center broke. That center of the bridge was formed by one, or possibly two, river boats that could be removed if ever the pontoon bridge needed to allow traffic through. Some accounts reckon the bridge broke because Fort Ragusa's defenders fired on the British pursuers and their roundshot shattered the boats, others reckon that the weight of the fleeing French proved too much for the craft, and others suggest the bridge was deliberately broken to prevent the British from crossing the river and attacking Fort Ragusa. However it happened, the result was that many fugitives drowned, and General Howard's forces were unable to cross the river to attack the second, smaller fort.

So long as Fort Ragusa remained in French hands, so long was General Hill's purpose unfulfilled. True the British could destroy the bridge with cannon fire, but they were far from Portugal, where the British army was located, and would be forced to withdraw before the French sent powerful reinforcements to drive them away. The bridge could be remade and Wellington's advance north of the Tagus would be threatened by forces from Soult's army. Fort Ragusa had to be attacked and destroyed, and the river crossing was gone.

Luckily the British force that had captured Fort Napoleon contained a Lieutenant Love of the Royal Artillery and twenty gunners. They manned the captured cannon on the ramparts of Fort Napoleon and opened fire on Fort Ragusa. The result was panic among the French, who simply abandoned the northern fort and fled. Some small boats had been seen on that northern shore and British infantrymen swam the river to bring them back and so enough men were able to cross the Tagus and occupy the abandoned Fort Ragusa, which, like Fort Napoleon, was slighted with powder captured from the French. The shattered remnants of both forts can be seen today.

It will be obvious from that account of the Almaraz expedition that I have taken great liberties to keep Sharpe occupied. The presence of twenty experienced men from the Royal Artillery would mean that Lieutenant Love had no need of Sharpe and his men to act as *matrosses*. More egregiously there is no mention in any of the accounts that the French had a small encampment at the old broken bridge, but it did not seem unreasonable to me that they might have had such a place from which they would attempt to repair the shattered span, and it would make a fine target for Sharpe.

I make no apology for including fiction in a novel that celebrates General Hill's achievement; my business is fiction. Equally fictional is El Héroe, who did not exist, and to many might seem a most unlikely character. The Spanish partisans, after all, are known for their visceral hatred of the French and their massive contribution to the expulsion of the French from Spain. Yet there were partisans who betrayed their own side, such as Josef Tris, El Malcarado, "the false-faced," who sold valuable information to the French and was eventually executed by the great Francisco Espoz y Mina, one of the most formidable partisan leaders.

Even without my fictional embellishments, the Almaraz expedition was a resounding success. General Hill had led his force deep into Spain, cut the only practicable link between Marmont and Soult, and then withdrew safely to the British lines. And he achieved that with an extremely light casualty list. The total British and allied casualties, either killed or wounded, were 189 men, while the French lost at least 400, while another 279 were taken as prisoners. The road into Spain and eventual victory was now open and, later in the same year, Wellington would lead his army to the stunning triumph at Salamanca.

Daddy Hill was one of the few generals trusted by Wellington, and he had rewarded that trust with his success at Almaraz. When in 1814 he was rewarded with a peerage, he chose as his title Baron Hill of Almaraz and of Hawkstone (the village of his birth in Shropshire). Three years after the battle of Almaraz, he was to be present at Waterloo, where, again, he distinguished himself. Hill's reputation was enhanced by the affection of the soldiers of Britain's army who recognized in Hill a man who prized them, admired them, and looked after them.

Sharpe is one of those soldiers and he will march again and, because he is a rifleman, that means he will march to victory.

ABOUT THE AUTHOR

BERNARD CORNWELL is the author of over fifty novels, including the acclaimed *New York Times* bestselling Saxon Tales, which serve as the basis for the hit Netflix series *The Last Kingdom*. He lives with his wife on Cape Cod and in Charleston, South Carolina.

DON'T MISS THE OTHER BOOKS IN THE
SHARPE SERIES!

"Excellently entertaining. If you love historical drama,
then look no further." —*Boston Globe*

"Richard Sharpe has the most astounding knack for finding himself
where the action is . . . and adding considerably to it."
—*Wall Street Journal*